TUESDAY
___

LOU GIBBONS

CENTULLE

A CENTULLE book
First edition June 2025
ISBN: 978-2-9594289-5-1
Copyright © 2025 by Lou Gibbons

———

All the characters in this book are fictitious and any resemblance to actual persons living or dead is purely coincidental.

All rights reserved. No part of this publication may be reproduced, distributed, transmitted or used in any other manner without written permission of the copyright owner and publisher. For permission requests, contact lou@lougibbons.com

Cover design by victoriaheathsilk.com

LET'S KEEP IN TOUCH!

I like to know my readers. If you'd like to stay in touch, join my Readers Club today to receive details of new releases and special offers.

An exclusive novella - The Shrewsbury File - is waiting for you as a free gift.

lougibbons.com

Sloth
/sləʊθ/

noun

1. the reluctance to work or make an effort.
2. a rarely-used word but one of the seven deadly sins, which quietly manifests itself as thinking your small contribution won't make a difference anyway.
3. a very slow tropical American mammal called Sid, immortalised in the film Ice Age.

CHAPTER ONE

Before the madness, it was a Tuesday that powered up like any other. Perched on the dining table, Dave's laptop announced it was World Blood Donor Day. *We're after your blood!* chirped the message to a burst of music. Dave's own blood drained from him as he glanced at the microwave in the kitchen. Quarter to eight. Early morning meetings were never good news, especially those organised on the spur of the moment.

He clicked on the invitation link.

'Not gonna lie to you, you look like shit on a stick,' said Carol, leaning in for a closer inspection. His wife's furrowed forehead filled the screen.

'Nice to see you too.' Dave snatched a handful of paperclips and dropped them into his lap and the sagging superhero boxer shorts that Secret Santa had gifted several years ago.

Carol lowered her head and tapped at her phone, affording an inspection of her roots. She'd done something to her hair. Dave hadn't noticed earlier. Probably something to do with her new job as Executive Personal

Assistant to their man at the top. Carol got the home office upstairs and he the kitchen-diner thanks to her illustrious career supporting many a rising star of Welsh politics. Big fish in little ponds, if you wanted his opinion. The lot of them, and this one more of a pillock than the rest. Or was that pollack? Dave smiled.

Carol looked up. 'Don't tell me you find this funny?'

Pillock, pollack. He was quick when he didn't try. Dave forced a frown and asked, 'What are you doing here, anyway?'

'Chairman's running late. Told me to prepare you. You could have had a shower at least.'

Dave's unvoiced anger at being left no hot water that morning disappeared into Carol's parting as she returned to her phone. He stared at the screen. She'd dyed it, that was it. Not that she needed different shades of blonde. Not that she would want his opinion.

'Let me see where he is.' Carol looked up briefly to roll her eyes. 'You know this is an important meeting.'

Dave strung paperclips together, scratching at his groin in passing. He *had* let himself go. That match Ellis had arranged at the Arms Park for the old team had been an embarrassment to say the least. One bang on the head and carried off. He ventured another look at Carol. As a rule, the Chairman was far too important to meet him. It had to be about what he thought it was. An empty mug beside the laptop beckoned. He might have time to make another coffee, grab a biscuit. Maybe not. He felt a bit sick.

The screen split into two. Dr Rhys-Wyn Llewellyn-Jones, the only person Dave had ever met with a double-double-barrelled name, burst into view.

'Morning everyone.'

Dave's tongue skimmed his teeth. No time for coffee. Fingering the metal daisy chain, he considered more

TUESDAY

paperclips. The longer it was, the easier it would be to hang himself with later.

'David! Hope me being late hasn't kept you from anything . . . important.'

Dave pressed on his trembling leg. That was Dr Double Barrel's way. Not overtly rude, he eroded any lingering self-confidence as if picking at a scab. No one liked him. He knew Dave's pipeline was empty. His days were too. Apart from that recent trip to the *World Mobility Summit*. That was what this meeting was about. It had to be.

Dr Double Barrel frowned. 'Bit off colour, are we?'

'No more hot water,' Dave mumbled.

Dave studied the on-screen petri dish that now housed him in a corner of the screen, waiting for a suggestion of some time off. Not that Dr Double Barrel was a real doctor, not a medical one. He had a doctorate in mechanical engineering and an MBA from somewhere French. McGill in Montreal, that was it. Spoke perfect Welsh and mastered the language of love. Too smooth by half.

While the Chairman muted himself, Dave reached for more paperclips. Spider-Man squatted on his retreating manhood, offering a reminder that with great power comes great responsibility. Dave tried to implore Carol with a stare. Meeting a steely eyed rebuff, his attention diverted to the bookshelf behind her. *Fifty Shades of Grey*, what the—

'We need a frank chat, David.' The Chairman expelled the contents of his lungs on returning to the meeting.

Dave relocked eyes with Spidey, increasingly doubtful of the power accorded to a middle-grade civil servant.

'It's hardly a great time to get arrested. Not with everything going on.'

There it was.

'Not technically arres—'

'*Oh! Carol.*' Dr Double Barrel burst into the Neil Sedaka

3

song that Dave remembered accompanying Carol's arrival on the dancefloor at their wedding reception. '*I am but a fool.*'

A giggle from Carol morphed into a glare in Dave's direction as a paperclip stabbed his thigh.

'The First Minister wants to know how the Agency tasked with promoting foreign investment into the Cardiff region can demonstrate it hasn't been . . .' the Chairman's eyebrows danced a knowing pause, his whiter-than-white teeth gleamed, 'pissing taxpayers' money up the wall.'

Dave's open-mouthed hesitation met with a raised hand.

'I don't need excuses, David. I need projects. Real investment projects. You know our strategy: value-added jobs. We want tech. You're the Head of America, aren't you? The *home* of tech. Where are these projects?' A hand tickled the air as if coaxing a Google R&D centre out of the sky to land in a disused Welsh warehouse.

'I had some good conversations at the Summit,' Dave muttered, remembering a bar on the Strip once the show had closed and a long chat with the son of the marketing whizz who had insisted Marathon be rebranded Snickers. His father had, by all accounts—

'Not conversations, David.' A knocking echoed out of the laptop. 'Are you actually listening? I want Gates, Bezos, all that lot on a plane coming to see what we're about.'

Getting anyone on a plane to Wales was never easy. The only real international connections were Lanzarote and Menorca and even those were restricted to six months of the year. Dave went to speak, this time meeting Carol's raised hand.

'You have three weeks to bring me something decent,' said the Chairman, his attention already out the door on its way to his next meeting. 'Or that's it.'

TUESDAY

'Three weeks?' shouted Dave.

'He's doing you a favour.' Carol's voice reverberated through the house before a giggle softened her face. 'Sorry, Rhys. I didn't mean to butt in.'

'*Oh! Carol*,' the Chairman sang back.

Dave's peripheral vision hazed. He was being hung out to dry and Carol was letting it happen. No one could muster a bona fide investment project out of thin air in less than a month. Dave dropped his head into a nod, trying to catch Carol's eye. So, she was calling the Chairman by his first name already. Single-barrelling it too, whilst he fixed Dave in his sights and aimed with both barrels.

'Silicon Valley, David, what's that about?' The Chairman scanned his phone. 'Wales *is* the Valleys and more than bloody one.'

Snatching a final clump of paperclips revealed the *Green, Green Tech of Home s*trapline adorning their latest marketing brochure. Dave sighed.

'Let's have a progress report in a week,' said the Chairman. 'See you next Tuesday?'

Dave's head shot up. The Chairman winked. C U Next Tuesday. How dare he call him that! Double-barrelled dickhead. Dave's cowardice groped to find its voice as he fidgeted in his chair. The Chairman disappeared.

Carol expanded to fill the screen. 'Jesus Christ, Dave! Not only do you turn up like the great unwashed. He thought you were tickling your bloody pickle. He's texted me to ask what you were doing under the table. Please tell me you put some trousers on.'

Anaemic thighs that had taken Wales to many a victory laughed back at Dave. He pulled the paperclip daisy chain into view.

'For pity's sake. I don't know what to do with you. You do realise your job's on the line?'

'I wasn't technically arrested, I was—'

'Cautioned, I know,' shouted Carol.

'Why haven't I had a shower?' said Dave. 'We both know who used all the hot water. And do you want to tell me how *Fifty Shades of Grey* made its way onto the bookshelf?'

The paperclip chain soared across the kitchen.

Carol's cheeks flushed.

Jesus Christ. Not Rhys.

'It's better than fifty shades of don't give a shit!' Carol's hand batted the air, Dave's eyes locked on the wedding band he'd placed there twenty-seven years earlier. 'I'm going into the office. I can't deal with you anymore.'

Alone in the online meeting room, Dave stared at himself. Hands abandoned tidying his hair to cover his face. A door slammed upstairs, followed by the front door. Whatever HR genius had invented remote working had overestimated the tenacity of the average Welsh home, not to mention his marriage. The house rattled as Dave let the chair dig into his back.

'Oh Carol,' he whispered.

CHAPTER TWO

He pulled the headphones to his ears, noticing a number he didn't recognise on the telephone screen. 'Good afternoon. CIA. Dave speaking.'

They were supposed to announce themselves in full, Cardiff Investment Agency, followed by the Welsh translation, *Asiantaeth Buddsoddi Caerdydd*. But using the ill-adapted mnemonic device *Asian teeth* invariably made Dave forget, hindering his feigned bilingualism. That, and the fact he couldn't be arsed.

'I'm calling to get advice on a business grant. I've got an invention, see. Hang on a minute . . .' A pause promised the habitual confusion engendered by Dave's laziness. 'Not *the* CIA?'

'The very same,' replied Dave, smiling at the fact it wasn't technically a lie and deciding a little bit of fun was just what he needed.

'Crikey. The CIA working with the Welsh government?'

Dave lowered his voice. 'That's right.'

'You don't sound American, Dave. Though to be fair, you don't sound Welsh either.'

You didn't have to *sound* Welsh to live in Wales. Dave had been through this more times than he cared to remember. Damn it. He'd slipped up by giving his real name though.

'Coming here, it's part of the training we get from Langley. That, and using false names.' That should do it. 'Are you alone, Mister—'

'Jones. Bryn Jones.'

Dave smiled as Bryn lowered his voice.

'The thing is, not many people know this, Bryn, but we use our diplomatic relations overseas to have our finger on the pulse of the latest technology.' Dave glanced at the brochures beside him. 'The green, green tech of home.'

'Green tech of home?'

'I mean, *it's not unusual.*'

'What's not?'

'The waste!' Dave's whisper broke into a shout. '*Forgive me, Bryn, I just can't take any more.*' He smirked, trying to recall other Tom Jones lyrics.

'Any more what?'

Dave straightened his face. 'Good Welsh ideas, Bryn, going to waste.'

A cough broke the silence that had graced the line. 'Well talking of waste, like I said, I've got an idea, in'it. An invention, like. It's going to put an end to—'

'Let me stop you there—'

'I—'

'The Russians.'

'What about them?'

'And the Chinese.'

'What've they bloody well been up to now then?'

'The question is not what, Bryn. It's why. *Why, why*

why?' Dave smiled, congratulating himself on 'Delilah' being an endless source of inspiration. 'They all listen in . . . *before they come to break down the door.'*

'My door?'

'Unless you have a patent?'

'Well, not—'

'Then, we must end this conversation for now.'

'But how will I—'

'Roath Park. I'm there every Monday at eleven o'clock. Third bench down from the Cariad Tea Rooms. Over and out.'

'Over and—'

Dave pressed the red button and pulled the headphones out of his ears. Misdialling happened, Dave's number similar to that of the Welsh Innovator Forum Coordinator: Owain something or other.

His laughter evaporated as he slid into the chair and slurped on his coffee. Stone cold, he spat it back into the mug. The conversation with Dr Double Barrel that morning played on repeat, denting the enjoyment of his humour. His wife flirting with the geriatric punched a bigger hole in his pride. Dave and Carol had drifted, that much was sure. When they'd met in one of the VIP boxes during the 1996 Five Nations tournament, he'd been the bright, young star of an ailing team and she a fresh recruit in the Welsh Government's Events and Marketing Division. She had smiled at his Mancunian vowels, questioned his place in the Welsh team and decided their mothers both being from Wrexham was fate uniting them. The future had looked bright.

Twenty-seven years later, she was comparing him to shit on a stick.

Dave's toes grasped at the woollen rug beneath his feet. Three weeks to find an investment project. Talk about a mountain to climb! He'd never been cut out for the job. A poster boy at first, he and a few of the old team had been plopped into positions here and there. Steve had been the face of Radio Rentals for years, until they went bust. Carol had pulled a string or two and Dave had been chosen to represent Wales abroad. It had been fun at first, flying to trade shows and helping Welsh companies export cheese. Now here he was trying to bring inward investment into Wales from North America with barely a degree in Sports Science, all to pay for a four-bedroomed house in Cyncoed.

Noticing he had new messages, Dave clicked on the email icon at the bottom of the screen and scanned his inbox.

Jolene Jones
Stolen tofu and beetroot wrap – 5th Floor
Hi, I hate to have to write this mail but it has come to . . .

Tofu and beetroot. Of course, that was Jolene's. If Dave was going to be labelled a thief, it wouldn't be for rabbit food. By the time he had realised it wasn't pastrami, it was too late.

Channel 4
Newly Released – *Forty and Forgotten*
Meeting the invisible men women no longer find attract . . .
Wales Online
Daily Headlines
First Minister announces government-wide audit in an . . .
George Walcott
Hip, hip hooray?
Dear Dave, I'm sorry to hear about your recent operati . . .

TUESDAY

Trying to remember a George Walcott, not to mention surgery, Dave clicked on the email, quickly realising it was one of the many he received for his namesake at Colchester Investment Agency. The other was David.W@cia.co.uk and he was David.W@cia.org. They had entered a sort of pen pal friendship, forwarding emails as and when. There weren't that many nowadays, just the odd promotion from the World Anglers Association. No need to forward this one anyway. Colchester Dave was off work for the foreseeable future.

Hang on a minute.

Dave extricated himself from the details of George Walcott's own hip replacement three years prior to return to his inbox, remembering skimming over something about a government-wide audit. He clicked on the Wales Online round-up and through to the headline article. So, the Chairman wasn't just having his fun. His own head was on the block, the First Minister cited as starting the audit with the Cardiff Investment Agency. It was attempting to trend on social media with the hashtag, #WasteFreeWales. Dave rolled his eyes.

'Dr Rhys-Wyn Llewellyn-Jones has been more than open, ensuring that all investment put into promoting Cardiff will soon reap benefits threefold,' Dave read out loud.

Threefold. No one used words like that. More to the point, there was the reason Dave wasn't being fired on the spot. It wasn't the time to be admitting they were having trouble meeting targets and a bad audit would need scapegoats. Rubbing his thighs to heat them, Dave glanced at the microwave clock. Half past four. So, the Chairman was setting him up to fail *and* making a play for his wife. Little—

Dave jumped as his phone rang. For someone who

navigated whole days without being called once, the day was proving busy.

Reaching for his headphones, Dave stared at the number, entering into a lengthy internal debate as to what country had a plus three hundred and fifty-four dialling code and whether there could be over three hundred countries in the world.

He pressed to answer. 'Good afternoon. Car—'

'Mr Welch?'

Dave ground his teeth. Hearing his name reminded him he would never quite be Welsh. Twelve caps hadn't been enough, nor the contract he had never signed to play professionally for Swansea, breaking his knee days before. A drawling Mancunian, Dave would have trouble selling Wales to the Welsh, let alone the Americans.

'Who's speaking please?' he asked, noting an accent he couldn't place but nevertheless praying it wasn't another Welsh inventor.

'Hel-ga Gun-nars-dót-tir.' The syllables danced in a straight line out of the phone.

Of the few calls Dave did get, a tiny minority were meant for him. The accent sounding Scandinavian, Dave assumed he'd been confused with Jolene, his only real work buddy, even if she was on the vegan, chakra-balanced end of the woke spectrum. He handled America, she Northern Europe. At least, she had done until recently, and that was when she was in the office and not living in a cave.

'Listen, I think you've got the wrong—'

'David Welch, Head of Am-er-i-ca for the CIA?'

'Don't tell me . . . you were looking for the FBI.'

'Pardon?' An awkward pause squatted the line. 'I'm looking for David Welch. Played scrum half for Wales. That try against Australia in the 1999 World Cup was unforgettable.'

TUESDAY

'Err. That's me.' Dave pulled his t-shirt over his belly. Intermittent fasting had put pay to two stone, but he had two more to go.

'We're running a conference in Reykjavik later this year. We hoped you could come as one of the speakers?'

'Reykjavik?'

'It's in Iceland.'

'I know where it is.'

He'd thought it was the capital of Finland, but it was all the same. So, Iceland had to be the three hundred and fifty-fourth country of the world. Dave stared at his phone. No one ever asked him to speak. About anything. Not even in their weekly team meetings.

'I'm not sure you have the right person,' he said.

'It's definitely you we need.'

No one ever said that either.

'Sustainable investment in a time of growth,' Helga continued.

'Listen, I—'

'The green, green tech of home.'

Dave's arm jerked, the tower of brochures next to him splurging out of shape like a half-eaten cake. Their marketing was only working! People were starting to believe the hype. Cardiff had no tangible investment backing up its vision. The last company that had moved into the docks made toilet rolls; recycled, but still.

'Listen, I'm actually Head of America.'

'It's a global event. It's definitely you we need.'

The line went quiet.

Dave liked any chance to get overseas, but the destination had to merit the effort. He'd pulled together a detailed business case to go to Las Vegas and Detroit. Got it approved eight months in advance. Wouldn't go to the same effort for a cold, lonely rock in the middle of the

Atlantic. Not that any more overseas jollies were on the cards, not with the caution. How could he have known the *Little Chapel of Love* performed ceremonies twenty-four-seven when, caught short, he'd weed against their wall? Anyway, it was unlikely he'd have a job in three weeks' time.

'Mr Welch? Are you still there?'

Dave rubbed his chin. Two-day stubble scratched back as he tried to find a polite exit. 'Helga, wasn't it? Listen, I can't commit to that now I'm afraid.'

'But it's definitely you—'

'You need, I know.' Dave stared at the microwave. Twenty-five to five.

'The land of fire and ice,' said Helga.

'Sorry?'

'Iceland, Mr Welch. It sits on two tectonic plates.'

'Like I—'

'Slowly being ripped apart by opposing forces.'

Dave frowned at the phone. 'Listen, send me an email,' he said, tapping the red button.

Dave sucked in his stomach. Fancy her remembering that try against Australia! Laughter erupted at the back of his throat. *Slowly being ripped apart by opposing forces!* Turning to his laptop, he quickly Googled 'land of ice and fire'. Skimming the search results, he pushed paperclips around the dining table, one by one by one. Unpredictable volcanoes, limited sunshine and a penchant for folklore offered confirmation, if any needed. Audit or no audit, the last place in the world he'd ever want to go was Iceland.

CHAPTER THREE

Dave gripped the steering wheel, his knuckles whitening. A door supported his elbow to the left, not the right. A gear stick sat to his right, not his left. Music, he could hear music. He knew that song. The 1999 World Cup, Bryn Terfel entering the pitch with Dame Shirley. The crowd roared; the pitch rumbled. Dave's arms vibrated. The ground *was* rumbling.

His head shot up.

Shit! The car was moving.

A solitary road unfolded before him. Dave gripped tighter, scanning the dashboard. Ninety! His foot pounded the middle pedal, screeching throwing him into the sun visor as the engine cut.

'Jesus Christ!' Dave rubbed his forehead. 'Not again.'

The doctor had ruled out concussion but closing the curtains was the only reprieve from the headaches. Regressing into adolescence to bond with their son, Carol said. Two million followers online, the last thing Seth wanted was Dad time.

'You okay?'

Dave jumped.

A man smiled from the passenger seat, a tightly-pulled red bobble hat covering his eyebrows and ears. Legs swung in the footwell, boasting a well-laced pair of walking shoes.

Dave checked the back seat.

'Only me,' said the man.

'Who are you?' asked Dave.

The red head fell back in laughter, eyes falling shut.

'Tell me who you are,' shouted Dave.

'Sal,' said the man, stretching an arm. 'Dave, when you call me, you can call me Sal.'

Dave checked the rear-view mirror as Sal's raucous laughter filled the car. Tarmac drew a straight line behind him. No signs of life. Ahead, the road led to a scattering of buildings and a hill rising like a soufflé out of surrounding green pasture. He searched the fields that rolled into a sea-squatted horizon. Oblivious to his predicament, sheep hugged the verge of the road, tallying an additional population of three.

'Where in God's name are we?' asked Dave, knowing, whatever the response, he didn't want to be there. He brought his attention back to Sal, his head sitting well below the headrest. 'Short for a bloke, aren't you?'

'English for a man who promotes investment into Wales, aren't you?'

'Touché. Hang on a minute. How—'

'Ready to climb that hill?' asked Sal. He opened the passenger door, thudded onto the road and slammed the door behind him.

Dave drove his palms into the upholstery encasing his thighs. Whoever this joker was, he knew all about Dave but Dave didn't know him from Adam. And yet his gut urged him to follow. He turned the key in the ignition. The engine roared into life and guided him around a bend in the road and into an empty car park.

Crisp air greeted Dave's exit from the car, silence peppered by a flag fluttering high on a pole. He marched over to a waving Sal to assess the hill before them. Dave hated walking anywhere, let alone up an incline. He craned his neck, deciding it couldn't be that high.

'Not even a hundred metres,' said Sal.

'Sorry?'

'The hill.'

'How do you always know what I'm thi—'

'This way!' Sal winked and turned on his heels.

Dave flexed his hands and pinched his face. He was here, wherever here was. So real and yet none of it made any sense.

'Be nice if everything in life did,' shouted Sal.

Dave shook his head, concerned by his new acquaintance's capacity to read minds but reminding himself that life rarely made sense. Whenever it started to, the rug was quickly pulled from under you. He pushed into the wind, catching up with Sal who had stopped before a white corrugated building. As red as his hat, a turret foisted a cross into the cloudy sky. Before it, stretched a picketed lawn and a scattering of headstones.

'Sad state of affairs,' said Sal. 'Never turn out well, do they?'

'What don't?'

'You don't read the Icelandic sagas?'

'Does anyone?' replied Dave, realising why Sal's accent sounded familiar. It was the same as whatshername who had called that morning. Dave scoured the rolling pasture, his eyes stopping on the flagpole. Wind resting, its colours remained hidden. 'Jesus Christ! Don't tell me we're in Iceland?'

Sal beamed at Dave. 'Last place in the world you'd ever want to go, am I right?'

Dave stopped himself from replying. No point in lying.

'Anyway, that's a good thing. Only works first time.'

'First—'

'Enough chatter.' Sal brought a finger to his lips. 'Now we walk to the top of that hill, stand in the chapel ruins, face east and make three wishes. Don't say them out loud. They only come true if you don't utter a word and don't look back on the way up.'

'Look back?'

'Like . . .'

'Like?'

Sal placed his hands on his hips. 'Do you read anything other than the rugby scores? Shh. It's not complicated. Walk, no talk and no turning back.'

Wind propelled Dave up a mud path that scribbled a line to the summit, urging him to keep pace with Sal's swift steps. His chest tightened. Not even a hundred metres. He used to run that in twelve seconds at his peak, but that was a while ago. And on the flat. As his breath quickened, Sal's words came back to him. Three wishes. They were climbing a hill to make three wishes. No harm in that. Grab hold of the reins and nudge life in a more positive direction. Like Aladdin and whatever he had wished for. Sal was right; Dave should read more, like when he was a boy. There had to be a clever way around this, somehow wishing for everything he ever wished for to come true.

'Careful what you wish for, Son.'

Dave's neck tensed as the words came out of nowhere. It was forbidden to look back. Long dead, it couldn't be Dad anyway. Never a man for ambition, he'd been found face down in his turnips at sixty-one. A lifetime toiling the fields rewarded by a massive heart attack. Dave's hand rose

TUESDAY

to his chest, grasping at his own fleeting breath. The wind whistled past as they came to a plateau and Sal stopped near a dry-stone wall. The question bubbled in Dave's throat whether they were at the chapel ruins but Sal shook his head to stop him from speaking.

As Dave steadied himself, he searched the distance. The sea he had glimpsed earlier stole what breath remained. He tightened his grip, the stone grazing his hands. Rivulets of water chiselled stories in a foreign tongue and whispers came to accompany the wind. Mothered by sugar-dusted mountains and coddled in cloud, the bay guarding the hill's secrets found its voice.

'Come,' it said. 'Learn to be free again.'

In that briefest of moments, Dave wanted only that. He closed his eyes and released the wall, arms falling to his sides. His muscles liquified as the bay called again, addressing him by name. Emboldened whispers invited him to leave everything and let the wind scoop him into the sky. He wanted to be free. Of course he did! Liberated from the pressure to be something he never could be. Free to follow a path he could call his own. Dave opened his mouth, dragging air into his lungs and trying to remember when he had last taken time to breathe.

His eyes sprang back open.

Sal stood before him, nodding.

Three wishes. Dave had forgotten.

Bile rose in his throat, that morning's meeting on replay. Double Barrel's whiter-than-white smarm, Carol's disappointment. Dave's insides churned, wind stabbed his eyes, his nostrils flared. Skittish words came thick and fast, pummelling his skull. He had to decide. Only three wishes.

Don't let Carol leave me.

Don't let Dr Double Barrel fire me.

There were two. He needed a third. Quick, quick . . .

'Really?' asked Sal, shaking his head.

'What's wrong?' Dave frowned, realising Sal addressing him mid-wish making meant he'd messed this up, like everything else.

'What does Jolene say?' asked Sal.

'Jolene?'

'People don't get it anymore, do they? Too busy asking for what they don't want to happen, rather than what they do. Reacting to circumstance, to what those around them are doing. Don't you ever think about what you, Dave Welch, want?'

'Well, I don't want to be here!'

Sal rolled his eyes.

Dave's teeth ground together. 'I never asked to come and now you tell me I'm doing it all wrong!' His hands rose with his voice. 'You really are a—'

'Come on, let's go.'

'But my third wish!' Dave shouted after him.

'You've already had three.' Sal bounced an annoyed path down the hill.

He'd wished to not lose his wife or his job. To keep his wife and his job, that was the same thing. Either way, it was two not three. Sal had no reason to be upset. It was Dave who had been marched up a desolate Icelandic hill for no bloody reason.

'Don't leave me here!' Dave shouted. 'It's freezing.'

'Your choice to spend your days in your underpants. And you think *I'm* strange.' Sal's anger carried into the wind as he disappeared out of sight.

Dave glanced down. Standing proud, the hairs on his legs looked back at him as blades of grass laced his toes. The wind returned to converse with him. As he closed his eyes, humming vibrated his entire being.

CHAPTER FOUR

'What are you doing sat in the dark?'

Dave opened his eyes. His toes grasped at the woollen pile, hardy Merino sheep unable to rid his legs of biting cold. Seth inspected him with the level of disdain that teenagers reserve for their parents.

'Well?' said Seth. 'Why are the curtains closed?'

'What?' Dave rubbed his thighs, casting a glance at the microwave. 'Nineteen nineteen! Shit! Is that the time?'

'No, Dad, it's an alien life form communicating with you the only way it knows how.'

A snigger drew Dave's attention to the hallway leading to the front door. Behind Seth stood a lanky silhouette as straight as a beanpole.

'So?' asked Seth. 'What *are* you doing sat in the dark?'

Dave looked to his lap, remembering his choice of novelty underwear. Spidey was no help now. He tried to cross his legs, the chair clinging to them. He could spend most of the day in his underpants but usually feigned normality for Seth coming home from school. It was gone seven o'clock.

'Working late,' said Dave, staring at a laptop that had long since signed off.

'Rodric is helping me with my Comp Sci homework,' said Seth, foraging in the kitchen cupboards.

The beanpole emerged from the shadows. Neck sausaged in a white shirt and burgundy tie, it nodded at Dave. He didn't look like Seth's usual buddies, their limbs as floppy as their sun-kissed hair. Rodric couldn't lift a surfboard, let alone ride one.

Dave's attention returned to his son, tieless and bearing a grin that would give a Cheshire cat a run for its money. 'Where's your mum?'

Wind tickled Dave's ears, humming a forgotten song. Endless sea and white-capped mountains. Dad had been there, and that strange little man. Dave massaged his head, pummelling the follicles to talk. A flag fluttered in the wind.

'Iceland?' mumbled Dave, eyes bouncing between Seth and the clock.

A dream, of course. He'd been asleep for hours. There had been that phone call, the conference . . .

'Yeah, that's right, Dad. Mum's gone to Iceland,' said Seth, armed with a pack of Gouda slices and a tub of chocolate spread. 'Let's hope she did. There's never anything to eat.'

Another snigger rumbled through the house.

'Enjoy yourselves, you two,' said Dave, impatiently.

'Doing homework?'

Dave needed to be alone, catch up on the day. He couldn't be taking three-hour naps when he had a project to find. Everything was coming back to him now. The First Minister wanted to know *how the Agency tasked with promoting foreign investment into the Cardiff region could demonstrate it hasn't been pissing taxpayers' money up the wall.*

TUESDAY

'Oh Dad,' said Seth, nodding towards Dave's groin. 'Don't forget, with great power comes great responsibility.'

Dave forced a smile.

'Nice to meet you, Mr Welch,' said a melodic voice from the bottom of the stairs, forcing, if Dave wasn't mistaken, the 'ch'.

'Don't slam the—'

Seth's bedroom door slammed shut, shaking the house.

―――

Clothed in a pair of tracksuit bottoms and nursing a cup of tea, Dave turned on his computer, his eyes never leaving his telephone. Two ticks confirmed Carol had received his message but as hard as he stared they refused to turn blue. Gone eight o'clock, she could be working late. The Welsh Assembly wasn't Westminster, but any job that hints at importance ensures the illusion with late nights and unwarranted travel. Dave fell into the chair. She might have mentioned she'd be away and he'd forgotten. Meetings in far-flung corners of Wales weren't uncommon. You could get to London and back twice, the time it took to drive to Bangor. That must be it. She was on a work trip and had no connection.

They had lost connection.

Dave thought back to the meeting that morning. She couldn't fancy Dr Double Barrel, could she? Dave knew little about Dr Rhys-Wyn Llewellyn-Jones. He had sprung out of nowhere a few months ago. Not your usual civil servant who had served in the trenches, but a fresh face armed with a background in international finance. *A valuable leader who we thank for bringing his private sector experience to the Agency and the benefit of Cardiff and its already thriving economy*, the internal memo had concluded. Or something equally sycophantic.

Dave encouraged the laptop back to life, rolling his eyes as he was reminded for a second time that day to *donate blood and do some good*. No time for saving others, he had his own skin to save. He clicked into his email. Five years on the job had relied on shapeshifting and massaging the truth: Internet research to uncover start-ups that had raised millions in venture capital and fabricated non-disclosure agreements preventing him from revealing any detail. The truth was, there was no transatlantic pipeline. No pipes, no oil.

Dave pulled at the waistband on his tracksuit bottoms. Noticing a pink wave tracing a line up his leg, he realised he must have pulled Seth's trousers out of the washing basket instead of his own. He sighed as he scrolled his new emails.

Wales Online
Weekly Round-Up
First Minister announces government-wide audit in an . . .
Jolene Jones
Mindful Tuesdays
Hi all, Just a quick reminder for those of you who mi . . .

It couldn't be Tuesday. No newspaper did a weekly round-up on a Tuesday. Dave double-checked his calendar, remembering his call with the Chairman only that morning. *See you next Tuesday*. Damn it. It *was* Tuesday and Dave should have been in the office. Their hybrid working plan had started out as future-of-work-flexible, whereby you chose whatever two days of the week you wanted to come into Cardiff House and worked the other three from home. The brainchild of Dave's lesser spotted boss, Digby Jenkins, Head of International, flexibility had soon morphed into a free-for-all and an acute reminder that Digby himself had become surplus to requirements. Starting this week, Digby had made Tuesdays mandatory office days for the International team, commencing with a two-hour team meeting. Jolene's proposition to follow the meeting with mindfulness had subsequently been endorsed by Human Resources. Dave set a reminder for the team meeting the following week, noting to mindfully invent a dental appointment straight afterwards.

Rhys-Wyn Llewellyn-Jones
Following our conversation
David, A productive conversation this morning, I think . . .

Dave deleted the email without reading it.

'Three weeks,' he said to Cyclops, who sprawled the kitchen floor, his torso at one-hundred-and-eighty degrees to his lower half. 'I know I have three weeks.'

Proud owner of two fully functioning eyes, Cyclops meowed a response that roughly translated as not giving a shit. It was the reaction he had to most things, including being named after an oval-shaped barrel wave off the coast of Western Australia.

A ping.

Dave checked the clock again and returned to his inbox to see a new email.

Dustin Harris
Future UK operations
Dear Dave, Our company works out of Michigan . . .

Dave stared at the email. American? He glanced back at the microwave. It would still be daytime over there. He didn't know any Dustin Harris. Future operations, that sounded positive. Nobody ever entitled an email like that. It had to be a generic mailing.

'Just open the bloody thing and you'll know,' Dave muttered to himself, clicking on the email.

Dear Dave,
Our company works out of Michigan in the automotive industry as a Tier One brakes supplier to major OEMs, notably feeding into ramped-up electric vehicle production in the States. We are currently looking to support our development in the European market by setting up a manufacturing facility.

It couldn't be! Dave had heard of projects falling into laps, but never his. At least, not in the past five years. Their marketing had to be working. He'd have to let Maya the marketing whizz know, not that he saw his younger sister much. The family high-flyer had made wiser choices, shipping herself off to France at a young age, avoiding marriage and children and rarely returning to visit. Dave leant in, absorbing his unexpected fortune. It was too good to be true.

We have heard a lot about your location from your recent marketing campaign and hope to schedule a visit with you soon.

Good God!

It's late where you are, and I'm travelling for the next couple of weeks, so not expecting an immediate reply. But I have your number from when we met in the States. Detroit, wasn't it? I will call you when I am back. In the meantime, please pull together for me what you can.
Yours,
Dustin Harris

TUESDAY

SVP – International Development – Great Brakes
+1 647 123 487

Damn, shit and blast! Dave had never met this guy. He'd never been to Detroit. It had been approved and booked for him to attend the *US Electric Car Show* but he'd developed a bad case of tonsillitis before take-off. He'd never told work he'd cancelled. You couldn't get the money back. *The Only Green Way is Essex* campaign had been launched there. It had been all over LinkedIn. The email was for Colchester Dave, it had to be. Having climbed to unexpected heights, the rollercoaster of emotion left Dave nauseous as it plummeted to the floor.

It *was* too good to be true.

Dave's back straightened, his mouth falling open.

Hang on.

Colchester Dave was at a private clinic, investing in a hip replacement the money he had saved to buy a static caravan in Leigh-on-Sea. He wouldn't be back for weeks . . . and Dustin's number was at the bottom of his email. All Dave needed to do was to call Dustin before he had time to put in a call to Colchester. Dave had no idea what he would sell him, but he had time to prepare as Dustin was travelling. Colchester, Cardiff . . . probably down the road for an American. Hardly a talented nation when it came to geography. Dave had once consumed three glasses of Moët & Chandon at the British Consulate in New York while trying to explain that he worked to bring investment to a small Celtic country, and not to the largest mammals known to man.

'Good night, Mr Wel*tch*,' said a voice from the hallway, as Dave reread the email, trying to remember if Michigan was on the East or West coast.

'Good night, Rod*ric*,' he replied, now convinced the

beanpole was intentionally putting emphasis on the last syllable.

The front door slammed.

'Haven't seen him before,' said Dave to his son.

'Bit of a nerd. Tried to get him to do my Comp Sci homework while I was talking to Jezz in Florida,' said Seth.

'Late, isn't it?'

'No school tomorrow. Some teacher training thing. Can't you remember a thing I tell you?' Seth's voice trailed off as he reached the landing.

'Don't—'

The bedroom door slammed.

Dave scratched his groin and returned to his laptop. If this email proved as promising as it sounded, it could save his job. A big win for Wales and Carol might see him in a different light too. When did wishes come true? Dave laughed. Wishes in dreams with strange little men at that! In any case, Colchester Dave would never be any the wiser. All's fair in love, war and saving your own lazy arse.

CHAPTER FIVE

'What's it this week, Dave? Doctor? Dentist? Hamster eat your mantra?' Hands on hips, Jolene stared at him.

Dave frowned, wondering whether he had ever seen an adult wear dungarees. 'What?'

'You're about to tell me you can't stay for mindfulness, when you of all people could do with it most.' Pity seeped through her Harry Potter spectacles.

Dave checked his watch. 'It's four o'clock.'

'Is there a better time of day to be fully present?'

'I mean—'

'Bet you thought you'd missed it again, running straight off after the team meeting this morning?' Jolene smiled. 'Lucky for you, it's been moved today.'

'Lucky old me,' muttered Dave, regretting his sarcasm. He needed Jolene on side.

'It's amazing you made the team meeting. Where were you last week? I'm forever covering for you. Are you okay?'

Dave offered a smile, grateful for the modicum of compassion. It made a change from being likened to shit on a stick, not that he'd seen much of his wife the past week. Team building in Aberystwyth accounted for two days; other absences remained a mystery. Dave shook his head. He needed to focus. Like an actor who has forgotten his lines – or never knew them – he'd been battling with stage fright and hadn't yet contacted Great Brakes. Coming to mindfulness might be his chance to appeal to Jolene's sense of compassion. What had she been spouting at Digby? Not compassion . . . the essential quality for productive teamwork . . .

'Empathy, Jolene. That's what I need from you.'

'Sorry?' Jolene pushed her glasses up her nose.

'You haven't been replying to my mails.'

'You haven't been attending my mindfulness classes. Anyway, I've been busy.'

Dave raised an eyebrow.

'You know I can't tell you.'

Jolene was involved in many an environmental cause, actions often involving criminal damage and pursuable in a court of law.

'Listen.' Dave pulled Jolene through the archway into the kitchen and dropped his voice. 'My neck's on the line. I need to find a project.'

He had a project. The problem was Dustin at Great Brakes had sent a second email containing a detailed information checklist. Dave couldn't pick up the phone and chat about the weather. If he was going to approach Dustin, he had to be well-prepared. He had one shot at swiping the project from under the nose of Essex. The problem was he knew very little about the *Green, Green Tech of Home*; Jolene did.

Laughter ricocheted around the eight square metres of black melamine.

'You've had five years to find a project and you haven't,' said Jolene. 'Why you getting your knickers in a twist this week? Anyway, we don't want to be bringing in any old shit to Wales now, do we?'

A lecture on the evils of greenwashing hung in the air. Using the first six months of her Head of Northern Europe tenure to fine-tune a sustainability matrix in Excel, Jolene had spent the following three years in no way inclined to be civil to any company crossing her path. Digby had resigned himself to Scandinavia not being a key market for Wales and decided Jolene's 'relentless drive and enthusiasm' more adapted to promoting the *Green, Green Tech of Home*. His decision had left the rest of the team aghast, but Digby was a keen golfer; the last thing he needed was a big foreign investment project to manage.

Dave reached for a lonely custard cream that had fallen out of its packet next to the kettle. It was quickly snatched out of his hand.

'No one ever speak to you about palm oil?' asked Jolene, the biscuit journeying the length of the kitchen to land on the European teabag mountain rising like Snowden from the food waste bin.

Dave stared at Jolene, debating whether he could tell her the reason he had a gun to his head. Even if Jolene collected cautions, hers were for worthwhile causes. In fact, he had no idea how the Chairman knew about Las Vegas. Carol wouldn't have told him, would she?

'It's Dr Double Barrel,' said Dave.

'What about him?'

'It's him who gave me the deadline.'

'So, tell him—'

'I think he's shagging Carol.'

'The smarmy little arsehole.'

'CB what?' asked Dave, admiring an aquamarine sky. His palms caressed the concrete beneath him, absorbing the impromptu June heat that had followed high on the heels of the previous day's deluge.

'D,' said Jolene, bringing the joint they had been smoking into his immediate eye line.

'And you're sure it doesn't have the same effect as weed?' he said as the ficus at his feet split into three. Three ficuses or was it three fici? Dave took the joint from Jolene, brought it to his lips and inhaled.

'Takes the edge off life, love. Looks like you need it.'

Dave questioned how, in that case, CBD was different to weed, or to what Jolene sold as mindfulness over many a coffee break. Mindfulness that today, without hesitation, had been pushed to next Tuesday. On elaborating on his suspicions regarding Carol's choice of *Mr Grey*, Jolene had snatched the forbidden custard creams and marched them out of the fire exit and up two flights of stairs to Cardiff House's little-known roof terrace. The last ten minutes had been spent listing Dr Double Barrel's failings as a Chairman – and human being – and rolling a rather large joint.

'He's got to be about eighty,' said Jolene.

'Fifty-seven,' replied Dave. 'Youngest man to ever be Chairman apparently.'

'Wouldn't be the youngest woman, would he?' Jolene rolled her eyes.

Smoke disappeared into the blinding sun, Dave allowing Jolene her daily five minutes on gender equality in the workplace. Of course, the Chairman was male, pale and stale. So was Dave, not that it advanced *his* career in the slightest. Lacking the Celtic or financial credentials placed him a hair's breadth on the wrong side of entitlement, a position surely as frustrating as losing the fight to *a narcissistic and stubbornly misogynistic patriarchy.*

'So?' said Jolene. 'What you gonna do?'

'Gonna do?'

'About double-barrelled dickhead.'

Dave laughed, smoke catching his throat.

'I'm going to find a project . . . make everyone realise I'm not the washed-up walkover they think I am.'

'Gonna find it in the rugby scores you spend your time reading, are you?'

Dave tried to sit up, realising his limbs no longer cared. Part of Dave, on the other hand, did. He needed to prove himself to both the Chairman and his wife. Get his career and marriage back on track. He'd let himself go in too many ways, fallen into laziness. He'd been thinking about it again last night, feigning sleep as Carol slid into bed at two thirty, smelling of grapefruit face wash and infidelity. At least she'd come home. This ship could be turned around.

Dave grunted as he hoisted himself onto his elbows. There was a five-hour time difference with Michigan, he'd checked. He was going to call Great Brakes before the day was out over in the States, front it and say he was from Cardiff. Dustin wouldn't care, but it would improve Dave's chances if he did it before Dustin entered into any discussion with Colchester.

'What time is it?' he asked, squinting at Jolene.

'Got a company meeting, have you?' Laughter bounced off the concrete.

'Would that be so much of a surprise to you?' Dave sat upright.

'Oh, come on! We always joke about you pulling your pipeline off the web ten minutes before the team meeting.'

'Doesn't mean I'm as useless as you're making out.'

'I never said—'

'Anyway, how's the *Green, Green Tech of Home* marketing coming on? Last time I looked, you weren't reaping in the projects either?'

'Touché,' said Jolene, passing the joint back to Dave. 'You hear what Digby said about the audit? There's no way we're all staying.'

Dave declined the joint with a shake of the head, reaching instead to touch Jolene's arm. His eyes danced with the swallows that inked a V formation up her biceps. 'Ignore me. I'm being a dick. Sorry.'

'You are.' Jolene held up the joint. 'Good job I brought the proper stuff.'

The atmosphere lightened and Dave thought on his colleague's words. If Jolene was concerned, like him, about losing her job, it could be his way in. Electric vehicles should be right up her street. It fell into one of the green boxes in the centrefold of the brochures they'd been unable to shift. To be fair, Jolene had insisted them a waste of trees. Four paragraphs summarised their target sectors, containing enough semantic obscurity to cover any potential investment project: data-driven world, e-health, sustainable living and . . .

'Decarbonised economy,' said Dave. 'That includes electric cars, right? I think I have something that could help us both out.'

Through a cloud of smoke, Jolene's face crumpled into a frown. 'In theory.'

'In theory what?'

'Electric cars are hailed as a panacea, love. Billions of them to hit net zero by 2050, but where's that electricity coming from?'

'Plug them in, don't you?' said Dave, returning to a horizontal position and closing his eyes. All greenwashing to her, he should have known Jolene wouldn't want to help.

TUESDAY

His body weightless, Dave floated back to the Icelandic hill from his dream. A pervading silence greeted him, followed by a whistling wind that swept him up, out over the ocean and past homebound birds. He pierced the clouds, rose further and further . . .

He opened one eye, digging his nails into his palms and tuning back into Jolene. With fervour and frustration, she explained how fossil-fuel power stations make most of the electricity powering electric cars, and would continue to do so for the foreseeable future. Dave relaxed back into the concrete. He was still in Cardiff. He'd simply slipped into another dream state, like last Tuesday.

'Hardly anything from renewables. It's a bloody farce!' said Jolene, sucking on the joint. 'And the heavy metals they use, don't get me onto the water pollution.'

Not intending to, Dave let his eyelids drop once more. He'd heard Carol texting in the dark once she'd finally made it home. They'd drifted over the past few years. Seth hadn't been easy. A bright lad – brighter than his father – but his grades had slumped.

'It's a curriculum for yesterday and not tomorrow,' Seth would say. 'When there won't be a tomorrow thanks to your generation screwing up the planet.'

So, Seth surfed – waves and the Internet – and talked to millions of people online. About surfing. That would pay a mortgage later.

Dave sighed.

'Right?' said Jolene. 'It's depressing, isn't it?'

Dave agreed, unaware of what had collectively depressed them.

'And there's that arsehole at the top getting us to chase bloody waterfalls.'

'Waterfalls?'

'Gigafactories.'

'You what?'

'The fast flowing, the exciting . . . the green, green tech of home. What's wrong with supporting our own businesses, our farmers, local supply chains. That's sustainability too, you know. But no, we have to seek money and glory on the other side of the world . . . just so it blows up in our faces later.'

Jolene lifted her head towards the sun, Dave spying an egress. He didn't need to retain the entirety of what she'd said to know it wasn't worth mentioning the brakes project again. He'd have to go it alone. Do a bit of swotting up this evening and bite the bullet.

'Sorry again about before,' he said, changing the subject to something they would be able to agree on. 'I don't want Carol to leave, that's all.'

'People don't get it anymore, do they? You're too busy asking for what you don't want to happen. Focus on what you *do* want.'

Dave frowned at the moment of déjà-vu. 'Maybe I'm not the man she wants me to be.' He prodded his distended belly.

'Why you always worrying about what others want you to be?'

Dave raised his head, remembering where he'd heard the same questions. 'What do y—'

The fire door slammed shut.

Dave fell onto the hot concrete. Who *was* Dave Welch? And what did he want if it wasn't to sink into the flagstones and disappear forever? No one would miss him. But this project had fallen into his lap. It was his chance. No one apart from Jolene contested electric vehicles. Anyway, Great Brakes just made the brakes, and great ones if you believed their name. What harm could be done with a brake? If anything, they saved lives.

TUESDAY

Dave squinted and checked his watch. Four thirty. A few more minutes, then he'd grab some sushi for dinner, dip into Jolene's files on the shared server, prepare himself and call Dustin. He could do this. People believed anything said with enough authority. And it wouldn't entail a lot of work getting them to Wales. After all, Great Brakes had come to him.

He wasn't being completely honest though, was he? It wasn't only stage fright. The curtailed conversation with Jolene had served as a loud reminder. Dave hadn't undertaken the proper due diligence, or *due militance* as he had coined it on discovering her thirty-five-page spreadsheet. It meant ensuring the company was financially viable, not embroiled in legal proceedings and not undertaking unethical practices such as bribery or child labour. It also involved ascertaining how environmentally friendly their operations were.

Dave couldn't be bothered. Even if he found the energy, imagine what he might dig up. Companies were asked to be whiter than white these days and allegations of pollution and greenwashing rife. There would always be something to sow the seeds of suspicion, Jolene would ensure that! Dave needed a project and one had been delivered to him on a plate. On paper, it ticked all the boxes. What more was there to discuss? The world needed electric cars and Wales needed investment. Governments had targets, so did he.

Dave closed his eyes and counted his breaths one by one by one.

CHAPTER SIX

Brisk air electrified his lungs and forced open his eyes. Dave lay motionless, stomach tensing and his body resting on something hard. Unable to hear himself think, he tilted his head.

'Aaaagh!'

Wrenched into a sitting position by his own screaming, Dave looked up at several basalt ledges, tapering the higher they stacked. Forging a merciless path from the heavens, water misted his face and pummelled his eardrums.

'Jesus Bloody Christ!' he shouted, his anguish meeting with a sigh.

The water that arrived with such gumption gathered in a crystalline pool around the boulder on which he sat, before carving a quieter route down the hillside. Breath seeped out of Dave as he edged his attention towards the inevitable. At the edge of the water, a red-hatted Sal gifted him a broad smile and a cagoule.

'Take this!' The turquoise coat landed on Dave's knees. 'You rarely come prepared. Have this idea you can waltz through life without a care in the world.'

TUESDAY

Curiosity — mixed with no desire whatsoever to converse with the strange little man again — pushed Dave to return to the noise behind him. Screaming long-held truths, the tumbling water demanded to be heard. Dave swallowed as his throat tightened and his eyes filled with tears. He hadn't cried since Dad died. He took a deep breath, leant back and tilted his head to retain the deluge. Higher ledges shying from view, it was impossible to see where the waterfall started or how high it rose.

'A hundred metres,' said Sal.

'Is that your answer to everything?' asked Dave, regretfully remembering the hill they had climbed together.

'Too close to see properly.' Sal laughed. 'Can't see the wood for the trees. Or is that the waterfall for the water! Look at those guys.'

Dave wiped his eyes and followed Sal's finger. Further down the hillside a family of camera tripods stood obediently in a row, a firing squad of lenses pointing at them.

'Enjoy the peace while you can. Timers on, they run up and stand in a line, like monkeys in a zoo. Too busy looking the part to be the part.'

Dave frowned as orders were shouted in a foreign tongue. Seven fingers pressed seven buttons and the same number of photographers started to sprint up the rocky path. Dave debated why they would need more than one photo and wondered where he was this time.

'Never seen a waterfall?' asked Sal.

Dave remembered Sal's capacity to read his thoughts, and penchant for sarcasm.

'Annoying, isn't it?' Sal threw his head back in laughter. 'Can't have any secrets from me! Come on, before that lot get here.'

Dave pushed himself off the boulder, stones crunching underfoot as he landed. Splashing through the glacial water and never questioning Sal's command, he reached the path that carved through the hillside's freshly plumped duvet of moss.

'This a different part of Iceland then?' Dave shouted after Sal, who bounced ahead, boots splaying outwards.

'Lots of fishing here. Big business. Must fish as much as possible and yet all the while we chuck whatever we like into the sea.'

Dave ran to catch up. 'But why are we here?'

Sal stopped in his tracks and turned around.

'Suppose you think this has nothing to do with you?'

Dave shrugged.

'Let's talk about this project you've found, shall we?'

'How do you . . .'

'You know there's something not quite right about it.'

'I don't know anything.'

'Because you won't follow up on your doubts.'

'It came to me when I needed it.'

'And that's more important than this?' Sal stretched an arm.

'My future more important than a waterfall in Iceland?' Dave noticed another ledge had come into view, making six. 'Well, yes!'

'Because the Chairman wants you to find a project so you can keep that job you hate? And by keeping that job you hate, Carol might love you again?'

'Bit close to the bone.'

Sal threw his hands in the air. 'Have you thought about what we talked about last time?'

Dave's frown met with a sigh louder than the gallons of water crashing behind them. He remembered his last visit and three wishes, of which he'd only been granted two.

'Oh no, you made three,' said Sal. 'Sure, the first one was a bit vague. Always helps to be clearer.'

TUESDAY

He'd wished for the Chairman not to fire him, for Carol not to leave. Then, he'd been stopped in his tracks by a tantrum not unlike this one.

'You said you wanted to learn to be free,' said Sal. 'Be what you want to be.'

'I *thought* it. I never *said* it.'

'Your thoughts are actions, Dave. They sow the seeds of what you become.'

'Maybe I want to be successful? Like my sister. Not the balding failure my wife, son and boss think I am.'

'And what if that's the problem right there?'

'The—'

Dave's voice disappeared into the wind as Sal continued down the path, a red cagoule descending all the way to his knees. Below it flapped a pair of hiking trousers.

Hurrying to keep up, Dave was soon hampered by the seven photographers. He slid to the edge of the path, greeting them as they passed. Seven heads bowed back. Tired with the edginess of the day's conversation and noticing Sal a good twenty metres ahead, Dave stopped. A flirtatious breeze caressed his neck, whispering in passing to pause, take stock, breathe. The hillside on which he stood rolled into a gaping bay and a sleeping sea, further questioning the need to rush anywhere. Dave closed his eyes, his nostrils flaring as one breath after another the tension flushed from his body.

He smiled.

His eyes sprang back open, an unexpected fear of being left alone gripping him.

Dave held his breath, noticing a figure stooping in the moss. Keeping one eye on the red cagoule further down the path, he tried to focus on the crumpled bundle of coat and wiry hair. He'd heard his voice last time. It couldn't be

Dad. Not Ted the Turnip King. Well, royalty until the squeeze had started.

Dave squinted. The huddled figure disappeared.

Of course, Dad wasn't there. Dying when Dave was in his twenties, Dad barely occupied his thoughts anymore. Alive, he had dominated them. His, those of the entire family and people in much higher places. Ted had vehemently opposed joining Europe back in the seventies, or the European Economic Community as it had been called. Said it would be the beginning of the end for the British neep. He'd shouted, protested and watched business slowly dwindle, diversification into other root vegetables unable to prevent the slide. A loathing for the French had manifested, Dad insisting to Dave's French teacher, Madame Beardsley, at every parents' evening that they'd always been a pushy lot.

'The only reason Concorde has an 'e' on the end is to please them,' Dad would say, the recycled joke humouring everyone but him.

Dave smiled, but the fear quickly returned. His stomach sank as he searched the hillside. Having arrived at the army of tripods, Sal placed lens caps on the cameras, one by one. Dave ran to catch up.

'You're not?' he winced, holding his side. He really was getting out of shape. He could barely do a flight of stairs anymore.

'Call me old-fashioned, but it's not about the photo. It's about soaking up the experience whilst you're here. Get it? Soaking up?'

A few metres away from the boulder on which Dave had been sat, the seven tourists blurred to twice their number. Dave waited for his vision to realign. 'But you can't—'

Above, arms and legs sprawled, limbs touching limbs to

TUESDAY

form a human chain. Successive flashes sent a misplaced cheer tumbling down the hillside.

'That'll teach them!' said Sal, laughing.

'You really are a strange little man,' said Dave, his voice peaking with what he recognised as Jolene's much-prized empathy for fellow human beings, who were *simply trying and failing*.

'I'm not!' said Sal. 'Well, maybe a little . . .' Sal reached for the bobble on top of his hat, paused and studied Dave.

'What's up?' asked Dave.

'What time is it?'

Dave checked his watch. 'Seven fifteen.'

'Wow, you were asleep for a while on that rock.'

Dave yawned, recalling the previous night. 'I do feel refreshed. Every cloud and all that.'

'That's eight fifteen back in Wales. It should be okay.'

'Okay?'

'Too late to do research and call now, isn't it?' said Sal, turning on his heels.

'What the—'

CHAPTER SEVEN

Dave's shouting woke him. His eyes snapped open and his torso jerked into a seated position. A reddened sky absorbed the sounds of a city evacuating lubricated clientele. Cardiff House . . . the roof terrace. Alone, apart from a solitary ficus that looked as bad as he felt. He rubbed his head, its contents rattling.

Dave reached for his phone that lay face down on the flagstone, stopping himself on knowing it was quarter past eight. A raspy inhale invited his tongue on a furry path around his mouth, the metallic taste making him wince. Bloody Jolene and her spliffs. He'd been out for the count, dreaming of Iceland again. There was no way it could be quarter past eight.

Dave turned over his phone.

'Shit!'

Dustin . . . Great Brakes. Dave pushed himself to his feet. It was gone three o'clock in the afternoon in Michigan and he still hadn't prepared any information. He wobbled towards the fire door, angry at Jolene for having delayed him on purpose. He stopped, remembering Jolene didn't

TUESDAY

know about the project. He hadn't told her in the end. For one, the project hadn't come to him by honest means, and two, from what he had retained, electric vehicles were the next scourge of modern society. For three, he hadn't researched the company or done any due militance. Due diligence! Jesus! They said that stuff made you paranoid.

In a sprint down to the seventh floor, Dave missed every other stair, the image of a hillside rolling into a welcoming bay flooding his mind. Why more dreams of Iceland? He'd never been there. Never wanted to. Not to mention imagining Sal and Dad again. He had to get his shit together.

Darkness lurking behind the glass-panelled door at the end of the hallway, Dave fumbled in his pocket. Coins tumbled to the floor as a badge emerged. He smacked it at a black box on the wall, a persistent red light flashing back.

'Let me help you.' Inquisitive brown eyes peered out from a plump face barely as high as his shoulders.

Dave tried not to grimace at the woman's bulbous nose. 'Sorry, do I—'

'The cleaner, love.' She wafted her badge in front of the black box. A click accompanied the red light turning green. 'Bit late isn't it?' She lisped the 's'.

'Could say the same to you.'

'Got a few jobs on the go, Mr Welch.'

'But how do you—'

'Know your name?' The woman readjusted her headscarf. 'Used to play for Wales, didn't you? Prop forward, yes?' The final letter loitered in the empty hallway.

'Scrum half.'

The woman pulled the door. 'You know what I mean.' She extended her arm. 'After you.'

Dave smiled as he strode to his desk. On rechecking the time, the semi-recognition of his previous success was soon forgotten. Twenty past eight. The thud of falling into his chair echoed through the empty office. He stabbed at the button to the top right of his keyboard, the machine sluggish thanks to a nap as long as his own. Dave slurped at cold coffee, eyes boring holes in the screen. *Today in 1919, Alcock and Brown took off for the first non-stop transatlantic flight* announced the Intranet homepage in a welcome message.

'Give a shit,' said Dave.

And remember here in Wales, we make wings for some of the world's best planes, continued the carousel. Dave wasn't sure who wrote this stuff. Tenuous as it was, he felt some sympathy. He'd struggle to craft five, never mind three hundred and sixty-five, chirpy things to say, let alone somehow link them to Cardiff.

A gurgling in his stomach reminded him he hadn't eaten and that it was probably too late to grab something. *Swshi Shack* next to the New Theatre would be closed. He'd have to spend his loyalty points another day. Customer of the month in May, at least he excelled in something. Dave went into the shared server, clicked on a folder called *Jolene*, another called *Green, Green Tech* and finally one called *Decarbonised Economy*.

'Right, let's get the show on the road,' he mumbled.

'Mr Welch?'

'Jesus Christ!' His hands grasped his chest.

Two nostrils hovered over him. A hand proffered a USB stick. 'Could I trouble you?'

'I'm—'

'It's for my son, he needs this printed off for school.'

'It's just—'

'His dad is such a fan. Shown him all your games.'

'Leave it with me.' Dave snatched the stick out of the woman's hand. She froze, not leaving his side. 'Shall I do it now?' he asked.

TUESDAY

Eager for her to leave, Dave clicked on the icon on the screen, then the only document on the USB stick and sent the Word document to print. He minimised the screen to get back to his research.

'It'll come off the—' Dave scanned the office but the woman had disappeared.

Arching his back, he stretched out the fatigue weighing upon him even though he'd been asleep for hours. He skim-read the files in the *Decarbonised Economy* folder, finally falling upon one called *Welsh Electric Vehicles Value Chain*. He yawned. He'd print it out to read tomorrow. Probably a bit late to make sense of it all now. He searched for the cleaner once more, the office still empty. Having forgotten to collect her USB stick, Dave saved a copy of the presentation on it so he could adapt it for purpose once he got hold of Dustin. No need to reinvent the wheel. On finishing, he noticed his mailbox had twenty-seven new messages. He scanned them, pausing on anything of interest.

Bryn Jones

About my invention
Dear Mr Welch, I believe this is your email. Just follow . . .

The persistent Mr Jones had Dave's email address. That was bad news. Where had he sent poor Bryn and his revolutionary find? A bench outside Cariad Tea Rooms. Dave shook his head. He had to stop pissing about. He deleted the email.

Rhys-Wyn Llewellyn-Jones

Our meeting today
David, A little disappointed you missed our catch up . . .

Shit! He'd missed the weekly *see you Tuesday* catch-up to

monitor where Dave was with his three-week ultimatum. How could he have forgotten? These 'trips' to Iceland were costing him. Dave clicked on the email.

David,
A little disappointed you missed our catch up. I can only assume you are working hard on a new project to have something to tell me about?
Rhys-Wyn

Dave pushed back his seat, the headrest dropping to dig into his shoulders. No more stalling, he had to contact Dustin tomorrow. He had a project in his sweaty little palm. Dave rubbed his hands together, realising they were indeed a bit clammy. He shut down his computer, trying to focus. All he needed to do was absorb some key lines about Wales as a location for a brakes factory, call and wing it. He could further develop it later. Remembering the presentation he had printed, he made his way to collect it.

Light glowed from the sleeping printer. Dave snatched a pile of warm sheets of A4 and headed back to his desk, lifting in passing a Ferrero Rocher from the open box on Digby's desk. Carol had pushed them into Dave's hand that morning to mark Digby turning fifty-five. With Digby unaware of the caution, or so Carol said, Dave hadn't shared the Chairman's ultimatum with his direct boss. In any case, even if the team meeting had opened with a dramatic Dylan Thomas citation, spittle forming at the corners of Digby's mouth as he encouraged the team to *rage against the dying of the light*, it had ended, to everyone's surprise, with Digby announcing his early retirement in two months' time.

Dave flipped through the papers in his hands, one falling on the floor as he approached his desk. A neon tube light flickered above him as he bent to retrieve it and read the title: *The water cycle*. Realising it was the paper he had printed off for the cleaner's son, he decided to look for her at the other end of the office but was quickly distracted by the illustration at the top of the page. Pulling the paper closer, Dave's certitude churned inside him as his eyes traced water cascading over several rocky ledges into a crystalline pool.

He dropped the presentation on his desk and himself into the chair. Pushing at the headrest to relieve his shoulders, he knew there was only one way to find out. He tapped one letter at a time, mouthing the syllables that formed his Internet search.

'Wat-er-falls in Ice-land.'

The tube light blinked its final breath. Plunged into semi-obscurity, Dave clicked to the image results. There it was, first row, third picture. Dave leant in, holding his breath. He clicked again, a mix of curiosity and dread leading him to a Wikipedia page.

'Dynjandi is the largest waterfall in the Westfjords with a total height of ninety-nine metres,' read Dave. 'Its name translates from Icelandic to "thundering noise".'

Sal had said a hundred metres, but it was close enough. The cursor hovered over the picture next to the description, Dave took a lungful of air and zoomed. Tapering basalt ledges stretched into the sky. Dave counted. Six. A lichen-covered boulder nestled in a clear, still pool. Exactly where he had been, except he had never been there.

As thundering noise filled his ears, the office fell into a deeper silence.

CHAPTER EIGHT

Dave stopped scratching his scalp on remembering the hair trapped in the shower plug that morning. What did his grandmother used to say? *Old age never comes alone.* He was forty-nine for God's sake. It was hardly ancient. A bushy tail tickled his nose. Dave coughed as white paws stomped over his keyboard.

'Cyclops!' He scooped up the cat, dropping it on the floor. 'Look where you're going!'

He rubbed his thighs and the jeans he'd put on, Carol having announced a furniture delivery. Luckily he was dressed, as Seth had also come home early, accompanied by Rodric. The furniture in question was a new sofa for the front room, a sofa they neither needed nor had been delivered.

'Ring the changes,' Carol had said with a laugh, Dave wondering if the resolution was limited to the upholstered furniture in her life.

Dave glanced at the microwave. Four thirty. He needed to work out what he was doing. He still hadn't called Dustin at Great Brakes, having convinced himself it wasn't

TUESDAY

such a big deal. With Dustin out of the office for another week, there was no real fear of Essex getting the project, and other worries plagued Dave, like waking up on a roof terrace with an innate knowledge of an Atlantic island he had never visited.

In trying to piece together recent 'sleep' episodes, he had started to note anything he could remember. He read the items once more on the A4 sheet beside the laptop:

– Sal (reads my mind)
– three wishes (of which I had two) on a hill
– what do I really want to be?
– Dynjandi waterfall – 99/100m
– Dad (careful what you wish for)

Rather than list items, he had circled them as he'd been shown in a team strategy session to develop something called a mind map. Connecting lines were used to show links between ideas.

'*We all hold a beast, an angel and a madman in us*. Embrace them in our vision for Cardiff,' Digby had shouted, scaring a freshly recruited Jolene enough for her to reach for her handbag before realising her new boss often quoted Welsh poetry.

Dave stared at words that had enough rings around them for a graphologist to infer sexual frustration but boasted no lines. Nothing to connect anything to anything else. Debating if he hadn't left both beast and angel on the rugby pitch with his sporting career, Dave had, in any case, abandoned scribbling. Noting Iceland as the common denominator he had returned to the Internet to engage in deeper research. Rabbit holes had led to marauding Vikings, folkloric trolls and Hidden People, not to mention volcanoes. The island was riddled with them. When they weren't erupting and bringing international air travel to a halt, not much else happened over there, apart from fishing. There had even been a set-to with the British over fish. Who picked a fight over cod?

Dave sighed. He might not have answers but he had come to realise there was more to his discussions with Sal. When he wasn't berating Dave on his general attitude to life, he was sending warning signals about the Great Brakes project. A project that had, after all, magically appeared out of nowhere. That afternoon, Dave had also used his time on the Internet to start what he had been avoiding: due diligence. Confirming his fears, the article he had found stared back at him from his laptop.

'Dave, where are you?' Carol's voice rippled through the house, the front door slamming.

Dave minimised the open browser window and crumpled the mind map into a ball.

'Hi honey. I'm home,' he shouted, immediately regretting the sarcastic greeting. 'Did you have a nice day?'

Carol marched into the kitchen-diner. 'Where's the bloody sofa?'

'Ask bloody IKEA,' replied Dave, deciding there was no better time for sarcasm.

Carol thrust a pile of letters at him. 'They said this afternoon. Rhys said they're always late.

'I *know* they're late. I've been sat here all afternoon waiting for them.'

'You sit here every bloody afternoon, Dave.' Carol peered over his laptop. 'Got dressed, I see.'

Dave gazed into blue hollows of eyes, querying if they voiced disgust, despair or contempt. But he had a project now, or did he? Going by the allegations in that article, he probably did need to research the company further before proceeding. He also needed to keep the conversation light.

TUESDAY

'Good day, love?' he asked, opening one of the envelopes, his mind still on the project. Life had become a rollercoaster way before the vivid dreams and lost hours. The Great Brakes project was a gift from heaven if there was one. A ray of sunshine after months of rain.

'Rhys was telling me about his time in Canada today.' Carol's red-soled shoes tapped their way into the kitchen.

This project would be the one thing to impress her, and Dr Double Barrel. In his second email, Dustin had shared it would create three hundred new jobs. An investment of ten million pounds, it would also regenerate brownfield land down on the docks. Dave had found everything he needed in Jolene's presentation. By some stroke of luck, it also contained a financial simulation for an electric vehicle Tier One supplier. And they could even offer grant aid, thanks to the Chairman's brainchild: the *Welsh Technology Accelerator Fund*.

'So?' Carol leant over the computer.

They locked eyes, Dave now sure the sentiment he had found difficult to decipher was contempt.

'Do you listen to a bloody word I say? What does the bank want?'

'The bank?'

Carol placed her hands on her hips. 'The letter in your hand.'

Dave unfolded the letter he hadn't had time to read. 'Five hundred quid! What the—'

Carol joined Dave. 'They're increasing the mortgage by how much?'

'"With interest rates rising to five point two this month,' read Dave, we are writing to inform you that your mortgage payments will increase by—"'

'Five hundred and fifty-six bloody pounds,' finished Carol. 'Thieving bastards. How can we afford that?'

By not buying sofas we don't need, thought Dave.

'Well, that's the end of all those trips for you!'

'Trips for me? Work paid for Vegas.'

'You've been all over the place since this *Green, Green Tech of Home* campaign started.'

'I never went to Detroit. Have you forgotten my tonsillitis? Was lucky not to have developed—'

'Septicaemia. How can we forget? What I haven't forgotten is your bill from some bar on the Strip.'

Dave eyeballed Carol. The words 'IKEA' and 'sofa' lingered at the back of his throat. 'Listen, don't worry.' He reached for Carol's hand as it pulled away. 'We'll find a way. We always have.'

Carol fixed him with a stare. Dave waited for a response. One blink for yes, two for no. He was losing her, if he hadn't already. He tried to remember a time they used to smile hellos and goodbyes, arrivals and departures accompanied by a kiss.

Seth burst through the door, breaking the staring contest. 'Anything to eat?'

'Hiya, love,' shouted Carol, her eyes never leaving Dave. 'Find a bloody project. How difficult can it be?' she whispered under her breath. She turned and tapped her way towards Seth. 'Got some of those biscuits you like.'

Dave watched, an observer in his own film.

A ping.

He glanced heavenwards, thanking whoever proffered the chance to come back to his computer.

Dustin Harris
Future UK operations
Dear Dave, Our company works out of Michigan . . .

TUESDAY

Wondering why the same email was being resent, Dave clicked.

We have heard a lot about your location from your recent Green, Green Tech of Home *campaign and hope to schedule a visit with you soon.*

Gratitude now seized Dave's chest. It wasn't the same email at all. Dustin was citing *their* marketing campaign. He read on.

I will call you next week. In the meantime, please pull together for me what you can.
Yours,
Dustin Harris
SVP – International Development – Great Brakes
+1 647 123 4876

Well, there you had it. It was a sign! Dustin was considering Wales anyway. He had reached out to Essex first, received no reply from Colchester Dave and decided they weren't interested. A sign, yes! Not from the other side, there wasn't one of those, but this project was meant to be. For Dave. For Wales. An extra five hundred quid a month, they couldn't afford that on Carol's salary alone. He needed to get the presentation ready and over to Great Brakes sooner rather than later.

In returning to his laptop, Dave reopened his Internet browser. The news article he had found about Great Brakes stared back at him.

Water pollution: Adrian's Creek wants answers.

Dave took a deep breath. So what if there was an accusation of dumping mercury? The company had never been formally prosecuted. And even if there was some truth to it, industry always dirties its surroundings a little. That's industry, and Seth was forever saying the Earth's surface is covered in about seventy percent water. A tiny bit of effluent would get quickly diluted. Refusing projects when they knock on the door is refusing progress. What jobs would they have, audit or not, if they decided Wales had enough investment? People had to pay their bills. Dave had to pay his mortgage. Further research could wait. He would get that presentation ready this evening, show it to the Chairman during their meeting tomorrow and send it over to Dustin.

'Good evening, Carol. Mr Wel*tch*.'

Dave lifted his head. A spindly figure ambled towards the front door.

'Bye Rodric, love,' shouted Carol.

'Little shit,' mumbled Dave, opening PowerPoint.

CHAPTER NINE

'Dave?' Digby's hand hovered over the whiteboard, brandishing a red marker pen. 'Don't suppose you have anything for us?'

'Anything for you?'

Dave had been miles away. The IKEA delivery had arrived at half past seven in the evening. Dave ready to return it and save two months of mortgage payments, Carol had produced burnt orange cushions to match the mottled grey fabric. Argumentative assembly had followed, leaving no time to finalise the Great Brakes presentation. Dave had come to the office early in search of respite and a chance to work, forgetting it was Tuesday and the team meeting.

'*He who seeks rest finds boredom*, David. *He who seeks work finds rest.*'

Dave exchanged looks with Jolene, who mouthed 'Dylan Thomas' across the windowless meeting room.

'Projects, do you have any?' asked Digby.

Dave straightened in his chair. The meeting with the Chairman was at two o'clock that afternoon, by which time his presentation for Dustin had to be ready. He might as well use this opportunity to counteract Jolene's cynicism and field the Great Brakes project to get some collective input. What did they call it? Not collective input, collective . . . intelligence. Digby had dragged them to a seminar on that too. Led by a Buddhist called Keith from Abergavenny, it had ended in smashed saucers and obscenities when his doodlings were inadvertently erased from the whiteboard during the coffee break.

'Actually, I do have something to share,' said Dave.

Digby pressed the marker onto the whiteboard, Dave unsure what he was about to write as nothing had been said. With a resounding crack, the tip of the pen snapped. Dave ducked. It flew over his head, ricocheted off the wall behind him and pursued a downwards trajectory into Pierre's coffee.

'*Putain*! I can't drink that now.'

Pierre was the French placement student who had joined their team to cover 'Europe' as part of their lead generation strategy. Recognising himself unfit for purpose, Dave wondered how someone grappling with puberty could manage a whole continent. Pierre achieved it with an uninterrupted display of disdain, frequent references to the *grande école* he had attended and a grandfather whose tennis partner had been Jacques Chirac.

'Dave. Would you mind getting me another pen from the stationery cupboard?' asked Digby.

'Why me?'

Digby stretched his arms. 'The last in, David, carries the weight of being the first out.'

That wasn't Dylan Thomas. If Digby was insinuating Dave's head was on the block, he had to know about the ultimatum. Dave stared at Jolene. He'd been there longer than anyone, including her.

TUESDAY

'Seen the size of this room, Dave?' Jolene's eyes widened. 'You're the closest to the door. Me and Pierre can't get out if you don't move. You might as well go.'

Dave nodded at the mere practicality.

'I'll be back in a minute,' he said, banging his head on the wall and clipping his knees on the table as he pushed back his chair.

He closed the door on muffled French despair and ambled towards the printer room. Inhaling the freedom of an open-plan office, he grabbed a Ferrero Rocher from Digby's desk, admiring a man that spent even less time in the office than him.

On entering the printer room, Dave remarked it empty. Silent. Even the printer was turned off. Strange, he thought. As he walked towards the back of the room, the door behind him slammed and the metal blinds jangled shut.

Dave jumped. Inspecting an empty room, he shrugged and resumed walking.

Counting his steps one by one by one, he continued towards the stationery cupboard, opened the door, pressed the light switch and entered. It wasn't until that second door slammed shut, a bright light flooded the room and he found himself facing Sal in what he later learnt was a Dacia Dokker that Dave screamed.

———

'There's a pair of lungs.' Perched on one elbow, Sal smiled at Dave. 'Ever think of singing for a living?'

Lying on something soft, Dave scoured the obscurity.

'Jesus Bloody Christ!' he said as he sat up and his head smacked the roof.

'Not quite.' Sal sat up. 'Anyway, thought you didn't believe in all that?'

'All what?'

Dave rubbed his head. The doctor had said to avoid any more unintentional impacts, making Dave question if any bang to the head was ever intentional. He had to get back to the meeting. What was this? *The Lion, the Witch and the Wardrobe?*

'Look like Narnia to you?' Sal threw his head back in laughter. 'Anyway, you hate those meetings.'

Dave looked around, conceding it didn't resemble how he might imagine Narnia and he did loathe team meetings, but for once he had valuable input. Metal clanged under his soles, his hands sank into a mattress beneath him.

'Are we in a camper van?' he asked.

'Cheapest way to see Iceland.'

Dave sighed.

'I know, I know.' Sal's eyebrows took cover under his hat. 'It's the last place you'd want to see, cheap or not. Look, I haven't got long.'

'For what?'

'That thing. What do you call it? Due militance.'

'Diligence?'

Sal examined the van roof. 'That makes less sense. Never mind. It means checking out Great Brakes, right? It's a process you're supposed to follow, however exciting the project. It includes all the environmental stuff?'

'How do you—'

Dave stopped himself from asking how Sal knew things. He just did, including Dave skipping due militance. Diligence.

'I mean, how much do you know about this company?' continued Sal.

Dave straightened his back. Seriously? His one bit of

luck in five years in the job and he had to explain himself? Even Digby didn't ask this many questions. Well, he wouldn't if Dave could get back to the meeting.

'Ha! When have you ever said that?' Sal laughed.

'Listen, it's a great fit for Wales. It can bring value-added jobs thanks to an essential contribution to sustainable net-zero transport.'

'Can you hear yourself?'

Dave could. He winced. He was quoting their *Green, Green Tech of Home* marketing brochure.

'You're rushing this for other reasons.'

Dave opened his mouth to speak, thinking better of it. Of course, he was rushing it. His job was on the line, his marriage too. And soon they wouldn't have a house to live in.

'Come on!' shouted Dave. 'Electric vehicles, everyone wants a piece of that pie.'

'Do they? Including the kids mining cobalt in Africa?'

'Bloody hell. It's like coffee with Jolene. Without the coffee!'

'Can't you see it's exponential growth disguised as a solution to problems caused by . . . well, exponential growth.' Sal smiled. 'Do we really need more cars?'

'It wouldn't have been sent to me if it wasn't meant to be.'

'The world revolves around David Wel*tch*, does it?'

Dave stared at Sal. 'Did you say—'

'Your dad would remember the European Union quoted as a great thing for the British people. Didn't help his turnips now, did it?'

'Times change, I suppose?'

Dave's head filled with a vision of Dad sat at the kitchen table, head in hands. Dave had resented him for not wanting to pass the rugby ball in the garden when he was a kid. Dave had been on tour when the neighbours found Dad in the field. It took two paramedics to release the turnip in his hand. Five days later he was buried.

'There are winners and losers,' continued Sal. 'Because everything is connected, any losers make us all losers.'

Dave let his head fall into his hands. This project had seemed too good to be true from the outset. He hadn't *needed* to speak to Jolene. He could have searched her files without consulting her first. It's what he had done in the end. They were on a shared drive, after all. Fishy, that was what Dave had first thought on receiving Dustin's email.

'Fishy?' shouted Sal.

Dave jumped. Sal stared at him.

'The due militance, Dave.'

'Diligence.'

'Do it! I have to go. Busiest night of the year.'

'Tonight?'

'Summer solstice.'

Dave recalled Jolene's discussion over coffee that morning about Scandinavians rolling around naked in morning dew. She and her friends were going to improvise down near the beach in Barry.

Sal edged down the van and flung the back doors open. 'Wanna see where I'm from?'

Light flooded the van as Sal dropped into a field of indigo. Towering over a smattering of meek buttercups, an army of purple-hatted flowers paraded the sun-dappled hillside.

'Follow me!' shouted Sal.

Fresh air lured Dave to follow. Once outside, he recognised the car as the one in which he had first met Sal, back seats removed and windows blackened. Ahead, squatting atop a slight incline, sat a red-roofed church. Two elongated top windows and a lower round window afforded the place of worship an air of surprise.

'I've always thought that too.' Sal laughed as he disappeared into the field, his red head barely taller than the purple residents. 'Not quite what you were expecting, eh?'

Dave shook his head, his hand caressing the tapering flowers. His third time and it was anything but a barren and desolate lunar landscape.

'Armstrong came here, you know.'

'Louis?'

'Went to the moon, did he? To play the trumpet? No, Neil! It's you that brought up lunar landscape.'

'You can read my mind, but there's no need to be sarcastic.'

Sal laughed. 'Anyway, check it out. These lupins were brought from Alaska to revegetate that lunar landscape. Look at it now. Our purple friends have taken over, forcing other plants out. The planet is an ecosystem built on many equally delicate ecosystems. Different but all connected. Now, stop following me. I told you, I have to go.' Sal turned on his heels.

'You really are a very strange man,' shouted Dave.

Sal stopped in his tracks. His back to Dave, a hand pulled at the bobble on top of his red woolly hat. One by one, two enormous ears revealed themselves. The other hand straightened his hair.

'I'm not a man. I'm an elf.'

Disrupting the lupins in their evening manoeuvres, Dave thudded to the ground.

CHAPTER TEN

'Jesus wept!' Jolene knelt beside him.

'What do you know about elves?' The untethered words raced out of Dave as, propped up against a wall, he stared at a Ferrero Rocher mashed into the grey carpet.

Jolene grabbed his chin and peered at him. 'You been smoking again?'

His eyes danced around the same stationery cupboard he remembered entering a few minutes earlier.

'Bloody hell, Dave. You only went to get a marker.'

Silently hoping Jolene hadn't heard what he had said on coming around, Dave searched an excuse for her finding him on the floor.

'I must have fainted.'

'Been here all the time, have you?'

'Where else would I have been?'

Not Iceland, obviously. Dave glanced at Jolene. He couldn't tell her about the dreams, if that's what they were as he hadn't fallen asleep this time. He'd entered a cupboard, probably fainted . . . and then entered a dream state. That sounded about right. The door had slammed

TUESDAY

shut, he'd seen a bright light and found himself lying face to face with that strange little man. Strange little elf. That would explain why he found him so short. No, it wouldn't! Elves didn't exist. Not even in dreams.

'Dave!' Jolene tugged at his arm.

Dropping his head into his hands, he tried to recall more detail.

'Lupins . . .' he mumbled.

'The flowers?'

Dave stared at Jolene, not remembering uttering a word and convinced she was reading his mind, like Sal. He prodded his forearm to check if he was really there.

'Stop it!' Jolene snatched his finger. 'And why are you talking about flowers?' She twisted to sit next to him.

'You heard that?' Dave looked around the cupboard.

He wasn't going entirely mad. Jolene *had* heard him. Shit! That meant she'd probably also heard the bit about elves. He needed to talk to someone but he couldn't mention Sal, even if Jolene did relive pagan summer solstice rituals in a field off the B4265.

'This about the Chairman and Carol?' Bespectacled eyes magnified bright blue eyeliner.

Wondering why Jolene appeared a touch angry, Dave remembered elves weren't his only worry.

'Shh . . . I don't want everyone knowing.'

Jolene let out a laugh. Dave frowned.

'Who's going to hear?' Jolene's arm pursued a circular path, reminding Dave of one of those game shows. *Look what you could have won. Several reams of A4 paper, a range of highlighter pens and a bumper pack of staples.*

'So, nothing else you want to tell me?' asked Jolene.

Dave exhaled. He could have mentioned any number of things on coming round, hopefully not the caution. He shook his head. He was getting paranoid.

'It's tough at home,' he said, trying to pull himself together, 'but listen, I haven't been entirely truthful.'

'That's better.' Jolene smiled.

'Better?'

'I'm listening.' Jolene hugged her knees.

'The Chairman has given me three weeks to find a project otherwise I'm . . .' Dave fumbled in his pocket. 'What time is it?'

'Half past one,' replied Jolene before Dave found his phone.

'Shit! My meeting is at two.' Dave went to push himself to a standing position. 'Hang on a minute. Our meeting was first thing this morning. I've been—'

'Gone for four hours.'

'Four hours?'

'So, what the hell have you been up to?' shouted Jolene.

Bloody Sal was stalling him again.

'Half past one, that's half past . . .' Dave stopped the conversion into Eastern Standard Time, the enduring secrecy around the Great Brakes project coming back to him. 'Look, I need to go.'

With a swivel of the hips, Jolene swung around to straddle him.

'Jesus Christ! What's got into you?' said Dave.

'Saw it on the wrestling channel. You're not going anywhere Dave Welch, not until you tell me what the hell is going on.'

Dave squinted as the cupboard door flew open.

'It's me that should be asking both of you that.'

The fragrant odour of money and power diffused through the room, cloying at his nostrils. As Dave picked up Jolene by the waist, Dr Double Barrel leant on the doorframe, sliding one hand in his pocket.

TUESDAY

'Chairman,' squeaked Jolene, dismounting Dave like a frog.

'Carol said you'd been disappearing for hours at a time. Who'd have thought it was to come to a stationery cupboard to—' The Chairman wafted a hand as if dispersing a bad smell.

'Nothing . . . I was . . . The marker pen . . . Dave . . .'

With an insistent stare, Dave attempted to inform Jolene she'd become incapable of constructing a sentence.

'You've got a good woman there, David. Wouldn't want to lose her.' The Chairman smiled.

'This isn't what it—'

'Every Tuesday and regular as clockwork. Little does she know you're not playing away but playing at home, as it were.' The Chairman chuckled. 'Done my best to console her, but when a woman comes home to find her husband not there, not even answering his phone . . .'

'I'm not . . . Every Tuesday?'

The first time Dave had dreamt of Sal, he'd fallen asleep at the dining table. Had that been a Tuesday? That time on the roof . . . definitely a Tuesday. Today was Tuesday. Dave rubbed at his temples. His head ached and his throat was dry.

'Suppose that's why you didn't make my meeting last week and I haven't heard anything from you since?' continued the Chairman. 'Lucky – or unlucky – for you I was popping by to tell you something has come up. It's me that can't make our two o'clock today.'

'You can't?'

'You've got until the end of the day. Now please make yourselves decent.'

The humming refrain of a Neil Sedaka song accompanied the Chairman's departure.

Dave glanced at Jolene. 'Shit.'

'Thought we were mates. Why've you been lying to me?' she said.

'I just told you he's given me three weeks to find a project. Well, one now.'

'I don't give a shit about your ultimatum, Dave.' Jolene glanced at the door and lowered her voice. 'I'm more concerned about being used as a shoulder to cry on. Making out you're hard done when you're the one dipping your wick elsewhere.'

'For Christ's sake, Jolene! You of all people would know I'm not sleeping with you!'

The temperature in the stationery cupboard plummeted. Dave ventured a laugh as Jolene stood and reached for the door handle.

'Fainted, you said?'

Dave nodded.

'Been here all the time?' Jolene stood in the doorway. 'You haven't though, have you? Digby told me to look for you when you first disappeared four hours ago.'

'But—'

'This room was empty. I only came back now because I saw the light under the door.'

Truth made way for silence as the door slammed shut. Damn, shit and blast. In what parallel universe did Dave not *dream* of Iceland, but *disappear* there every Tuesday?

CHAPTER ELEVEN

Unable to face an irate Jolene, a Digby full of poetry and a Frenchman who was judgemental on the best of days, Dave escaped via the accounts department at the other end of the floor. Any work to be done that afternoon would be from home.

The bus ride offered time for reflection. As with the greatest of life's unanswered questions – Why is the sky blue? Is there a God? Why are the French so bloody good at rugby? – Dave couldn't explain a disappearing act every Tuesday. Jolene must have simply missed him when checking the stationery cupboard and the Chairman misunderstood Carol's comments. Where would he have been otherwise? Certainly not in Iceland! His original theory had to hold true that his 'travels' were nothing more than dreams.

That said, if Dave wasn't disappearing, he *was* losing hours of his life to these dreams. What's more, he now found himself in a stranglehold. The cockerel strutting around his wife had decided Dave was having an affair with his one and only ally and that ally was convinced Dave was playing away. A cruel irony when Dave hadn't had sex for thirteen months.

'Erectile dysfunction affects approximately forty percent of men aged forty and nearly seventy percent of men at seventy,' Dr Banks had chirped, coincidental number patterns blinding him to the grim prognosis.

The bus ground to a halt at the Motorpoint Arena, a motorcade transporting the Scottish First Minister across town. Dave sank into the itchy velour seat, unnerved that nothing from recent weeks made sense, not least the Great Brakes project turning up out of nowhere. Dave rested his head on the window recalling his last conversation with Sal. Moon landings and lupins? Dave didn't need a mind map to confirm those two things shared nothing in common.

He pulled out his phone and typed *Neil Armstrong Iceland* into the browser. A news article popped up, accompanied by a picture of the astronaut salmon fishing. Thirty-two astronauts had trained in a northern Icelandic fishing community for the Apollo 11 mission, its 'magnificent desolation' comparable terrain according to Aldrin. Wondering how he could have known the anecdote troubled Dave, but the story offered nothing else.

He googled *lupins in Iceland*. Again, all true.

The planet is an ecosystem built on many equally delicate ecosystems. Different but all connected, that's what Sal had said. And yet some Icelanders seemed more than happy with the purple flower. Dave shook his head and clicked on a message informing him of new emails.

Wales Online
Daily Headlines
Scots in town to talk fish. What does Wales want . . .

TUESDAY

Digby Jenkins
And now gentlemen, I must leave you
Dave, Never did see you after your trip to the stat . . .

He'd better read that.

Dave,
Never did see you after your trip to the stationery cupboard.
As the great Dylan Thomas would say, And now, gentlemen, like your manners, I must leave you.
Jokes aside, I hope everything is okay. I hear the Chairman cornered you?
Digby

'Not the time for poetry, Digby,' mumbled Dave. 'Never the time.'

Rhys-Wyn Llewellyn-Jones
Between us
David, Let's agree that what happened today . . .

'Agreeing on what?' Dave clicked.

David,
Let's agree that what happened today between you and Jolene will stay between us. An unfortunate incident indeed. Sorry about having to miss our meeting. You were no doubt keen to share your new project(s) with me. I imagine postponing the meeting very frustrating. I'm around all evening. Call me on my cell.
BR,
Rhys

His cell? He sounded less Welsh than Dave. And how lazy did you have to be to not spell out 'best regards' in full? Nothing had happened with Jolene to *stay between them*. Judging by Digby's email, however, whatever the Chairman thought he saw was already common knowledge anyway.

Damn, shit and blast.

———

Dave slammed his laptop shut on hearing the front door do the same. He had finished the presentation for Great Brakes. All that was left to do was send it. High heels marched a direct route to the kitchen.

'So, you're here?' said Carol, dropping a carrier bag on the kitchen worktop.

'Where else would I be?' Dave crossed his arms and straightened himself in the dining chair.

'Don't you have to be in the office on Tuesdays? My meeting was cancelled. Rhys let me off early, suggested I pop in to see you on the seventh floor.'

'Did he now?'

'You weren't there.'

'Because I'm here.' Dave guffawed, quickly coughing to subdue his enthusiasm. Rearranging the papers next to the computer, he noticed Seth and Rodric flanking Carol.

'Good evening, Mr Wel*tch*.'

Dave's eyes met Rodric's. 'Dave, Rodric. You can call me Dave.'

Seth rolled his eyes.

'Right, you two,' said Carol. 'Up you go. Don't you have computer science homework?'

'Of course, Carol,' said Rodric.

Seth rummaged in the shopping bag, pulling out a bag of mini-Snickers.

TUESDAY

'Goodbye, Mr Wel*tch*,' said a voice as the boys made their way upstairs.

'What's that kid's problem?' Dave asked Carol.

'Problem?'

'He talks to me like we're in *Downton Abbey*, not you.'

'Well, I see him all the time, don't I?'

Dave frowned at the ironic response that seemed to suggest he wasn't home enough.

'That's you all over,' said Carol. 'Should take a leaf out of his book rather than whinging about him being too polite. And what have you said to Jolene now? Could barely look me in the eye.'

Dave re-opened his laptop, hoping it would swallow him whole. 'Don't worry, it's just the summer solstice.'

'Summer—'

'Energies, she loves that stuff. Listen, I have to . . .'

Dave didn't have time to finish his sentence. High heels tapped their way back into the kitchen, Carol muttering about it being a fine time to start doing some bloody work.

Elbows either side of the laptop, Dave's head fell into his hands. Focusing on the Great Brakes presentation that afternoon had momentarily distracted him but he hadn't forgotten his other, now more immediate, problems. The sweat of a guilty man gathered at his hairline and yet he had done nothing wrong. He certainly hadn't done anything with Jolene, or any other woman for that matter. His only crime was disappearing – dreaming – for long periods of time, and always on a Tuesday.

If it was all in his head, he could stop it. He ruffled his hair. Enough with lupins, Armstrong, waterfalls, hills, wishes . . . elves!

Dave had googled them in more detail too, revealing parallel existences, or so the story went, elves occupying traditional professions like fishermen and fishwives. Sal had mentioned fishing when they'd met at the waterfall, but never said that's what he did. And this time the main topic of conversation had been due diligence. Sal had been insistent, even angry. Dave dug his nails into his scalp. Sal didn't exist! None of it existed! Remembering what Digby said about everyone containing beasts, angels and madmen, Dave wondered if the madman was consuming him whole, or . . . He lifted his head, realising it was the only explanation left.

He stared at the browser's search bar, fingers hovering over the keys and wondering how to formulate the request. *How to know if I'm the chosen one?* Dave fell back into his chair. A vessel to communicate messages from the other side? Dave Welch, a slightly overweight, washed-out rugby player in his late forties was *not* the Second Coming! Anyway, there was no other side and even if there was, what possible reason would there be for conferring on anyone an innate knowledge of Iceland?

Dave looked up to the Murano droplights, their reflection staining his skin yellow. That left one explanation. The one he had been avoiding: madness. In fact, wasn't the definition of madness, doing the same thing over and over?

How could he check he had all his mental faculties?

Dave thought back as far as he could in his childhood, deciding that recalling the names of their dogs growing up a good way to check. Without much effort, they came to him in order: Moriarty (a perfect storm of a name as Dave had idolised Welsh rugby captain, Richard Moriarty, and Maya had been an avid Sherlock Holmes fan), Pelé (Dad more of a football fan) and the self-explanatory, Farty.

Too easy. Maybe he could test himself by listing all the caps he'd received or women he'd slept with.

Reliving match by match in his head, he counted the

caps, remembering the scrums, the tries, the post-match parties. The women? Dave paused. An alcohol-fuelled period of his life, it proved more difficult, but could be put down to the simple excesses of youth.

Something else? What about lines from *Hamlet*? He'd studied that for English GCSE.

Dave addressed Cyclops. 'Though this be madness, yet there is method in it.'

No, Hamlet wasn't mad and neither was Dave. The dreams had to be, well, dreams, and their content pure and absolute coincidence. Like the Great Brakes project dropping into his inbox. Pure chance. A bit of lesser spotted and bloody brilliant good luck.

What if . . .

Dave typed *most lucky person in the world* in the search bar as he reached for a California roll next to his laptop. He'd cashed in his loyalty points at *Swshi Shack* on the way home. He scrolled the search results.

'America's Contest Queen?' He chewed as he leant in.

A certain Helen Hadsell was cited as having won the greatest number of contests in a lifetime. To be fair, she'd entered a shedload, which had to improve your chances. Dave scrolled, smiling as he read that she'd gone on to host lectures on positive thinking. He clicked through to her book, hesitating to order it but coming back to the original page, knowing he'd never find time to read it. In any case, the article gave the gist. Helen had won so many prizes simply by channelling enough positive energy into what she had wanted to happen.

Dave's mouth dropped open, half-chewed rice falling into the cracks between laptop keys. Hang on! Sal had mentioned that! *People don't get it anymore, do they? Too busy asking for what they don't want to happen, rather than what they do.* That was it! Dave had *manifested* Great Brakes into his life when he needed a project. He didn't need the book. He was doing it already! The dreams were to tell him it was meant for him, not Colchester Dave. The email arriving in Dave's mailbox first time around was no accident, nor the second time. The Universe was insisting, wondering when he'd actually sit up and listen. He had the presentation. There was no need to get caught up in this other stuff. This project had been sent to him. The wheel was turning.

Ping.

A new email.

Dustin Harris
Future UK operations
Dear Dave, Just reaching out as I still haven't heard fr . . .

A shiver coursed Dave's spine. He glanced at the microwave. Six thirty. Great Brakes wouldn't keep turning up if it wasn't meant to be. He clicked, read the message and pressed on the reply button.

Dear Dustin,
Please find attached a presentation about the Green, Green Tech of Home *and why Wales is the perfect location for your future UK site.*
Let's talk once you've had time to read this.

Dave hesitated, unsure of how to sign off. After dipping back into Dustin's email, he finished with 'Yours', his name, title and mobile number. He went to press the send button, remembered the Chairman's ultimatum and added him on copy. Two birds, one stone. It would save another email.

The whoosh of the departing email sent Dave rolling into his chair. What would be, would be. Dave came back

TUESDAY

to the Internet browser, closing the page about the Contest Queen and returning to the *Daily Herald* article he'd found the other day. *Water pollution: Adrian's Creek wants answers.* He'd read it several times. He clicked on the cross to the top left of the screen. Probably fake news. That's the term the Americans used nowadays.

CHAPTER TWELVE

Diced beetroot mingled with cherry tomatoes, multi-coloured beans and some worse-for-wear avocado. Pea shoots and a solitary walnut part-covered the misery. Dave squinted to read the logo on the brown paper bag beside them. A *Vegan's Dream*; his nightmare.

'Remind me why we order from there?'

'You can't eat maki every day, Dave.'

Jolene had refused his suggestion of sushi. Something about a whole city in Japan struck down in the fifties. Dave had stopped listening.

'Fish is good for you, isn't it?' asked Dave.

'Tuna is the hoover of the sea.'

'The what?'

'Eats all other fish, and the shit they've swallowed.'

Jolene was never happy. Dave, on the other hand, was currently more than happy. An excuse of a lunch would not dent his good humour. Having sent his email to Dustin at Great Brakes, he had received a reply the next day talking about serendipity – whatever that was – and informing Dave that tickets to the UK were already booked. Today was the final day of Dave's three-week ultimatum, the Chairman well aware of a potential three hundred new jobs for Cardiff. With Dustin scheduled to visit the proposed site on Thursday, Dave still had two days to iron out final details.

Dave felt Jolene staring at him. He resolved to work on his resting face, deciding he must seem overly depressed by lunch.

'How about explaining yourself, rather than whinging?'

Dave shovelled a conciliatory forkful of lunch into his mouth, a kidney bean making a dash for freedom. He softened his face with a smile, remembering he had also been avoiding Jolene for the past week, unsure how to address the elephant – or the elf – in the room. He couldn't shapeshift his way out of her being unable to find him in the stationery cupboard the other day, let alone offer credible proof he wasn't having an affair under Carol's nose.

'Whatever you think is going on,' said Dave, catching another errant bean, 'it isn't.'

He dropped the cutlery in the recycled cardboard container and glanced around the kitchen to see what biscuits he might pilfer later.

'All I know, Dave Welch, is the Chairman thinks it's me the harlot because of your disappearing acts.'

'I'm not sleeping around, Jolene.'

'I know that much, Dave.' Jolene let out a laugh.

Dave frowned.

'Look at you. You can barely get dressed in the morning.'

'Harsh.' Dave's shoulders sank.

'Anyway, overheard your conversation with Dr Banks.'

Please to God, no. He hoped they weren't going there.

Jolene patted his arm. 'Happens to forty percent—'

'Of men in their forties, I know,' Dave whispered, eyes

bouncing around the kitchen on confirming the conversation's direction.

He pulled at the rubber band on his wrist that he'd found it in the kitchen drawer that morning. It stopped him drifting into somnolence, his trips to Iceland – apart from that time in the stationery cupboard – having occurred when he was nodding off. Dave pulled harder, wondering why. There was no chance of sleep now.

'Your sex life,' Jolene indicated Dave's groin, 'Or lack thereof, isn't what concerns me. What I want to know is how these disappearing acts tie in with you making up a bloody project. You really think lying will save your skin?' She stared at him.

'For God's sake, Jolene. It's a real project.'

Sweat gathered in the small of his back. Dave pulled at the band. On announcing the Great Brakes project that morning in the team meeting, the tension had been as palpable. While Digby hadn't even pretended to give a shit, Jolene had been full of questions. Rather than citing the company by name, Dave had quickly invented a file name, claiming the competition with Essex made it highly sensitive.

'Project America?' Jolene raised an eyebrow. 'You're taking the piss.'

Dave sighed, realising it did smack of a presidential campaign and berating himself for not having been more inventive.

'Fell into your lap, did it?' Jolene frowned.

Dave couldn't share the company's real identity to convince her. His real motivation behind the file name was to prevent Jolene from undertaking any of her own due diligence. The article in the *Daily Herald* had alluded to other incidents, notably an old legal battle with a community somewhere in Asia. It had sent Dave into yet another

TUESDAY

rabbit hole of research, but he'd found nothing to incriminate the company. Instead, money had been donated to the inhabitants of a local coastal village as part of a regeneration project.

Dave needed Thursday to go well. He needed to change the subject. He looked over Jolene's shoulder to the printer room.

'You know, I've been thinking. It must have been dark that first time you came in the stationery cupboard to find me.'

He wouldn't be stepping foot in there today in any case. It was Tuesday and so far, so good. He was taking necessary precautions like accompanying Carol to the office, his *dreams* only happening when he was alone. The journey had been full of effusive praise and talk from Rhys of a promotion. How the tables had turned.

'I must have been hidden in the shadows,' Dave continued, forcing a laugh and remembering Carol kissing him on the cheek as he got out of the car.

Cutlery slammed onto the table.

Dave jumped.

'Stop changing the bloody subject!' shouted Jolene. 'If you're not playing away, and this project is as real as you claim, what *are* you up to every Tuesday?'

Elastic smacked into Dave's wrist.

'And what the hell is that?'

'Oh, just something . . .'

To stop me seeing little men, thought Dave.

'Looks like . . . Hang on, that's it, isn't it?' asked Jolene.

Arms beneath the table, Dave twisted the band.

'You should have said.'

He frowned.

'We all have problems with self-worth. It's a tough world out there. Finding your place is hard. Being who you want to be even harder.' Jolene placed a hand on his shoulder. 'Nothing to be ashamed of, taking time out to see a therapist.'

'Therapy!'

Dave didn't need therapy. That was Jolene all over, always in some kind of session. Last time, it was a cellular memory thing, the lives of her ancestors feeding into her current inabilities. Hang on a minute . . . Cowardice regained control as Dave spied a way out.

'Nothing to be ashamed of,' he said, nodding.

'That woman who won *Masterchef* last year, she says her therapist introduced her to the elastic band thing. Pulled it whenever the anxiety kicked in. Stopped that little voice inside her, raising questions she didn't really want to hear and asking if she was good enough. Saved her soufflé in the semi-final.'

Dave wasn't suffering from anxiety. Slightly on edge, but who wouldn't be with everything going on? He continued to nod as, in the distance, a short woman entered the printer room carrying a bucket. As she turned, a large nose came into view. Dave's eyes narrowed. It was the cleaner from the other night. He held his breath, his chest tightening. *Very* short, a headscarf covered her ears. She couldn't be, could she? Dave pinched his thighs. He felt awake. This wasn't a dream.

'That woman,' he whispered, grabbing Jolene's arm. 'You see her?'

Jolene turned. 'Course I can bloody see her. Are you listening to me at all?'

'She's the cleaner, right?'

'All the gear, probably no idea. Don't know when the toilets last had a proper going over.'

The woman entered the stationery cupboard, closing the door behind her.

TUESDAY

'You okay?' asked Jolene. 'You've gone all white.'

'Gotta go,' replied Dave, standing and knocking over the remnants of a vegan's dream.

Closing the printer room door, Dave stood facing the stationery cupboard. He played with the band on his wrist, wincing as it entangled itself in his arm hair. The cleaner had to be in there and she had to be one of them. He had entered the same place when he had disappeared, fainted . . . whatever you wanted to call it. But how could she be? They weren't in Iceland, they were in Wales. Dave pulled at the elastic as hard as he could. It snapped back with a crack and he grabbed his wrist to numb the pain. He wasn't asleep. Why would an elf appear when he was awake? Why would another elf appear at all?

'Elves don't exist!' mumbled Dave, snatching at the handle and yanking open the door.

'Jesus Christ!' shouted the woman. Hands rose to her chest, spittle spraying the cupboard. 'Don't go giving me a fright like that.'

'What are you doing in here?' Dave frowned at the mountain of pens, pencils and marker pens at her feet. Closer, he tried to gauge her height. Four foot eight, ten at most.

'What does it look like?' She wafted a cloth and a bottle of cleaning spray in his direction. 'Giving this place a once over.' She lisped the 's'.

'You're a real cleaner?'

'Why? You fancy doing it?'

Dave edged into the stationery cupboard, ensuring he kept the door open with one hand. He lowered his voice, noticing the woman shrink back. 'But why in here?'

'Clean the stationery cupboard in the kitchen, do you?' The woman threw her head back in laughter.

Dave examined the far wall against which Jolene had found him, deliberating whether the room could be some kind of portal. He shook his head. He had to put an end to the nonsense he was thinking. This wasn't *Back to the Future*. He never *travelled* in time. He *lost* time. In Iceland. Dave reached for his elastic band, belatedly remembering he had been holding open the door.

The door slammed shut.

Dave held his breath, his eyes screwing together. He pulled at the elastic band. Once, twice, three times. His wrist stung.

He listened. Silence. You could hear a pin drop.

He edged open an eye.

The cleaner smiled. 'Everything okay?'

Dave coughed as alcohol fumes ambushed him. He pulled at the band, examining the four walls. He hadn't gone anywhere.

'We all need something to numb the pain, don't we?' said the cleaner.

Was she talking about the band or the booze? Was she reading his mind? It was like talking to Sal. What *was* she doing there?

'Not much fun, I'll admit, cleaning shelves.'

She *was* reading his thoughts.

'You're one of them, aren't you?' Dave shouted.

'One of what?'

'Come on! What's under the headscarf?'

'My head.' The cleaner laughed as she sprayed the empty shelf with the bottle in her hand. 'What we want to do isn't always what we need to do.'

'You *are* one of them!'

As Dave reached for her, the door flung open.

TUESDAY

'Dave!' shouted Jolene. 'What the bloody hell are you doing in here again?'

Dave pulled at the elastic band. It snapped, flew across the room and hit a young man he didn't recognise stood next to his colleague.

'We were just—' Dave addressed the ceiling.

'Talking about Mr Welch having a lot on his mind,' finished the cleaner. 'But he took the time to help with my son's homework the other evening.'

Dave inspected the woman's smile, ignoring what she meant. He reached for his empty wrist, remembering with confusion that he'd been on the verge of ripping off her headscarf.

'Pleased to meet you, Mr Welch,' said the man next to Jolene, stretching out a hand. 'Sorry to turn up like this.'

Dave recognised an American accent. It was only Tuesday. The man was dressed in shorts, a shirt covered in lotus flowers and an orange t-shirt illustrating the evolution of man, its final iteration a demigod carrying a surfboard. He appeared too young but it had to be him.

'You must be Dustin? From Great Brakes?' Dave smoothed his hair, inhaled deeply and shook the man's hand. 'Our visit isn't until Thursday, but no problem.'

Jolene's eyebrow jumped a notch, a smile lighting up her face as her attention ping-ponged between the two men.

'My name's not Dustin, I'm Jedd,' replied the man. 'I'm your son, Mr Welch.'

CHAPTER THIRTEEN

'Your son?' said Jolene.

'My son?' said Dave.

'Bloody hell,' said the cleaner. 'Think I'll leave you to it.' She dropped the cloth and spray inside the bucket and picked it up. 'What happens on tour doesn't always stay there, Mr Welch,' she lisped, squeezing past.

'This not a good time?' The American voice pulled Dave away from the stench of gin flooding his nostrils.

'What do you mean my son?' replied Dave.

Curly black hair flopped over a tanned face. Dave's hair, what was left of it, was curly, but brown. That lacklustre, mousy brown reserved for British people. Jedd was American, probably in his twenties. When had Dave been in America twenty years ago?

'Wales Rugby Union Tour of the States and Canada,' said Jedd.

Dave's eyes narrowed, trying to decipher if Jedd could also read minds.

'1997. San Francisco,' continued Jedd.

Dave had tried to forget that tour. Demoralised by a

TUESDAY

knee injury that had prevented him from joining the British and Irish Lions in South Africa, he'd spent most of it pissed. Part of him had always known his knees would one day get the better of him. He replayed the matches in his mind. One had been at a baseball ground in North Carolina, another up in Canada and, Jedd was right, they had played in San Francisco.

'Bal-bo-a Park,' muttered Dave.

The name had made him and Ellis laugh, reminding them of the *Rocky* films and encouraging them to shout it like a ring announcer. Dave wasn't laughing now.

'My mother, Grace, worked at the stadium,' said Jedd. 'Met you in a bar afterwards. She said you . . .' He searched for a diplomatic way to summarise his conception, 'hit it off.'

'Hit it off?' asked Jolene, her face barely hiding a whirring mind that was no doubt attempting the same calculations as Dave. 'But how long have you and Carol—'

'Jolene! Don't you have work to do?' shouted Dave.

Dave didn't have to do the math, as the Americans say. He knew full well he had toured the US and Canada *after* he had met Carol. There had been late nights, fans in bars, comforting shoulders. Jedd had to be twenty-six.

Dave tried to displace Jolene from the printer room with a firm stare.

'Jesus wept, Dave,' she muttered, before flashing a toothy smile at Jedd. 'See you around here again soon?'

Dave nodded at her to leave. She wouldn't be seeing this guy anytime soon.

The printer room door closed. Dave examined the young man in front of him, realising he had to be a surfer, like Seth, to wear such a t-shirt. The Great Brakes project offered a hopeful flicker of light at the end of an interminable tunnel. A surprise son would extinguish that. Not to mention that once Dave and Carol had got married, they'd waited a long time to conceive. So long, they'd had only Seth. He had turned up eight years later, a welcome but complete surprise when they'd given up.

'How did you find me?' asked Dave.

'Mum says you were such a great player. Cut down in your prime. When I started asking questions, we found you on the net.'

'But how can she be . . . sure I'm the father.'

'Are you suggesting—'

'No, no, not at all.' Dave reached out a hand to touch Jedd's arm. This wasn't going well. Even if Dave couldn't remember who he'd slept with, suggesting Jedd's mother had notched up as many conquests wasn't helping. He needed time to think. Remember, but most of all think. 'Listen, Jedd wasn't it?'

'That's right.'

'Are you staying in Cardiff? Give me your number and I'll call you tomorrow. I've got this visit I need to prepare and—'

'It's all a bit of a surprise, I understand.' Jedd held out a card.

'Private investigator?' asked Dave, reading it and admiring Jedd's flowered shirt. 'Like Magnum?' He laughed.

'The ice cream?' Jedd frowned.

Jesus. He *was* young enough to be his son. Dave shook his head. Taking Jedd's arm, he guided him out of the printer room and off the floor via the accounts department.

'Bet people find it funny you're Welsh and your name is Welch,' said Jedd, softening the 'ch' to a 'sh' as he disappeared out of the door to the elevators.

TUESDAY

Dave peeked around the wall. Jolene was at her desk. Of course she bloody was. Straightening her neck like a meerkat at the slightest sound, she awaited his return. Despite an air conditioning upgrade the previous summer, sweat trickled down Dave's arms. He rolled up his shirt sleeves, double-checking for wet patches.

'What now?' The nasal disdain came from behind.

Dave smiled at the familiar hair loss pattern, the Frenchman's crown barely reaching his neck. Even a *grande école* couldn't guarantee a hirsute future.

'I need my briefcase,' said Dave.

'So go and get it?' Pierre shrugged.

'I don't—'

'Want to see Jolene?'

'Jolene?'

'You've been watching her for at least ten minutes.'

Their eyes locked, Pierre entering a hurried negotiation that left Dave thirty quid out of pocket. On returning, Pierre stuffed the briefcase and a sheet of paper into Dave's hands.

'Found this too,' he said. 'Next time, keep me out of your lover's tiff. Heard about you in the stationery cupboard. *Mon Dieu.*'

Denial collided with suspicions of misplaced jealousy, leaving Dave speechless but sure his life was going from bad to worse. Pierre sauntered back to his desk, cashmere sweater draped over his shoulders. Dave retraced the exit route he had shown Jedd to the other side of the seventh floor, starting to read the sheet in his hands. Expecting a memo, he was surprised to discover a school worksheet.

LOU GIBBONS

The Water Cycle

The water cycle is the continuous movement connecting all water on Earth. It joins the oceans, land and atmosphere and began about 3.8 billion years ago when rain fell on a cooling Earth to form the oceans. A complex system, it includes many processes. Liquid water evaporates into water vapour, condenses to form clouds and precipitates back to Earth in the form of rain and snow.

Dave stopped in his tracks, his attention jumping to the waterfall at the top of the page. He'd seen this sheet before. He pressed on the button to call the elevator.

'Hurry up,' he muttered, the display panel announcing it was on the tenth floor.

Dave returned to the sheet, now remembering the cleaner having given it to him. It had to be the homework for her son she'd been talking about in the stationery cupboard, meaning she could be a real cleaner, after all, even if there was something odd about her.

He continued reading.

Water is used directly for bathing, drinking and cooking, while indirect purposes include its use in the processing of wood to make paper and in the manufacture of steel for car parts. Most of the world's water is used for agriculture, industry and electricity.

It was basic, primary school level. What was so important about the water cycle? Dave held his breath, making the glaringly obvious link with Great Brakes and the allegations of water pollution.

It had to be a warning!

Dave looked up and down the corridor but the cleaner was nowhere to be seen. He placed his briefcase between his feet to reach for the elastic on his wrist, remembering it had snapped. This was the best project to cross their desks

TUESDAY

in the past five years, probably ever. How serious could those accusations be? He looked up at the display. Lift on the tenth floor, an arrow flashed downwards.

Ping.

The elevator doors slid open. Dave picked up his briefcase and dashed inside. He'd had enough. The Chairman, Jolene, mystery sons turning up out of nowhere. He had to focus on getting a project win. Dustin would be here in two days and it was Dave's time to shine.

The doors slid shut. The floor rattled. Numbers on the display screen turned one by one by one. Bright light flooded the elevator. As Dave covered his eyes, he realised the elevator couldn't have been on the tenth floor moments earlier. Cardiff House was only nine storeys high.

CHAPTER FOURTEEN

'You're British, you should know about the Cod Wars.'

Dave opened his eyes and screamed.

'Hello is a more common greeting,' replied Sal, who no longer wore a red bobble hat but a flappy leather one. Thankfully, it also covered his ears.

Dave's stomach churned.

'You're an elf. You don't exist.'

'If you're talking to me now, I'd say I do.' Sal laughed.

Dave grabbed both sides of a wooden hull. His knees touched his chin as he tried to steady the sway. Sea stretched before him and extended back as far.

'Anyway, the Cod Wars—'

'Cold? There was only one,' Dave answered, insisting on the 'l' and questioning why he got drawn into these conversations.

The swell subsided. He let go of the sides and straightened himself. Shivering, he unrolled his shirt sleeves.

'There's no such thing as bad weather, only bad clothes.' Sal's head fell back in more laughter. 'And I said cod, not cold. Not a fisherman though, are you?'

TUESDAY

Sal wore a smock made of the same leather as his hat, gathered at the waist thanks to a cord that passed between his legs. To his side, in a sheath, hung a knife. Dave cast his eyes around a boat no more than a few metres long. Of course! Dave had read Icelandic elves were often fishing folk.

What was he saying?

'Elves don't exist,' mumbled Dave.

He looked out to sea as droplets of water splashed into the boat. Fish traced rainbows in the low sky, their skin absorbing the sunlight unable to warm him. Dave's shoulders dropped. He knew how these things worked. He was in it for the long haul. Damn, shit and blast. If only he hadn't got into that lift on his own.

'Thought you'd made it through the day, eh?' Sal laughed again. 'I'll always catch up with you, even when you don't want it. Most of all when you don't want it! Anyway, the Cod Wars ran from the late fifties until the seventies. All because your lot weren't happy with us extending our waters.'

Dave frowned. 'My lot?'

'The British,' said Sal. 'But here in Iceland, our herring fisheries had collapsed. Classic case of overfishing. Weren't going to let that happen again.'

Dave shook his head. The last thing he needed was an obscure history lesson.

'Still don't get it, do you?' said Sal as he picked up the oars and started to row. 'It is all connected. Everything always is.'

Air lifted from the sea to caress Dave's face. Open-mouthed, he inhaled, oxygen flooding his body for the first time that day. A day that had been spent ducking and avoiding. Questions, people . . . the organisation of the Great Brakes visit in two days' time. The same thought still niggled Dave: a project appearing out of nowhere had to be too good to be true. Dave Welch didn't wish things into existence. He was no Contest King. If he could positively influence the future, he wouldn't have forfeited his rugby career to end up a useless cog in the Welsh government. The other accusations against Great Brakes insisted on a blatant disregard for the environment. Nothing was proven but where there's smoke, there's fire. Great Brakes felt like his saviour and his executioner. He wouldn't be hiding the company's real identity from Jolene if he didn't have doubts.

Silence swaddled them as Sal rowed, his eyes never leaving Dave's and harbouring words Dave already knew. Above, birds danced, cawing at the quilted curtains of cloud hiding the sun.

All Dave wanted to do was breathe.

'Our nation was built on fishing, you know,' said Sal after a long moment. He stopped rowing, letting the boat float. Dave scanned the horizon, looked behind him. They must have arrived but arriving would suggest they were heading somewhere.

'It's here, right enough,' said Sal.

'So, what happened after these Cod Wars then?' asked Dave, remembering Sal had said everything was connected.

'Quotas,' said Sal. 'Issued annually for every stock. Apparently, we lead the way in sustainable fishing now, cutting-edge fish-processing technologies reducing waste. Wonderful, isn't it?'

'Isn't it?' asked Dave, suspecting a hint of irony.

He'd read something about sustainable aquaculture in the *Green, Green Tech of Home* presentations. The Wales Online article about the Scottish First Minister's visit the other day had spoken of it too. Offshore fish farms, that was the Scottish thing. The Welsh had developed a vision as part of their *sustainable living* strategy, preaching against overfishing that left nothing for future generations.

'Three quarters of the quotas are with a handful of big companies. Sustainable is it, putting smaller companies out of business because they are deemed less efficient?' Sal's voice gained in speed as he spoke.

Memories came back to Dave of listening to Dad talking to Mum at the kitchen table, whisky in front of him and head in his hands. Dave would sit with Maya on the stairs, consoling a sister nine years his junior by lying and saying she had nothing to worry about. Fish, turnips . . . it was all the same. In pursuit of tomorrow, today was quickly sacrificed. What was it Jolene had called sustainability strategies the other day? *Corporate profiteering in sheep's clothing.*

'Villages used to thrive on being close to fishing grounds. Nowadays you land a catch over here and transport it way over there to be processed.' Sal's hand traced a line over an imaginary Iceland.

The sky, bigger than before, weighed on Dave. His head ached. As Sal continued to talk, Dave debated the overriding importance of what he had to say given his more immediate problems.

'They call them sustainable targets,' continued Sal, 'but they're pulling huge amounts of fish out of the sea at any one time. The seas, the oceans, water on Earth; it's a delicate ecosystem.'

Dave lifted his head. 'The water cycle!'

Sal smiled. 'The water cycle,' he repeated.

'But that cleaner gave me a sheet about that. The one with the big nose who stinks of booze.'

'Harsh,' said Sal, a smile escaping him. 'But you're starting to piece it together.'

Clouds parted, the sun's rays hitting the boat's flaking green paint.

'Piece what together?'

'Everything, Dave. It's all connected. I'm sure we've spoken of that before.' Sal offered another smile.

Above, birds cawed.

'Everything's connected,' repeated Dave. 'Like Jedd turning up today.'

'Jedd who is or isn't your son?' asked Sal.

Dave dropped his gaze. Jedd wouldn't have any reason to lie. Why would you track down a spent excuse for a Welsh civil servant if he wasn't your dad? Dave had revisited the North American tour, at least the bits he could remember. Pissed off he wasn't gallivanting with the Lions, his knee had pulled for most of the first half at Balboa Park; he'd been substituted in the second. The physio had talked about an altered gait. They'd got shitfaced that evening, Ellis calling over a table of girls to sing with them. The journey back to Heathrow had been full of turbulence, dread and the realisation that alcohol engendered bad judgement. Hitting the tarmac at Terminal Three, Dave had rushed through baggage control into Carol's arms, asking her to marry him.

'Another delicate ecosystem by the sounds of it,' said Sal.

Dave raised an eyebrow. When it came to good or bad judgement, Sal had an infinitely better grasp on Dave's life than he did. Dave pulled at the elastic on his wrist. 'Hang on a minute. Didn't this—'

'Looks like you needed a new one.'

'Why are we here?' asked Dave, plucking the band further. He wanted it to hurt. He deserved to hurt. He'd messed up years ago and it was coming back to bite him.

TUESDAY

'Everything and anything comes back around. Like your water cycle,' said Sal.

Dave raised his head.

'Everything you say and do disperses into the sea of life. It flows back around, as it were. Comes to find you.'

Dave tacitly agreed he being was an arsehole, busying himself with saving the house of cards that was his life when Jedd's arrival was about to bring it tumbling down anyway. But what if the Great Brakes project could be an opportunity to start afresh? A chance to succeed where he had failed. Jedd would have to stay quiet for the time being, but once the project was claimed as a win and he slid into Digby's job, Dave would introduce Jedd to Carol, play with his age, say he was twenty-seven, twenty-eight.

'More lying then?' said Sal. 'What was that about starting afresh?'

'Jesus Christ! Will you stop doing that?'

'What?' Sal smirked.

'Making me face up to my contradictions. It's bloody annoying.'

'You know why you're here, don't you?' said Sal. 'In the middle of the Atlantic in a flimsy rowboat.'

'It's not to talk about sustainable fishing, is it?'

'Corporate profiteering in sheep's clothing,' said Sal.

'It's about the rubbish Great Brakes is pumping into the sea,' replied Dave.

'What's the point of developing so-called sustainable fishing if we are poisoning the oceans? Poison that makes its way through the water cycle.'

'And I need to stop it,' shouted Dave, grabbing the sides of the boat as it started to wobble.

His knuckles bulged as paint chipped off the hull into his hands. Clouds fused together, incarcerating the sun and forcing a gust of wind under the hull.

The boat capsized.

Icy currents froze Dave's scream, dragging him into the watery darkness. Fish ambushed him, their skin sliding off his. As Dave sank deeper, thousands rose heavenwards. Their glassy eyes watched him, one by one, as if infecting him with the sickness that was dragging their dead, bloated bodies to the surface.

CHAPTER FIFTEEN

Dave woke to his own screaming.

'Hello is a more common greeting.' A body dropped next to his on the bench.

Dave frowned. That couldn't be Sal, not again. His eyes opened onto a crowd blurring into a congealed mess. The day's heat met with evening excitement. It was evening, wasn't it? The air felt somehow tired with the day.

'What's with the screaming?'

'Seth?' asked Dave, wiping his arms, then his face. 'Jesus Christ! All those dead fish.'

'There a reason you're sat halfway up Queen Street rambling nonsense?' replied Seth.

Queen Street. That would explain the crowd. Sweat inched down Dave's back, his shirt clung to him. Paint chips dug into his hands as they gripped the wooden bench, reminding him he'd been on a boat. He seemed to have disappeared with Sal again and now he was sitting on a bench with his son.

'You been drinking, Dad?'

Unsure, Dave bent forwards and pulled the sodden shirt off his back as he scanned the high street. Dimmed shop lights framed throngs of people bulging in and out of bars, imbued with happy hour *joie de vivre*.

'What time is it?' asked Dave.

'Gone seven. Jeez. Sounds like a right sesh.'

Dave ran his hands through his hair, then dropped them to cover his eyes, trying to recall his last memory. He'd been in the elevator, seen a bright light. He dug his nostrils into his palms and exhaled. He could do with a freshen up, but he didn't smell of booze. He had no recollection of leaving the elevator, remembered only the tenth floor.

There was no tenth floor.

'What's going on, Dad? This all 'cos you and Mum are getting divorced?' Seth pushed his hands into his pockets, slouching into the bench.

'Why would you say that?' The words shot out of Dave, his chest tightening as his current non-elf-induced problems reappeared one by one. He lowered his voice. 'Did your mum say something?'

Seth shook his head.

Dave studied Seth, realising you didn't need to be Sherlock Holmes to deduce things were bad at home. Seth was a worried little boy. All he wanted to hear was it would be alright, that other parents split up but his stayed together. Forever and ever. Dave's arm twitched to hug his son.

'You've been acting weird for ages.' Seth tucked a lock of hair behind his ear. 'That's what happens before a split, right?'

'Weird?' Dave wondered whether the 'you' to which Seth referred was plural or singular as he stared at an orange poster in the shop window opposite him.

Three-for-two books. Did anyone read books anymore,

proper paper ones? Wasn't everything online now? Bite-sized chunks of life containing minimal words, no chewing required.

'Mum said people fall out of love.'

Dave's attention sprinted from the poster back to his son. 'She said that to you?'

'To Aunty Heather.'

Carol had told her sister she'd fallen out of love before she'd thought to mention it to Dave? His hands grabbed the bench. Carol's bloody sister and her opinions, that was all he needed. Like gherkins in a burger, you never asked for them but were always served twice too many. After three divorces, Aunty Heather was left with one overriding belief that ninety percent of men were toxic. From what Dave could make out, it equated with a bastard majority of which he formed part. Dave forced his hands into his pockets, his belt gouged his insides. The writing was on the wall and good old Heather the counter signatory. Something else Dave could rack up to failure.

As Seth sank further into the bench, Dave realised the courage it must have taken for his son to broach the subject. This was about Seth, not him. When was the last time they had sat side by side?

'Look, I know I'm not a great dad,' said Dave.

'I don't need you to be great.'

Dave shrugged.

'We used to do stuff together.'

'Me and your mum—'

'It's not all about you, you know.'

'But you said you were worried about the divorce.'

'Get divorced! Stay together!' Seth threw his hands in the air. 'Just be happy. Once you've sorted out your own shit, you can take a moment to try and get me.'

Dave drove his back into the bench, realising Seth's

disappointment was in no way linked to a possible divorce, more a classic egocentric teenager move. Try and *get* his son, what did that mean? Accept he spent days online, never leaving his bedroom? Fathom the interest in chatting with faceless followers? Agree with a blatant lack of ambition in life? Dave had never sat down at the dinner table and asked *his* dad for understanding. Dad had told him rugby wasn't a proper job from the beginning. He often wondered what Dad would make of Maya if he was still alive, his little sister that had gone on to climb the corporate ranks to secure a very 'proper' job. He probably would have overlooked the million-pound marketing campaigns feeding into globalisation and mass consumerism. Dad would have forgiven his little girl anything. Dave rubbed his face as the memory of sea mist caressed him. He had bigger problems than an adolescent crisis, like how, with no recollection whatsoever, he had been transported from an elevator to a bench. He'd been in a boat. All those fish.

Dave shivered.

'Can't you just get your head down in school?' he asked.

'Like you did?' shouted Seth.

'What does that mean?'

'You've got a third in Sports Science, Dad.'

Dave went to speak but stopped himself. Dad had told Dave to get his head down but Seth was right. At Seth's age, Dave was already playing in the Under-18s, had been told he was heading for national caps, the Lions. They'd promised him the Lions, following on from sponsorship that had paved a path into university.

'Intend to surf your way through life, do you?' asked Dave.

'At least I'm enjoying myself. Anyway, how is my surfing any different to your rugby?'

'That's my point entirely!'

'But you played for Wales. You were the best.'

'Were. Was. You said it right there.'

'Really, Dad?'

Dave was only trying to share fatherly advice, let his son learn from a well-trodden path. He could never put a foot right with that boy. Failed as a husband and as a dad. Dave rolled up his sleeves. He went to strum the blue elastic band, remembering it snapping and hitting Jedd.

Dave had almost forgotten. Not one but two sons.

He evacuated the air from his lungs to see Seth's face frozen in expectation.

'Really what?' shouted Dave.

'We make the life we want, Dad. It's you that decided yours is going to be miserable.'

'I didn't decide to ruin my knees! To get kicked out of the only thing I could do before hitting thirty. To end up middle-aged, balding and useless, with an equally useless job trying to peddle a country no one has ever bloody heard of!' A crowd slowed before them and Dave dropped his voice. 'I didn't ask for any of this.'

'Shit happens, Dad. To *everyone*. You surf the wave whilst it's there. You don't cry when it breaks, you just find a different one. What happened to you? We used to have fun.' Seth shrugged. 'It was you that got me into the sea. All those trips to the Maritime Museum.'

'You remember them?'

'There was that special exhibition—'

'About octopi?' A smile tickled Dave's lips on feeling all wasn't lost and remembering their trips to the museum and the childhood days Seth would spend stuffing Carol's tights to make tentacles, leaving no toilet paper for its rightful intention.

'About European islands,' said Seth.

Dave's back sprang straight. 'What islands? I've never been to an exhibition about islands!'

'No need to shout. Of course, you have. That's where I learnt all about sneaker waves, the power of the ocean. It's awesome how . . .'

Seth continued to talk as Dave's mind flipped to a windy hill, fields and fields of lupins, waterfalls, Louis Armstrong – no, not Louis, Neil – Sal, elves and fish. Dead, rotting fish. If he had been to an exhibition on European islands, part of it could have been about Iceland. But it was so many years ago and wouldn't explain it all coming back in technicolour now. Mind you, since his first visit, he had done a lot of Internet research, now he thought about it. He'd recognised those worn leather clothes when he was last with Sal . . . he hadn't *been* with Sal. Elves didn't exist. So, how had he entered an elevator and ended up on a bench? What possible—

'Dad!'

Dave jumped.

'You're not listening, are you?' Seth stood in front of him.

Dave opened his mouth.

'Don't bother! You want us to be all father and son and you can't even be arsed to listen. Aunty Heather is right.'

'Listen, your Aunty Heather—'

'Thinks you're having a mega midlife crisis.'

'She thinks what?'

'Can see why Mum thinks you don't love her anymore.'

'She thinks *I* don't love *her*?'

Dave searched for words, answers to long-buried questions, as a man approached from behind Seth, his hair lifting in the evening breeze and wearing a t-shirt illustrating the evolution of man into surfer. Jedd's gaze locked with his. Dave shook his head. In any case, it was the briefest of moments before Jedd turned his full attention to Seth.

'Hey man! I don't believe it. You're Surfer Seth off TikTok right?'

CHAPTER SIXTEEN

The sweet smell of former times flooded Dave's nostrils as he leant over the North Terrace's blue barriers. The grassy expanse beckoned him. He hadn't played in weeks, doctor's orders merging into the chaos of recent Tuesdays. Interrogations as to why Tuesday and no other day had woken him at four o'clock that morning. The more important question as to why he was being transported to Iceland – rather than the punctuality of those visits – had prevented him from going back to sleep.

In the absence of answers, Dave had pondered the one thing he could try and resolve: whether Jedd's claim to be his long-lost son was true or not. It was odd to turn up out of the blue after all this time. On his way out of Cardiff House, Jedd had said his mum had spoken about Dave throughout his childhood. Why wait until now to find him? Time was also against Dave, his original strategy of stalling until after the Great Brakes visit scuppered by Jedd being Seth's greatest fan. What were the chances of that? Probably equivalent to those of disappearing to Iceland every Tuesday.

TUESDAY

Realising he needed help adding meat to the skeletal memory of a rugby tour three decades ago, Dave had waited for a godly hour to call Ellis. Misplaced hope had met with a recollection of Iestyn drinking seven pints out of Dave's sock but not much more. However, Ellis had been good enough to suggest the Arms Park a secret enough meeting place. They needed to get blood tests, he had insisted. Dave could make decisions once he had the facts. In the meantime, mum, not dad, was the word.

Dave looked up at the boxes, thinking back to when he and Carol had first met and wondering where the years had gone. The empty stadium was deafening in its silence. Despite waking up like a student after a three-day bender and the ensuing abuse from his son, the upside to the previous evening was discovering his marriage might be retrievable. The thing was, Carol thought Dave had fallen out of love. Dave had also debated whether he still loved his wife in the early hours, concluding no one really felt the same after decades of marriage. He and Carol were hardly a perfect match but he wasn't at an age to be starting out afresh, certainly not when surprise offspring had decided to rock up, or considering current mortgage rate spikes. He prodded his belly, doubting anyone else would want it anyway.

Dave pulled his phone out of his pocket to check the time. Twenty past eleven. The on-site nurse was doing the blood draws. A friend of Ellis, she was going to take them to the laboratory at the hospital. Dave had arrived early and had already done his, Janine talking incessantly about some Detroit rapper she'd seen at the Millennium Stadium the previous evening.

'Read in the paper he trashed his room at the Hilton,' she'd announced, Dave watching the blood drain from his lower arm. 'Says it was his brother. Loves a bad boy, me.

Like Griff Stevens in sixth form. Stevo, we called him. Could have had any girl he wanted, him. Chose me though, didn't he?' she had triumphantly concluded, her stare wandering sadly out of the window.

Dave scanned the terraces once more, annoyed at Jedd's tardiness. Pressing on the blue icon with a white envelope on his phone, he noticed he had new messages. With Dustin arriving later that afternoon and the visit to the site at the docks scheduled for tomorrow, there couldn't be any hiccups.

Jolene Jones
Fwd: Is Great Brakes becoming the shame of the . . .
Begin forwarded message: From: Jolene.J@cia.org
Jolene Jones
Fwd: Mercury in the water: 40% of Europe's lakes . . .
Begin forwarded message: From: Jolene.J@cia.org
Channel 4
Newly Released – *No Hard Feelings*
When the sex is gone, is the relationship over? Meet the women . . .
Jolene Jones
Fwd: Water pollution: Adrian's Creek wants answers
Begin forwarded message: From: Jolene.J@cia.org

Damn, shit and blast.

Jolene knew the company he was meeting was Great Brakes, even though he'd managed to keep it under wraps for a whole week, referring only to Project America. But how could she know? Only the Chairman had been informed of the company's real identity. He wouldn't have told Jolene. He had no reason to.

However she knew, she knew.

Damn, shit and blast.

Dave rescanned his inbox. Jolene had read the same

articles as him concerning Adrian's Creek. Dave clicked into the top email and scrolled an article entitled: *Is Great Brakes becoming the shame of the Great Lakes? The greenwashing phenomenon.* The reportage, published the previous day, was new to him and outlined more accusations. A not so pretty picture was forming of recurrent bribery and corruption as Great Brakes facilities had developed across the world. Rising competition from places like China meant their prices remained competitive by ignoring regulations to reduce metals in brake pads, leading to the more recent accusation of intentional pollution closer to home in the States. Dave sighed. It didn't make for great reading, but it didn't prove anything. He scrolled up to the publication name. *Earth Day Warriors?* He sighed again. Hardly mainstream media. Dave skipped to the article's conclusion.

With sources close to the Adrian's Creek factory insisting the recent spill may not have even been an accident but intentional mercury dumping prior to a recent inspection, how much more evidence do we need before our water cycle becomes even more heavily polluted?

Dave recalled a bulbous nose, a gin-infused stationery cupboard and him semi-assaulting a very short woman.
The water cycle.
The cycle of water.
The continuous movement connecting all water on Earth.
Everything. It's all connected.
I'm sure we've spoken of that before.
Dave shivered on remembering Sal's big ears. Supposed to stop all this, was he? Because he'd been told to by an elf?

'Elves don't exist,' muttered Dave, wondering if he could reframe Sal as that little voice everyone has in their head, the one that tries to guide you right.

Even then, would it be reason to listen? After all, it could have been an accident at Adrian's Creek. Wasn't it better for Dave to go with what he knew . . . and the only thing he knew for sure was that he needed this project to save his career and his marriage. The little voice in his head would be the first to say that, wouldn't it?

The water cycle.

The cycle of water.

The continuous movement connecting all water on Earth.

Dave's phone vibrated. Two text messages had appeared on his screen.

Jolene Jolene
We need to talk about Great Brakes!

Dustin Great Brakes
Caught the earlier train. In Cardiff at midday

'Shit!' said Dave, checking the time.

Twenty to twelve.

He glanced around the stadium. No sign of Jedd. They'd said eleven o'clock. He hadn't even shown up. The whole secret son routine couldn't be a wind-up by one of the lads, could it? Ellis seemed to take it seriously enough. Dave replied to the two messages and pushed his phone back into his pocket. Taking one last look around the stadium, he saluted the aitch-shaped post. The try was his. Now it was time for the conversion.

―――

As Dave opened the door to the eighth floor, the Chairman slapped the back of a ball-shaped man in an oversized suit and banana-coloured tie. The lobby filled with laughter as a mounted television screen announced: *Croeso i Green, Green Tech*, offering a reminder that their new slogan was so bad it was untranslatable.

'David!' The Chairman looked him up and down.

Dave wiped his brow with the back of his hand and smudged the sweat into his trousers. Having taken the stairs two by two, removing his suit jacket beforehand would have been a good idea. He couldn't take it off now. He'd worn a red shirt. Idiot. Red for Wales. Red for sweating, out of shape—

'Head of Americas here at the Cardiff Investment Agency,' said the Chairman, introducing him.

'America,' corrected Dave, hoping the plural had been a slip of the tongue and knowing bridging continents would overstretch his limited capacity.

'David!' The man thrust a hand into his, patting his shoulder with the other.

Dave's shirt sleeve glued itself to him. The lift *was* working and it *was* Wednesday but he'd decided not to take any chances.

'Dustin, I assume?' Dave flashed a smile. 'Made it in a bit earlier, I see?'

'Early bird and all that, David. Ain't that so?'

Dave pulled his shirt sleeves at the wrists.

'Everything in order for the visit tomorrow?' The Chairman smiled.

Everything. It's all connected.

The water cycle.

The cycle of water.

The continuous movement connecting all water on Earth.

'You okay, sir?' The American drawl broke Dave's chain of thought.

'Okay?' Dave reached for his head, feeling a little dizzy.

'Not as outta shape as me.' His tie slopping to one side,

Dustin patted his stomach as it strained at his shirt buttons like a scene from *Alien*.

'Fine. I'm fine,' said Dave, gazing at his own belly and wondering if he'd been staring.

Dave may have lost two stone since he'd started dieting two months ago but was feeling more unfit than ever. As he rued his laziness at not trying to get back in shape, Jolene's string of emails played on repeat. *The recent spill may not have even been an accident but intentional mercury dumping prior to a recent inspection.* He'd 'white lied' saying he was out of the office all day, but she'd catch up with him at some point.

'I have a quick question about Adrian's Creek if I may?' said Dave.

'Adrian's where? Aren't we here to talk about Wales?' The Chairman stretched an arm. 'Come on, David. Let's get you a glass of water, shall we?'

The Chairman led the way towards four leather chairs and a glass coffee table adorned with tall blue bottles of Welsh water, a swirl of Welsh cakes and a copy of the *Western Mail*. Dave pulled the new band on his wrist. Sweat-laden, it slipped through his fingers. If Dustin could simply confirm it *had* been an accident at Adrian's Creek, he could tell Jolene she had nothing to worry about. Everything could proceed, without a care in the world. The visit to the docks, Dave's career, his marriage, his life.

The Chairman sat opposite Dave. He pushed the plate of Welsh cakes across the table. 'Just telling Dustin he isn't the only American in town, David.'

Their eyes locked. A smile spread across the Chairman's face as the suspicion taunted Dave he had to be talking about Jedd.

'We Americans do like Europe, don't we?' Dustin thumped his pulsating stomach as he reached for the plate.

Dave swallowed. Here he was worried about paci-

TUESDAY

fying Jolene when she'd only gone and told the Chairman Jedd was his son. It had to be Jolene. No one else knew.

'You sure you're okay?' The Chairman's face dropped into a frown.

'Can't choose your family, eh?' Dustin laughed.

'What?' Dave shot him a look, any lingering benefit of the doubt replaced by the certitude that they were indeed talking about Jedd.

'Sure you're still up to this visit tomorrow?' insisted the Chairman, a glint in his eye reminding Dave of his ultimatum and the worthlessness of the Great Brakes project if it failed to land.

'Tomorrow won't take long.' Crumbs scattered Dave's trouser leg as Dustin leant in. 'Let's see those green, green valleys of tech!'

'Green, green tech,' said the Chairman.

'Of home,' finished Dave, a raisin bouncing off his shoe as he pulled away from the Chairman's gaze and dragged a finger inside his shirt collar.

Dave tried to reason Jolene speaking to the Chairman, knowing how much she hated him. But it had to be her . . .

Of course! Dave sat upright, realising that shared confidences between Jolene and the Chairman would also explain how she knew the identity of Great Brakes, as the Chairman was the only person who could have told her. But why would they be sharing secrets? She'd called him smarmy . . . but only when Dave had said old Rhys was having it away with Carol.

'Jesus Christ!' mumbled Dave, deluged by the conclusion that Jolene and the Chairman had to be sleeping together.

'David!' The Chairman's voice rose as he grabbed his arm. 'You *do* have everything ready for tomorrow?'

'Of course!' Dave forced a smile and shook off the Chairman's hand.

Trying to bring his attention back to the meeting, Dave clenched his fists, silently berating Jolene for having gone too far by attempting to scupper his marriage to stop the project. She was trying to get at Carol, jealous of her for also sleeping with the Chairman. An idea Dave had stupidly planted but now recognised as false because Seth had said Carol still loved him. Knowing ahead of time the audit was on the cards, Carol must have used her influence with the Chairman to orchestrate the ultimatum as a safety raft. She hadn't been against him at all in that meeting. She was on his side. Dave kicked another raisin off his shoe and relocked eyes with the Chairman. Dave may have misjudged the situation but it was as clear as day now, even if the old dog played a very good game. He was jealous! After finding Dave in the stationery cupboard with his girlfriend, old Double Barrel was set on vengeance.

'Why don't you head off. We'll get down to business tomorrow, David,' said Dustin, slapping him once more on the back. 'I'm a bit tired myself.'

Dave examined the Chairman, hoping he respected Carol too much to upset her by telling her about Jedd. On scouring the finely combed hair and inhaling the expensive cologne, he decided otherwise. The only thing worse than a woman scorned is an entitled man who doesn't get what he wants.

The Chairman smiled. 'Our David knows to focus on what's important and not get sidetracked, don't you?'

Dave nodded, winded by a conclusion no one in their right mind would have seen coming, but now knowing it was every man for himself.

CHAPTER SEVENTEEN

The car had been cleaned inside and out. Dave sported the same new suit as the previous day, changing red shirt for white. He'd cleaned his teeth. Twice. He pulled into an expanse of concreted wasteland, as grey as the Bristol Channel onto which it looked.

'So, this is it?' asked Dustin.

'Right here and waiting for the right company.' Dave smiled.

Dustin admired Queen Alexandra Dock and a crane stacking a container on top of two others. 'I'm liking what I see, David.'

Dustin had insisted on sharing breakfast at his hotel that morning. Unwavering when it came to his intermittent fasting plan, Dave had sipped on tea and regurgitated sales arguments he'd learnt parrot-fashion, watching Dustin consume the bounty of three trips to the buffet. Checking his reflection in the rear-view mirror, Dave wondered how to refashion those same arguments during the next ten minutes, otherwise visit commentary would be sparse.

'Let's take a walk about,' he said, smiling.

He could do this. The Chairman's thinly veiled threats were one thing. The fact everyone was in cahoots against him, another. Jolene and the Chairman! They were laughing at him behind his back. This was his one chance to show everyone Dave Welch didn't fail at everything he turned his hand to.

They exited the car into a steady breeze and the cries of hungry seagulls who had strayed from the eateries at Cardiff Bay. Dave winced as a train screeched in the distance. Multimodal connectivity, had he mentioned that over breakfast? Road, rail and sea. Perfect for European export. He felt for his phone and pulled it out of his pocket.

Jolene Jolene
Why aren't you in the office?

Jolene Jolene
The visit is still this afternoon, right?

Jolene Jolene
You spoken to him about Adrian's Creek yet?

Jolene Jolene
Are you ignoring me?

Having got the measure of things, Dave *was* ignoring her. Faced with a colleague determined to save the planet but also raging with jealousy and ready to stop at nothing, he'd moved the site visit from afternoon to morning. Lunch at Giovanni's near the New Theatre had also been moved to Dave's back garden, that on a sudden whim of Carol.

'Americans bloody love a burger,' she had insisted. 'Leave it with me.'

She had flown out of the car before Dave had found time to reply. Dave let out a laugh. Absurd now to think he'd decided Carol and the Chairman lovers! Not that he would have imagined in a million years the Chairman and Jolene.

'How many square feet again?' asked Dustin.

'Ten thousand,' said Dave. 'Planning approved. Industrial, storage and distribution usage, of course.'

B something or other. B2 or B3, maybe eight. Dave smiled. It didn't matter.

'Sounds about right,' said Dustin.

Dave shielded his eyes from the sun. His head pounded. What did they say? The sun shines on the bold . . . God smiles on the bold . . . No, fortune favours the bold.

'Sits directly on the water I see. That's good, isn't it?' Dustin smiled at Dave.

Dave dropped his gaze, unsure if Dustin wasn't somehow referring to the allegations made against Great Brakes, maybe checking him out. Now regretted having mentioned Adrian's Creek at their first meeting, he had to change the subject.

'Multimodal connectivity, Dustin,' rushed Dave. 'Road, rail and air. Perfect for European export.'

'Air?' Dustin frowned.

'Sea, I mean sea.' Dave squinted. 'And of course, we have a very affordable workforce here in Wales.'

Dave relaxed, knowing it safe to highlight an affordable workforce. It was always part of the main sell. Dave had attended a training session in Amsterdam on first starting in his current role. He'd met people from Marseille, Turin, somewhere in Switzerland and a whole team recruited to help companies *see Crewe anew*. Develop your unique selling proposition, they had been promised. A city where money grows on trees or a town where fountains contain the elixir of eternal life, they would be unique selling propositions. A scrap of land with planning permission, a low sky and the odd skanky bird; you get that everywhere. By the end of the three days, Marseille, Turin, Crewe and the nameless Swiss canton had all become *a central location with excellent transport links, available land and an affordable workforce.*

'And how much is this going to cost me?' asked Dustin.

'Cheaper than the southeast of England,' replied Dave, reminding Dustin he knew Colchester was also on the cards, even if he'd made out he'd never heard of Essex between two hash browns that morning.

'You mentioned that over breakfast. But how much?'

'Forty percent,' replied Dave, pushing a stone around the floor with his foot.

He'd made that up. Well, not entirely. Everyone knew investing in Wales was more affordable. Forty was a nice round figure. Once Dustin was hooked, Dave would reel him in with his trump card during the presentation: the *Welsh Technology Accelerator Fund*. The Chairman had called last night, during Dave's many attempts to align paragraphs in PowerPoint, asking if they were on the same page.

'A misunderstanding, Chairman. I know what I should be doing . . . and what I shouldn't,' Dave had replied, determined to alleviate any misunderstanding around Jolene and reassure the Chairman he wasn't after his girlfriend. 'Whatever doubts you may have had about me, please forget them.'

An email had followed, leaving the negotiations to Dave and giving him permission to offer up to fifty percent in grant funding. Winning the Chairman's trust meant he wanted this project as much as Dave did, reassuring Dave further that the Chairman had no interest in telling Carol about Jedd.

TUESDAY

Dave's phone buzzed in his pocket. At some point Jolene would work out the visit had been pulled forward. Before that, Dave had to make a detour.

On their way, Dustin had revealed himself a Shirley Bassey fan and started asking tricky questions about the area's insalubrious past as Tiger Bay. A keen fisherman, he also wanted specifications on the Cardiff Bay barrage development. Unable to compensate for years of playing *Candy Crush* in briefing meetings and feeling like an ill-prepared contestant on *Mastermind*, Dave had resorted to more agenda changes and relocated their post-visit meeting from the Hilton to Cardiff Bay Visitor Centre. It meant an unintentional double bluff for Jolene, or triple if you counted lunch, and made Dave's 'specialist subject' delegation.

Dave turned to the car, hoping a quick quarter of an hour would be enough to sate Dustin's curiosity before dazzling him with his presentation.

'Let's go and see where Dame Shirley grew up, shall we?'

———

'Today, Cardiff only has three operational docks capable of handling ships of up to 35,000 tonnes deadweight: Queen Alexandra Dock, Roath Dock and Roath Basin. Owned by the port, Roath Basin is now only used as a hospitality berth.'

The microphone thudded on every 't'.

On arriving at the Cardiff Bay Visitor Centre, Dustin's enthusiasm had carried them immediately into an eleven o'clock presentation called *Cardiff: Coal Capital of the World*. Not unlike the crane in the picture behind him, a man towered before them. He had to be at least six foot five.

Dave wondered what might invent itself to carry them back out and get to more important business. He glanced around the darkened room occupied by him, Dustin and a row of high school children.

'Let's start our story right back in 1794,' said the crane.

Let's not, thought Dave, pushing down on his bouncing leg.

'. . . When the Glamorganshire Canal was completed, linking the then small town of Cardiff with Merthyr . . .'

Jesus Christ! They had centuries to get through before Dave could deliver his trump card. Never had he been given this much responsibility. With Digby's position up for grabs, preparing for the visit had made him see his potential. What had Seth said? You make the life you want. Dave had already lost two stone. He could lose two more. He could get that promotion, make his family proud. Why couldn't he and Carol be happier?

'By the 1830s, Cardiff was shipping almost half of British overseas iron exports,' continued the crane. 'Between 1840 and 1870, the volume of coal exports increased from 44,350 to 2.219 million tonnes.'

Confronted with too many numbers and noticing one of the kids in front of them skinning up, Dave looked for his exits. Waiting outside would also give him the opportunity to run through his presentation on his phone one more time. He scrunched his face to signal needing a wee, standing making him realise he did indeed have to relieve himself.

Descending a flight of stairs and entering the toilets, Dave's nostrils flared on inhaling air-freshened freedom. He inspected his reddened face in the mirror and shook the weakness out of his arms, remarking it hot upstairs. He had just unzipped his flies, was aiming at a shying blue pastille in the white porcelain and enjoying the pressure in his bladder dissipating, when a voice came over the tannoy.

'Will a Dustin Harris come to the welcome desk please?'

Dave's head shot up. His face questioned him in the mirror. Was that a lisp on the 's' or an aging microphone?

'Come on!' he shouted as he watched a steady stream swirl below him, before shaking off the final drops and scrambling to zip his trousers, his fingers numb.

Outside, he pulled on the door to the stairwell leading upstairs. Finding it locked, he hesitated before stabbing at the elevator button.

'Come on!' he shouted at the elevator doors.

They opened, he edged inside and closed his eyes.

Ping.

The doors slid back open, as did one of Dave's eyes, relieved to see he was still in Cardiff Bay Visitor Centre. He edged out of the elevator and scanned the hall, attention landing on an empty welcome desk. He tucked a finger under the blue elastic band, ran circles around his wrist. No sign of Dustin, Dave decided he must have returned to the presentation. They had only got to the late eighteen hundreds, after all. Whatever had called him out couldn't have been that important. Dave turned towards the room that told tales of Cardiff's heyday.

Then, he saw the nose.

Dave's eyes narrowed. He'd recognise her anywhere. It *had* been a lisp over the tannoy. He knew it! He watched the cleaner from Cardiff House enter a room to the other side of the hall and rushed to follow her, glancing at the panel beside the door on which was written *The Cardiff Blitz*.

In a darkened room, words flickered, announcing a film about to start. Newsreel footage filled the screen, illuminating the room. Dave's eyes bounced from wall to wall, seeing rows of chairs but no one in them. He had been sure she'd come this way.

Music trumpeted. Dave jumped.

Black and white buildings crumbled before him, people searching the rubble for what had been lost.

'One of the biggest coal ports in the world, Cardiff was a strategic target for the German Luftwaffe.' A lilting Welsh voice surrounded Dave. 'The city got used to being regularly targeted between 1940 and 1944.'

Sirens wailed. Dave walked towards the screen. People scurried, masks in hand, squeezing themselves into makeshift bunkers. A poster filled the screen. *Listen for the sirens. Turn off the lights and seek shelter*, it advised. *Handbells signify the raid is over. Rattling announces poisonous gas.*

'As the German forces tried to disable the port, over two thousand bombs fell on Cardiff,' continued the commentary.

Swastika-painted planes glided through a night sky. Burring filled the room. Dave rubbed his head as he watched the cumbersome machines relieve themselves, bombs tumbling like oranges from a shopping bag. He fixed the dots splattering into houses, schools, lives. One by one by one, dust clouds rose into a sleeping sky.

'A most poignant example of humankind's capacity for self-destruction,' concluded the lilting narrator, as the room exploded in light.

Then, the lights went out.

CHAPTER EIGHTEEN

His jacket weighed on him, the air tropical. The ground trembled. Dave opened his eyes. Knees buckling, he stretched his arms to steady himself, noticing the flesh on his hand bulging between the straps of a contraption that resembled a mutant fly. Two breathing vents eyeballed him.

'For emergency situations,' said a familiar voice.

Listen for the sirens, rattling announces poisonous gas.

Dave lifted his head, the fear he was indeed now time travelling quickly replaced by a more immediate threat.

'Jesus Christ!' he shouted.

A world away from war-torn Wales, the blackened hillside before him spewed its insides. Oozing molten flesh and blood, a disembowelled Earth pleaded for help. Smoke rose, dirtying the clouds and shrouding the sun before lodging itself firmly in Dave's throat. He coughed.

'Volcanic gases can be dangerous if the wind is blowing the wrong way,' said Sal.

Wondering if wind could ever blow the *wrong* way,

Dave grabbed the gas mask on his wrist, unravelling the strap.

Sal placed a hand on his arm. 'Not today!' He thrust a black box towards him. 'Look, it's blinking green. Never understood that expression either, wind blowing in the wrong direction. I mean, it blows whatever way it wants to. As if there is a right and wrong way.' Sal shrugged, a giggle lingering at the back of his throat.

Dave frowned. Not Iceland. Not again. And stood face to face with a volcano in mid-eruption if he wasn't mistaken.

'Certainly is. That's Fagradalsfjall,' said Sal.

'Fa . . .'

'Fa-gra-dals-f-jall.' Sal hovered over every syllable.

'Bloody active volcano.'

'Fa-gra-dals-f-jall. Means "beautiful valley mountain" in Icelandic.'

'Ac-tive-vol-can-o! Why the hell are we here?'

'You still don't get it, do you?' Sal shook his head in a manner akin to most of Dave's teachers at comprehensive school.

Dave eyed the volcano. Orange gloop traced an unrelenting path down the hillside, confirming it a bad idea to let it out of sight. Wobbling, Dave shook the gas mask from his wrist. As it dropped, he crouched to retrieve one of the grey rocks at his feet. His thumb slid over its holes, the cold refreshing him.

'Is this a lava field?' he asked.

Sal nodded.

'What if the volcano erupts on us?'

Sal watched the sloth-like ooze and laughed. 'Don't you think we'd see it coming?'

'Isn't that what they said in Pompeii?' Dave stood and

TUESDAY

thrust his hands in his jacket pockets, the rock he'd collected thudding against his hip.

He had to get back. The crane would be finished soon, that was if Dustin was still listening to him. Then, Dave would deliver his *pièce de résistance*: fifty percent grant funding. This was his one shot. He didn't trust Sal's faith in the volcano, but Sal was right about one thing: Dave didn't get why he was here. Not today of all days. But today was . . .

Wide-eyed, Dave addressed Sal. 'Hang on, it's not Tuesday.'

'No, it's Thursday.'

Of course, it was Thursday. Dave had made sure Dustin's visit hadn't been programmed on a Tuesday. 'But I've always seen you on Tuesdays.'

'Something special about Tuesdays?'

'It's me that should be asking you that!'

'You see me when you need to see me.' Sal rolled his eyes. 'Kinda funny it's always been the same day of the week though.' He threw his head back and laughed.

'This is *not* funny!' The air cracked. Dave jumped. 'What the hell was that?'

'Don't get your knickers in a twist. It's just molten lava breaking the hardened stuff as it moves forward.'

Sweat trickled down Dave's back. Bile rose in his throat, along with the certitude that there was no way such proximity to a volcano was safe. He ran his tongue around his mouth to rinse the metallic taste and wondered how to convince Sal he had to leave. He checked his watch. 'Look, I need to get back.'

'To seal the deal?'

'It's my way out of this mess.'

'Mercury in rivers, seas and oceans, you don't care about that mess?'

'Come on! Most of the world is made up of water. So what if there was a little accident over in the States.'

'Accident?'

'Nothing's been proved.'

Dave stared at Sal, his face as red as the hat once again covering his head. He must know he'd have more chance of convincing Dave when hiding his hairy ears. Dave rubbed his nose, tears trickling down his cheeks as smoke engulfed them. No smoke without fire, that was the saying. Something about Dustin's comment down at the docks *had* bothered Dave, that smile when Dustin had realised the site sat right on the Bristol Channel. Dustin had brought up Adrian's Creek again in the car.

'Maybe you've heard things?' he had asked, shuffling in his seat and rearranging his trousers. 'Nothing's been proved, David.'

Dave could have called a halt to the project there and then. He knew grant aid was a driver when it came to Dustin's final choice. All he needed to do was not offer the fifty percent funding. His decision could align with current rhetoric.

'Find us companies that aren't motivated by financial incentives but are driven by other reasons to come to Wales. The money must be the cherry on the cake. Those are the orders from on high,' Digby had already reiterated several times that year.

Find Dave a company unmotivated by money, especially free money. If they didn't want companies seeking cash support, why set up a fund? Anyway, what city wasn't interested in three hundred jobs? If the factory wasn't built in Wales, it would be built somewhere else. That was the name of the game. Everyone wanted manufacturing investment, new jobs, sustainable futures . . . green, green bloody tech. He was hardly going to save the world by

TUESDAY

saying no to Cardiff and watching it happen in Colchester.

'This newfound son of yours, think you can sweep him under the carpet too?' asked Sal.

'Do we need to talk about him now?'

'You tell me?' Sal rolled a rock in the palm of his hand.

'He might not even be mine. He didn't turn up at the stadium, did he?'

'You know he is though, don't you?'

'Jesus, Sal! Let me go back. I need to find Dustin and close this deal. This is my way out of the shower of shit they call my life!'

'You're the one stalling. You wouldn't be here otherwise.'

'Stop saying that!' Dave's cry echoed into the lunar wilderness. 'I don't want to be here. Why would I want to come here?'

'Maybe it isn't as simple as grant funding?'

'Give me a break, will you?' Dave hands splayed in anger. 'I'm doing everything I can to save my job, my family, my marriage.'

'The woman you married nearly thirty years ago out of guilt. Was she ever really the one? Head of America, that the job you always wanted, is it? And what about Seth? Do you have the relationship you want with him or are you pushing your son to end up like you? In a life full of choices that were never his own.'

Dave sank to a crouch, his head dropping into his hands.

'I'm not here to beat you up, you know,' said Sal.

'You're doing a pretty good job.' Dave's head burrowed between his knees. Searching elusive silence, he stared at the black ground.

'Tell me what you know about tectonic plates.'

Dave sighed. 'Iceland sits on two that are slowly being ripped apart by opposing forces.'

Sal squatted beside him. 'Tectonic plates interact with each other because of the Earth's internal heat.'

Dave didn't need to hear this. He needed to get back. His head returned to his knees. Why wouldn't the little elf go away?

'Elves don't exist,' he whispered.

'The Earth's internal heat moves material beneath its crust, the energy release coming in the form of earthquakes and volcanoes,' continued Sal. 'Any form of friction creates energy, energy that can't be contained. It's the same in life. Create friction between your thoughts, your words and your actions and wait for the tremors. Sooner or later, they always come.'

'Go away, go away, go away!' Dave covered his ears with his hands, his nails scraping his scalp.

He didn't want this. He didn't need this. He knew this project wasn't great on paper but let him run with it for God's sake. Everything in his life was on the line here.

'Think about it. You've known Jolene long enough to know she's not messing around with the Chairman.' Sal's muffled words reached Dave. 'This is your last chance. Otherwise, it will be taken out of your hands.'

'Out of my—' Dave lifted his head.

Sal had disappeared.

Dave scanned the rugged landscape. Empty, it laughed back at him. He had what he wanted. He'd told Sal to go away and he had . . . and now he was all alone, with no way of getting back to Cardiff Bay Visitor Centre. From the floor, the gas mask stared at him, its eyes full of pity.

Dave leant back on his hands, resolving he'd wait for the wind to change. It didn't matter if he was gassed to death, he'd only screw up if left to live. Win or lose this

TUESDAY

project, there was no way Carol would accept an illegitimate son from a past rugby tour. Jedd had to be his. There was something that would never go away. Dave inhaled, urging invisible gas to come and take him. Tremors rattled his arms, numbing his shoulders, then his head.

Wait for the tremors. Sooner or later, they always come.

On the horizon, Dave locked eyes with molten flesh and blood spurting higher than before in incandescent freedom.

Up until now, danger had whispered to him. 'Get the hell out of here. What idiot sits and gazes at an active volcano? Are you out of your bloody mind? You've got more important things to be doing, like sorting your life out.'

Now, not a bone moved, muscle twitched or tiniest of thoughts came to play. Smoke attacked Dave's eyes but he couldn't miss the conflict being waged before him. A confrontation that had long been brewing, a war between opposing forces and a battle with only one victor. Letting go of fear came with the promise of deliverance. Intoxicating, it spoke in a new tongue, promising the freedom that accompanies accepting control as nothing more than an illusion.

'Be in awe,' it said as Dave's eyes watered. 'Come closer, watch me, respect me. I am Mother Nature. You don't mess with me.'

CHAPTER NINETEEN

A crooked eighteen stared at Dave. The slightly off-centre eight had always annoyed him. The handle wrenched out of his hand as the front door swung open.

'What took you so long?' said Carol, sounding unusually concerned.

Dave searched for facial clarification, his wife's stone-like forehead suggesting recent Botox. Smoke tickled his nostrils. Fa . . . fa . . . that volcano. He scanned the porch. He'd been in Iceland a few seconds ago and now he was on his own doorstep. Wondering how many hours he'd lost this time, Dave pulled his phone out of his pocket, catching sight of a string of texts from Ellis, the last one asking him to call as soon as possible.

'Jesus Christ!' said Dave. 'One o'clock.'

Carol prodded his cheek. 'You okay? You're a funny colour.'

At the end of the hallway, a crowd mingled in the back garden. The Stereophonics poured out of the speakers, wishing Dave a nice day. It would be a lot nicer if he knew what the hell was going on.

TUESDAY

'I said you wouldn't be long,' said Carol, stroking his arm.

Dave examined his wife, wondering when she had last touched him with such affection and remembering he'd been with Dustin until he had disappeared. There had been an announcement. That ugly little woman. So where was—

'Bet you shit yourself losing your wallet like that?'

Dave froze. 'My wallet?'

'At the stadium.'

'The stadium?'

'You going to repeat everything I say?'

Dave thought on his backlog of texts. Thank God for Ellis. He must have assumed something had happened with Jedd and covered for him. Dave craned to look past Carol as the music made an impromptu departure to 'The Sound of Silence'. He loved Paul Simon.

'Who's here?' he asked.

'Most people.' Carol sighed. 'No Jolene, though. Hope she's not in a strop.'

'A strop?'

Carol tried to frown, Botox holding firm.

Dave forced a smile, realising he was repeating himself again. His skull ached.

Carol's voice dropped to a whisper as she leant in. 'Don't know how you forgot to invite her. When I called trying to find you, I made up some excuse, agreed she could bring her new fella.'

'Bring her new fella?'

Carol sighed. 'Stop it!'

Dave had no idea Jolene had a new boyfriend. That said, how would he? He'd been avoiding her. It didn't make any sense to bring her boyfriend to a barbecue at which her lover, the Chairman, was likely to make an appearance . . . not unless she was trying to make him jealous . . . still thinking he was also having it away with Carol . . .

'Dave?'

'What?'

'I said, you must not have noticed losing your wallet yesterday what with today being the big day.' Carol laughed.

Dave nodded, forgetting about Jolene and returning his attention to what might have happened to Dustin. He pulled at the elastic band on his wrist, recalling a gas mask and debating whether he had been gassed to death as requested. A spider crawling out of a dirty corner of the porch confirmed it too shitty for the afterlife, introducing another option: some kind of parallel universe.

'Don't tell me you'd forgotten about the barbecue?' Carol's forehead strained.

Dave looked down the hallway, snippets of schedule coming back to him. Carol had invited everyone to their house for a barbecue. He *had* forgotten. Not a parallel universe at all. More a nonparallel continuation of the day and him very much alive.

'It's Thursday, right?' Dave's attention snapped back to Carol.

'Dave! Focus!' Carol poked his cheek again.

'Get off!' he said, batting away her hand.

'Of course it's Thursday. I'm trying to save your sorry skin here. Told Dustin you were on your way. Now, get rid of that bloody thing.' She pulled at the band on his wrist, snapping it. 'It's stopping circulation to your head. No wonder you're making no sense.'

'What's wrong with you?' said Dave, rubbing his wrist and kicking the broken band across the doorstep, unintentionally dismembering the spider.

TUESDAY

He was missing hours of the day. Again. At least he hadn't missed the barbecue. He still had his presentation to deliver. There was time to claw it all back.

Carol buffered for a moment before regaining use of her arms to readjust her hair. 'Look, I'm sorry. It's just Rhys has been telling me what a great job you've been doing.'

'He has?' Dave lifted his head to see his wife smile.

Perfume cloyed at his nostrils, reminding him of the charred mountain. Beautiful valley mountain. *Come closer, watch me, respect me.* Dave shook away the thought. He couldn't remember the last time they'd been this close. Carol stroked his arm again, his groin stirred.

'The Head of International is yours. There's even talk of the job relocating to Paris.' Carol's lips moved into Dave's neck. 'I know we've had our ups and downs lately, but—'

'David! Great little place you have here.' Dustin appeared in the hallway.

'Panic over! Dave found his wallet,' said Carol, straightening herself.

'Awesome. Sorry I had to dash off at the Visitor Centre. Some mix-up.'

Dave went to ask for clarification, remembering the tannoy announcement and foolishly following that strange little woman. He stopped himself, deciding it didn't matter. Carol was right. He had to focus. In the distance, he saw Digby and Pierre exchanging pleasantries. He inspected the cornices that, according to Steve from Happy Homes Estate Agents, added an inexplicable amount of value to their home. Remembering their monthly payments had shot up with the interest rate spikes, he resolved to push any Iceland nonsense out of his mind.

'Come on then, love,' Carol gripped his arm. 'Time to finish that conversation with Dustin over a burger.'

'Well, well, well, there's Wales's answer to Houdini.' Jolene poked Dave in the ribs as she pushed past him.

She stretched out a hand to Dustin. 'You must be Mr Harris from Great Brakes. Been dying to meet you. I'm Jolene and this is my boyfriend, Jedd.'

Digby's lips moved in time with words. Dave had no idea how much Lidl four-for-three Italian wine it had taken for his boss to slur so heavily. In any case, he wasn't listening. Dave's position was strategic, his eyes never leaving Jolene and Jedd as they intertwined limbs near the gazebo, hanging off each other's every word. Dustin rushing to play master of ceremonies hadn't yet afforded conversation with Jolene, the sheer amount of cow he was grilling equally incompatible with her veganism.

Jolene caught Dave staring, smiled and glanced towards Carol who had been discussing Parisian landmarks with Pierre for the past half an hour.

Double jeopardy.

Dave slurped his gin and tonic, glancing around the garden and confirming the one small mercy of the day: the Chairman wasn't at the barbecue. Carol had said he couldn't make it, filling Dave with gratitude as too many of his secrets had already congregated for lunch.

'*When one burns one's bridges, what a very nice fire it makes.*' Digby leant in, the olive in his hand pausing *en route* to his mouth.

Dave's mind flashed back to smoke clouding over the volcano, the molten ooze of conflict. What was it Sal said about thoughts, words and actions aligning? He'd been hiding his doubts around Great Brakes from everyone, trying to keep it from himself, but Digby seemed to know something.

Wait for the tremors. Sooner or later, they always come.

'Sorry?' Dave asked.

This project was his chance. It was only a little bit of mercury, after all. He needed this job. Wales needed jobs.

'Bit jealous, are we?' Digby pointed his cocktail stick towards the gazebo.

'Jealous?'

'You haven't taken your eyes off Jolene. Pierre was telling me about your tryst in the stationery cupboard.'

Shit. Dave had forgotten about that. This was all he needed, assuming tryst was a poetic version of the Chairman finding Jolene straddling him. Dave had enough truths to hide without adding fabricated rumours.

'You've got it all—'

'I'm not one to judge, David. Your personal life is none of my business.'

As Dustin started distributing burgers to Pierre and Carol, Dave dug his nails into his palms, knowing Jedd and Jolene would be next.

'Jolene's sleeping with the Chairman,' said Dave, wondering how and why the words had flown out of his mouth.

Digby threw his head back in laughter. 'I hardly think so!'

Dave turned his attention to Digby. 'What do you—'

'Gay as you like, that one.'

'Not sure you can say that.'

'*You* can't. You'd be cautioned. Again.' Digby slapped Dave on the shoulder. Waves of wine swelled in his glass.

Wait for the tremors. Sooner or later, they always come.

'As a gay man, however, I can. Why do you think I'm being pushed out?'

'Thought you were retiring?' Dave studied Digby.

'From a job that affords me the time and contacts to reach a 10-handicap? I was *asked* to retire. Someone didn't like me saying no to his dick being pushed up against me over the photocopier late one night.'

'The Chairman?' Dave closed his gaping mouth, wondering if he didn't prefer incomprehensible Dylan Thomas renditions. 'You didn't report him?'

'A gay man crying sexual assault, you think that would be taken seriously? Them's the rules, my friend.'

Dave's shoes absorbed the wine sloshing out of Digby's glass. The rest of him had a harder time taking in what he'd been told. 'But the Chairman's married.'

'Think Oscar Wilde.'

Dave's frown deepened.

'That daytime TV presenter then,' said Digby. 'You really think old Rhys will come today? Bricking it I might spill the beans before I leave.'

Dave steadied his boss who poured another glass of Pinot Grigio and downed it in one. The stress of the day starting to show, Dave stretched his fingers, trying to rid the numbness seizing them, and wondered if he had ever seen Digby so drunk or deploying vocabulary not structured in stanzas.

Debating if the day couldn't get any worse, raised voices drew Dave's attention back to the other side of the garden. Framed in rows of pink fairy lights, an angry portrait confirmed it was indeed about to deteriorate and that, in listening to Digby, Dave had taken his eye off the ball. The entire conversation incomprehensible, words like 'greenwashing' and 'bastard' sailed across the garden.

TUESDAY

Jolene waved her arms, forcing Dustin to retreat into the hedge.

Dave and Digby crossed the lawn, Carol and Pierre doing the same.

'*Viens. Calme-toi,*' said Pierre.

'Don't patronise me, you little French prick.' Jolene was puce.

Carol stared at Dave.

'Go on! Tell everyone about Adrian's Creek, Dustin,' shouted Jolene. 'Don't you think they should know you're going to be flushing mercury into our water too?'

'Mercury?' asked Jedd.

'Jolene!' Dave tried to silence her with a hard stare.

'Dave,' shouted Carol. 'Sort this out, will you?'

'Used to things being kept secret, aren't you Dave?' Jolene glared at him.

'And what the hell is that supposed to mean?' replied Carol.

'Listen, let's all calm down, shall we?' Dave's head span. 'Why would the Chairman be offering money from our Welsh Technology Accelerator Fund to a company wanting to pollute our water?'

'Funding, David?' Dustin slapped him on the back, knocking him off balance. 'That's excellent news.'

The gazebo swayed in the breeze. Carol nodded at Dave to seal the deal. What were those figures again? If only he had his presentation. Remembering it was on his phone, Dave tried to find his pocket.

'Welsh Technology Accelerator Fund, you have to be kidding me,' shouted Jolene.

'What the actual . . .' Jedd eyeballed Dustin. 'Polluting the water. No way, man. That's so not cool.'

Dave wobbled. His hand slid down his trousers. All he needed to do was find his pocket. These trousers had pockets. All his trousers had pockets. As his hand slid again, the fairy lights fused into a candyfloss mess. He staggered forward. Light flooded the garden. This couldn't be happening. It wasn't Tuesday, it was Thursday . . . but it had already happened on a Thursday. It had happened earlier that day. He stretched open his eyes, knees buckling under his weight. Oh God, it *was* happening. Twice in one day? Not back to the volcano.

'Fa . . . Fa . . . Fa-gra . . .'

Wait for the tremors. Sooner or later, they always come.

'Dave?' Carol's face got bigger, then tiny, tiny, tiny.

Lemon and rosemary danced out of the gin in which they swam, glass smashing at his feet. Dave reached for the gazebo, a chair and finally Digby on his own journey to the floor. Rarely had Dave commanded such respect as his head hit the flagstone, silencing the garden. Faces fused into one, a handful of seconds allowing time to note an incident of enough severity to disrobe Digby of any poetry the Pinot Grigio had spared.

Then, for the second time that day, the lights went out.

CHAPTER TWENTY

Barefoot, Dave hopped from rock to rock. Water whistled past; the wind gushed. In the distance, birds waltzed through ash plumes as the Earth spewed everything it had been trying to hide. White-hot exasperation spurted from craters to flood the valley, filling Dave with calm.

'Rage, rage!'

Dave stopped, the voice catching his attention. On top of a boulder, a man in a red neckerchief balanced a glass of Pinot Grigio on his head.

'Dylan Thomas?' asked Dave.

'Who else?' replied the man, stretching out his arms to balance himself, his gaze focused ahead. *'Rage, rage against the dying of the light,'* he cried, his curls and jowls rolling on the 'r'.

'What the hell are you doing in Iceland?' Dave searched for Sal. For once, he wouldn't mind seeing the little fella. 'Hang on a minute, aren't you dead?'

'Doesn't a bit of us die every time we continue to put up with this shit?' asked Dylan Thomas.

'Living the life everyone else wants,' replied Dave.

'You're a prime example. You don't even like Paris. Full of bloody French.' Forgetting the balancing act, the poet threw back his head in laughter, glass splintering behind him.

'Carol does though,' said Dave.

'You're scared of change, that's all. Don't like the friction, like with those tectonic plates.'

'Maybe I've changed?'

'Maybe you were pretending to be someone else.'

'I'm disappointing.'

'To her?'

'To myself.'

'It's impossible to feel such disappointment if you're honest with yourself.'

Dave shivered. An icy stream lapped his knees.

'Why are you here anyway?' he asked.

'Early retirement, is that what I really want?' The poet jumped from the boulder to land facing Dave. 'I likes the tremors, see. When you think about it, it's that friction you're avoiding that makes life move forward.' He grabbed Dave's arm and shook it.

'Sooner or later,' said a voice, Dave noticing his new friend's lips not moving.

'They always come,' replied Dave.

'Looks like it is sooner rather than later,' said the same voice.

Beep, beep, beep, beep, beep.

Unable to recall the last time he'd heard a rocky stream beep, Dave tried to move.

'He's awake!'

A scurry of feet approached.

Beep, beep, beep, beep, beep.

Dave opened his eyes. Above, several heads crowded in.

'This isn't Iceland?' asked Dave.

TUESDAY

The heads exchanged worried looks.

'You're at Heath Hospital, Mr Welch,' said a white coat, if Dave wasn't mistaken, placing the emphasis on the final syllable.

Dave waited for the man who had introduced himself some minutes earlier as Dr Bete to finish reading the clipboard he had unhooked from the foot of the bed. A poker face confirmed ignorance of the latent humour in his name. Dave tried to rid his thoughts of Gloria Estefan as she played on repeat and the room swayed in time to the music.

'We ran a number of tests whilst you were asleep,' said Dr Bete finally.

Doc, doc, doc, doc, Doctor Bete.

'Lucky you were admitted when you were.'

Won't you help me, Doctor Bete?

'You have a severe case of mercury poisoning.'

'Poisoning?' Dave tried to straighten himself, his arms collapsing.

'Stay where you are, Mr Welch.' Dr Bete shouted from the end of the bed. 'If you're feeling woozy, it's the medication. Anyway, where was I?' He returned to the clipboard. 'Double the level indicative of toxic exposure. Do you work in manufacturing? Have cause to handle the metal?'

Mercury. Adrian's Creek. Great Brakes. Dave rearranged his arms, wincing as the tube running from the back of his hand caught on the bed rail. The factory wasn't in Wales yet. Absolutely impossible to have been exposed to anything.

'Mr Welch?' insisted Dr Bete.

Dave shook his head, staring at the drop of saline about to fall from his drip. 'I'm the Head of America.'

Dr Bete pulled what Dave soon realised to be a torch out of his breast pocket. With a whoosh of white coat, he moved to the side of the bed, pinned Dave's eyes open and blinded him.

'Bloody hell!' shouted Dave.

'What year is it, Mr Welch?'

'What?' Dave squinted, batting away the light.

'You sure you're the Head of America? The President of the United States?'

'President? I work for the CIA.'

'So, Langley, not the White House?' Dr Bete beckoned the backing group of interns arranged in a semi-circle behind him, deploying what Dave interpreted as international sign language for a patient losing the plot.

'At Cardiff bloody House. The Cardiff Investment Agency,' replied Dave.

'Cardiff Investment Agency?'

A skeleton of a boy who looked no older than seventeen stepped forward. 'Can I help you, Dr Bete?'

Doc, doc, doc, doc, Doctor Bete.

'Ah! Read about the audit in the paper.' Dr Bete wafted the intern away, adding an eye roll for good measure.

'We bring foreign investment into Cardiff.' Dave sighed.

'That's you?' Dr Bete frowned. 'Waste of taxpayers' money if you ask me.'

Dave hadn't asked. Jesus Christ! Akin to every taxi ride he had ever taken in Cardiff, the golden rule was to never mention you worked for the Cardiff Investment Agency. Dave had taken to introducing himself as a central heating technician. On cheekier days, a male escort.

'When you think what we could do with that money in

the National Health Service.' Dr Bete shook his head. 'Crying shame.'

'Don't suppose we could get back to my mercury poisoning?' asked Dave.

'Indeed,' Dr Bete reverted to his clipboard. 'It's extremely rare to have such levels in your blood without some kind of chemical accident.' He flipped through the sheets in front of him. 'Twenty-one nanograms per millilitre, to be precise. Talk me through the last few weeks. Noticed any anxiety or mood swings?'

Of course he had, what with everything going on. Who wouldn't be shitting themselves at the thought of their wife leaving them and losing their job?

'No more than normal,' he replied.

'Numbness?' Dr Bete pulled at Dave's fingers.

Dave had been having trouble feeling his fingers, now he thought about it. And his legs were more tired than usual, clumsy at times.

'Just general tiredness. The odd sign of stress.'

'Lack of coordination, muscle weakness, hair loss, metallic taste in your mouth? Any nausea? In any case, Mr Welch, you have mercury poisoning, that much we know. How you got it is what we need to work out.'

'But you can get rid of this mercury?' asked Dave.

Dr Bete searched the air, Dave doubting answers were airborne. 'One step at a time.'

Examining Dr Bete, Dave wondered how he could be so perplexed given his big head. Big head, big brain. Not big . . . his head was *massive*. How had Dave not noticed?

Dr Bete raised an eyebrow.

Conscious he had been staring, Dave averted his attention to his own hands. Jesus Christ! They were enormous too. He wiggled his fingers. Dr Bete was right. He could barely feel them.

'How much do you weigh, Mr Welch?'

'Sixteen stone . . . probably more like fourteen now,' said Dave, correcting himself on remembering his fasting.

'You've lost weight recently?'

Dave nodded.

'In a short space of time?'

'Suppose so. Still need to lose a stone more from here.' Dave pinched at his belly as best his comedy hands would allow. Whatever drugs he was on, it was good shit.

'Hmm,' said Dr Bete, rubbing his chin.

'What?'

'Oh nothing. Just thinking you sound very English to be promoting Wales.'

'And you have a very big head to be a doctor.'

Dave frowned at his retort making no sense, let alone being impolite.

'My head looks big to you?' Dr Bete leant in.

'To be fair, the closer you get, the bigger it looks. Sorry, I didn't mean to be rude. Must be the drugs.'

Dr Bete rubbed his chin again. 'Anything else look bigger than normal?'

'My hands?' Dave ventured his answers as questions. 'That nurse over there?'

Dr Bete followed Dave's finger to two buttocks squeezing down the side of a vacant bed on the other side of the room 'Oh that's Craig.' He lowered his voice. 'Big fan of the old Magnum. The ice cream, not the PI.'

Dr Bete sniggered, offering an unexpected olive branch in a common love of dad jokes and making Dave question if he was as bad as he had first thought.

'So, doctor?'

'You banged your head when you fell, that's right?'

Dave nodded.

'And I see in the files you were in here not long ago

TUESDAY

after a rugby injury. I'll book you in for an MRI and an EEG. Let's have a look at that head of yours. Could be some answers there.'

Dave smiled to himself. No one had ever said that.

'I'll run some more blood tests too. Get settled in, Mr Welch.' Dr Bete's head fell back, laughter erupting like machine-gun fire. 'How funny, just noticed your name isn't quite Welsh, just like you! I'll let your family know they can see you now.'

Dr Bete and his backing singers disappeared. Dave snatched his phone from the bedside table, displacing water from the jug next to it. The two ticks still hadn't turned blue. Dropping the phone into the sheets, he played with the buttons he'd been told made the bed more comfortable. The mattress inclining and reclining, his toes continued to tap the melamine. What it really needed was an extra foot in length. He remembered Brendan from Treorchy saying family could ride alongside as he hoisted Dave into the back of the ambulance, but nothing after that. With no visitors allowed, Carol had to be in the waiting room. She probably simply had no connection.

As he continued to stare at the four bars on his phone, a familiar face popped around the side of the curtain. Seth fell into the chair next to the bed.

'It's all they had downstairs,' he said, dropping several packs of Hula Hoops at Dave's feet. 'You okay, Dad? How did you manage to get mercury poisoning?'

'The doctors told you?'

'Mum called the hospital.'

Dave craned to see past the curtain.

'Said she'd be here later. She's sorting out stuff first.'

Dave's stomach churned.

Seth shrugged. 'Sorry, Dad.'

'Sorry?'

Tears welled in Seth's eyes. 'Rodric's dad dropped us off. When we came into the garden, I heard Digby saying someone had gone down like a sack of shit.'

'Bloody Digby!' Dave attempted a laugh. 'Wasted on Pinot Grigio.'

'Then I saw you on the floor.' A tear rolled down Seth's cheek. 'I thought you were dead.'

'Sorry to give you a scare, Son.'

'Sorry for being a shit, Dad. I knew you weren't right when I found you on that bench the other day. I've been waiting all this time.'

'You came in the ambulance?'

Seth nodded. 'What will they do with you now?'

'Don't worry, they'll sort me out.' Dave rested an arm on Seth's shoulder, doubting the veracity of his words, Dr Bete having been less than encouraging.

'Best you're off work for a while anyway,' said Seth.

'How's that, Son?'

'As they were carrying you out, Jolene called your boss an effing disgrace.'

Dave winced. 'Digby was pissed as a fart but that's going a bit far.'

'Not him. Your other boss.'

'The Chairman was there?'

CHAPTER TWENTY-ONE

Slats opened and closed on a setting sun. Of the ten buttons on the handset, four related to bed position, two controlled lights and two activated the blinds. The other two presented more of a challenge. Dave stabbed at the plastic box, his attention tracking the room for any sign of change.

Seth had left on the arrival of a meal cart delivering a lactose-free, meat-free, gluten-free lasagne, accompanied by the apologies of an auxiliary nurse called Maureen.

'Not your lucky day, is it?' she'd said, slamming a plastic tray onto a table and wheeling it towards him. 'I'm not being funny, but who makes lasagne with no cheese, no meat and no pasta?'

'Not *Swshi Shack* is it?' Dave had replied.

'You're right there, love. Bloody loves a maki, me.'

Maureen gone, Dave had pushed the table away, a decision he now rued as his stomach whined from neglect. His eyes followed the tube connecting the drip to the back of his hand, his veins standing proud in a way he would have difficulty doing once released, whenever that might be. His thoughts returned to the barbecue and him passing out at the eleventh hour, just as the Chairman graced everyone with an appearance. Something didn't add up. Digby had been sure the Chairman would keep a low profile. Dave had been so close to closing the deal. He had to get out of hospital. Surely, they wouldn't keep him in for much longer. The NHS was short of beds.

He stared at the empty bed opposite.

Dave rubbed his face, wondering what more could have happened once he'd been stretchered away and what mess he would come back to. For Jolene to let rip at the Chairman as Seth had described, the conversation must have degenerated. Had she accused him of knowing about the mercury incident in the States and the trail of allegations levelled at Great Brakes? Dave had kept his doubts to himself. Smarmy though he was, the Chairman was in no way implicated. If the shit hit the fan, as the expression went, it would be more a question of Dave convincing everyone *he* had been blissfully unaware.

He hadn't been though, had he?

Sinking into the pillow, Dave closed his eyes. He'd had doubts all along, doubts he'd refused to hear in order to keep his marriage and career on track. Now, here he was, hauled up in Heath Hospital with mercury poisoning, having turned a blind eye to a company flushing the *same* toxin into the sea. It was too much of a coincidence. Sal said everything and everyone was connected. Busy trying to make his bit of the world flow smoothly, Dave had ignored other bits of the world flowing into his. Technology pushing the human race to instant gratification, this was its equal and opposite: instant comeuppance. Even if he feigned ignorance, it had been his job to undertake further due diligence. He hadn't. He was screwed either

TUESDAY

way. And to top it all off, here he was, believing the words of an elf! Dave hadn't mentioned that part of the past few weeks to Dr Bete. Once in a medical institution, it was ill-advised to talk of seeing little people or disappearing to Iceland for hours on end. He'd never see daylight again.

Dave reached for his phone and asked Google what seeing elves meant. Hundreds of search results gathered in milliseconds, the algorithm interpreting *seeing* as *dreaming* because, let's face it, who did *see* elves. Dave read about dreams of elves representing situations requiring wise decisions (he'd messed that up), indicating the arrival of someone important in your life (Dodgy Dustin?), or being blessed with good physical and mental health (you had to be joking).

He made a fresh search on Icelandic elves, having read about them briefly but deciding it was time to dig deeper. The results were no better, yet somehow consoling. On devouring an article in *The Guardian* declaring a staggering fifty-four percent of Icelanders believed in them, Dave decided that if he hadn't been dreaming and ever saw Sal again, he'd relocate. A stranger, lonelier rock than he could have imagined, Iceland could offer safety in numbers.

Sal wasn't real. He couldn't be. So why did Dave recall with such clarity everything they had discussed?

'Knock, knock.' Carol stood at the door. 'Room to yourself?' she asked, examining the bed opposite before approaching. 'You look like shit on a stick.'

'Mercury poisoning does that to you, Carol.'

Dave glanced at the time on his phone. Nine thirty.

'Sorry, love. I tried to get here earlier.' Carol dropped a box of Jaffa Cakes on the bed. 'It's all they had downstairs.' She hovered at the side of the bed. 'Jesus, Dave. Mercury poisoning?'

Dave shrugged.

'How did you get that?'

Dave shrugged again, wondering why she hadn't sat down.

'Can they make you better?'

'I hope so, love.'

'Suppose it explains a few things?'

'Sorry?' Dave reached out a hand, knowing he would need her support to do what he had to do.

Carol's gaze danced around the room before catching his eye, dropping her hand into his and finally sitting down. 'Let's not worry about what's been and gone, the past.' She stroked his fingers. 'Focus on getting better, the future.'

Dave pulled away from Carol's stare, remembering Jedd, a six-foot piece of the past going nowhere. Sal didn't have to be real for everything he said to hold true. All that talk of thoughts, words and actions aligning. Dave had been thinking and saying one thing and doing the exact opposite for weeks, months, most of his adult life. It was suffocating. He had to tell Carol about Jedd, and Adrian's Creek. It was time to be honest. He'd start with the latter. Carol was dead set on this promotion to Paris, but she'd understand why they weren't going if she knew what Dustin and his lot were up to.

'I need you with me.' Dave squeezed her hand.

Carol looked to her knees. 'I just needed to get my head straight.'

'Head straight?'

'Sort things out, you know.' Carol traced the stripes on her trousers with her forefinger.

'Sort what out?'

'This afternoon, I mean. I had to sort things out this afternoon.' Carol's eyes met Dave's. 'Digby punched the Chairman.'

TUESDAY

'He did what?' Dave sat up in bed. 'Seth mentioned something, but why was he—'

'Then locked him in the shed. Said he'd taken him hostage but we said that didn't work because we knew where he bloody was.' Carol's hair bounced in time with her explanations.

'Bloody hell!'

'Kept saying he had skills that made him a nightmare for people like Rhys.'

Laughter shot out of Dave on remembering Digby's other Pinot Grigio-laced confession of a Liam Neeson fetish.

Carol stared at him, not sharing his mirth.

'And what about what Jolene said?' asked Dave, realising he could be in a position to unmask the accusations against Great Brakes without admitting he'd known all along.

'What do you mean *what Jolene said?*' Carol wrenched away her hand.

'Well, she called him an effing disgrace, didn't she?'

'Rhys?' Carol frowned.

'Because of what happened with Digby?'

'Well, of course because of that,' shouted Carol. 'You don't go thrusting yourself up against anyone you want, now do you?'

'Okay, okay. Calm down.'

Carol returned to tracing lines down her trousers.

Dave took another glance at the time on his phone, something telling him Carol could still have been there sooner. His eyes bore into the top of Carol's head, searching for answers.

'I'm sorry. It's been a right day,' said Carol as she sank into the chair. 'Not to mention Jolene getting fired.'

'Jolene getting fired?'

'She went ballistic. Left not long after, before the police got there.'

'The police?'

'You're doing that thing where you repeat everything I say again,' said Carol, sighing.

Dave mumbled an apology. 'Go on,' he insisted.

'Well, there was no talking Digby down from the garage roof. He'd padlocked the shed and swallowed the key by then.'

Dave opted for a nod as he wondered if anyone could have imagined Digby's response, let alone Jolene being fired. His stomach sank. He should have listened to Jolene. She'd been right all along. Carol's shoulders hanging low with the weight of the day, he questioned how to broach the subject of Great Brakes.

'Bet Dustin thinks we're a right lot,' said Carol as if reading his mind. Forcing a laugh, her gaze floated out of the slatted blinds into the car park.

'Suppose that's put the kibosh on the factory down the docks?' said Dave, hopefully.

'Not at all!' Carol's attention came back to him. 'You remember Dustin was called away at the Visitor Centre?'

Dave remembered a bulbous nose and his decision to never mention seeing elves.

'Well, it was the CEO back in Detroit,' continued Carol, in full swing, 'saying investors were putting on pressure to close the deal.'

'What?'

'Dustin is more convinced than ever by Wales, especially since you promised the grant funding.'

'I'm not sure I prom—'

'The Chairman has pushed the file straight up to the First Minister.'

TUESDAY

'This afternoon?' asked Dave, realising he was screwed.

'Well, once that young sergeant got him out of the shed.' Carol leant in, grabbed Dave's hand in hers and whispered, 'Rhys says Paris is ours! He's so pleased with you.' Her gaze floated back into the car park. 'Things have been complicated but we could try to put everything behind us and start again? For Seth.'

Dave forced a smile. Up that godforsaken Icelandic hill, the two things he had wished for were to not lose his wife or his job. Here he was, wishes granted and more alone than he had ever felt.

Be careful what you wish for, Son. Dave stared over at Dad perched on the end of the bed opposite, smiling. Life was about winners and losers. Ted had been on the losing side of a common agricultural policy; Icelandic fishermen had been sacrificed to big fisheries pushing a sustainable technology agenda. Dave had a third in Sports Science but he was beginning to understand Jolene's browbeating since her arrival at the CIA. True sustainability has no losers. Dave had to break his silence on Great Brakes, especially now it had gone up to the First Minister.

Carol continued to talk about the Marais, almond croissants and the B she had been awarded in A-Level French. Dancing in abandon, her words regrouped to pin Dave to the bed, pushing him into a future he didn't want. He sank back into the pillow and closed his eyes. A fancy life in Paris would not come off the back of poisoning the seas and oceans. As he'd looked out from the top of that hill, he'd also asked to be free. Free from the lies, the pretending, the life everyone else wanted for him. A wish so silenced, he hadn't heard himself say it.

His breath quickened. Emotions, thoughts, words, actions, aspirations fought for air, suffocating his screams.

Tell her, tell her, tell her.

'And to think Dustin hadn't heard of Wales until you contacted him out of the blue with that email,' said Carol. 'You've pulled a bloody blinder with this one, love.'

'Out of the blue?' asked Dave, confusion forcing his eyes back open.

CHAPTER TWENTY-TWO

'So, when will you know?' Seth sat on the end of the bed, biting Hula Hoops off his fingers one by one and reminding Dave of his own childhood pastimes.

'As soon as they do. You know my doctor's called Dr Bete?' Dave laughed.

'So?' Seth smiled.

The music reference was before Seth's time but his attitude towards Dave had softened since yesterday's tears. Anger gone, the complicity they had shared when Seth was younger was making a return. Dave reached for the bag of crisps and placed hoops on his own fingers. He thought back to that morning and the series of corridors he had been wheeled down by Magnum-loving Craig to get to the radiology department. A chatty enough bloke but gifted with limited spatial awareness, Dave's legs had scuffed two doorframes and a fire extinguisher.

'Do you have any metal in your body they need to know about?' Craig had asked as Dave rubbed his knee and the technician excused himself to nip to the toilet.

'Several nanograms of mercury,' Dave had replied.

'I think they mean more like shrapnel or a pacemaker.' Craig's laughter had broken into coughing. 'The "M" is for magnetic.'

Minutes later and alone in a plastic tube, Dave had debated whether he should have mentioned two aging lead fillings in his premolars but respected the sole instruction to stay very still. A whole playlist later, he'd decided the 'RI' in MRI stood for Ruddy Interminable.

'You'll never guess what music they had on in that MRI machine.' Dave said to Seth.

'Gloria Estefan?'

'So, you do know that song!' Dave threw a Hula Hoop at his son. 'No, it was Chumbawamba. That one about getting knocked down but getting up again.'

Seth laughed. 'That's mad.'

Seth reloaded his fingers with Hula Hoops as Dave's thoughts lingered on his son's last word. Silence replaced laughter. Never mind inappropriate music choices, what if Dave *was* mad? No one had evoked that eventuality but it lingered in the room like a bad smell since his admission. Yesterday's conversation with Dr Bete had focused on the mercury in his blood. It was only during the sleepless night that followed that Dave had considered the effect of such high levels on his brain. Between the MRI and the electrodes stuck to his head earlier that morning, madness had to be what they sought. Thank Goodness he hadn't mentioned his recent *travels*.

'I brought your computer by the way,' said Seth. 'What do you need it for?'

'Work stuff.'

'Shouldn't you give it a swerve 'til you get better? Not gonna lie, your place sounds like a madhouse.'

There was that word again. Dave stared at Seth. Skipping over the detail about elves and Iceland, could he confide in his son about the rest? He needed to bounce his doubts around with someone. Carol's words from the previous evening rang in his head. *Out of the blue?* Dave had never contacted Dustin out of the blue. He had received an email from Dustin. Two, in fact.

'Listen, remember that American at the barbecue?'

'The one eating his body weight in cow?' Seth smiled. 'Wondered when he was going to start munching his way through the whole garden.'

Dave laughed. 'Seriously, I'm not sure the company he works for is legit. I need to check something.'

'Let me help you then?' Seth pulled the laptop out of his rucksack. School books tumbled to the floor.

'*A Christmas Carol*?' asked Dave, noticing a sour-faced man and cursive *Charles Dickens* adorning one of the covers.

'English lit,' replied Seth.

'Why you reading it in the summer?'

'Not actually reading it. Found someone on BookTok talking about it.'

'Book what?'

'Social media thing, Dad.' Seth laughed as he picked up the books one by one. 'Anyway, not sure you have to read a book in the season it's set? You sure you should be working?'

Dave made a mental note to stop with the questions. They raised more questions. 'Right, let's see.' Dave powered up his laptop. He drummed at the metal below the keyboard as the Intranet welcome screen announced *Happy Middle of the Year!*

'Jesus Christ. Here we go,' he mumbled.

It's the one hundredth and eighty-third day of the year! continued the red-and-white carousel. *With one hundred and eighty two days behind you, today is about taking a deep breath, reflecting on your achievements so far and planning out the next one hundred and eighty two days.*

Today was about clearing up his mess, thought Dave. Today was about getting to the bottom of Dustin Harris and Great Brakes. He clicked into his mailbox, noticing a raft of emails. Nothing too important. That Icelandic woman inviting him to the conference again. Dave paused for a moment, stared over at the bed opposite.

'Dad?'

'What, Son?'

'Who's Hel-ga?'

Dave shook his head, realising he must have said her name out loud and that everything had started with her call. 'Right, let's look at these emails.'

Dave entered 'Dustin' into the search bar of his mailbox. It compiled several results. He read through the dates and titles. The later ones all related to Dustin's visit schedule. Dave scrolled until he found an email entitled: *Future UK Operations*. That had to be one of the first emails he'd received from Dustin. He clicked and read.

Dear Dustin,

Please find attached a presentation on the Green, Green Tech of Home *and why Wales is the perfect location for your future UK site. Let's talk once you've had time to read this.*
Yours,
David Welch
Heat of America
+44 7792 765345

Yours? Dave wondered who signed off like that before realising the email was from him to Dustin and not the other way around. He'd even spelt his own title incorrectly,

TUESDAY

making him sound like a reality TV dating show winner. He clicked back to the search results, unable to find any earlier emails from Dustin. Dave tried again, entering 'Harris' and 'Great Brakes' in the search bar, having a vague recollection of Dustin using a different email address when travelling. Still nothing. Working back from the date of his email to Dustin, Dave scoured his inbox line by line. He made it to May the twenty-fourth, already knowing he'd never heard of the Great Brakes project before June.

'Emails don't just disappear,' said Dave.

'Can't find what you're looking for?' asked Seth.

'Those emails.'

'From The Very Hungry American?'

'Dustin.' Dave raised an eyebrow. 'Seriously, Seth. They've gone.'

'Maybe you deleted them?'

'I didn't!' shouted Dave.

Seth frowned. 'I told you working was a bad idea.'

Dave fell into his pillows. He couldn't have imagined the emails and pulled a company out of thin air. He couldn't second-guess email addresses. He'd met Dustin for God's sake. Three trips to the breakfast buffet, that was very real. Great Brakes was real. Why was Dave questioning himself? This was getting ridiculous. He remembered those emails.

Dave sat upright, searched again on 'Dustin' and gathered the same results.

'You okay, Dad? You've gone a funny colour.'

'How do you make emails disappear?'

'What?'

'Seriously. If I haven't deleted them, how have they disappeared?'

'Someone else deleted them?' Seth gaped at Dave, a Hula Hoop mid-air.

'But who?' Dave shouted as he reached for an imaginary elastic band.

'You've got to calm down, Dad.' Seth craned his neck to catch the attention of anyone passing by.

Dave had to get it together. He was worrying his son. He took a deep breath. 'Sorry. It's that American . . . Dustin.'

'Mum said you'd landed that project. Good news, no?'

This was it. Dave hadn't mustered the courage to tell Carol, but he needed to come clean about Great Brakes. He would start with Seth.

'This project,' he said. 'They're claiming to be all sustainable making these electric cars but there are suspicions around Great Brakes dumping toxic waste in lakes and seas.'

'And you're bringing them here?'

'I've messed up. I was warned but didn't follow through. Thought I needed the project at any cost to save my own sorry arse.'

Seth's face lost all expression as he lifted the computer away from Dave. Forgetting his fingers were adorned with the last of the potato snacks, crumbs broke into the folds of the bed. 'Warned by who?'

Dave looked out of the window, regretting his use of the word 'warned'. He couldn't mention Sal, Seth was worried enough.

'You know, a little voice inside my head.'

'You have voices in your head?'

'Shit! No! Not voices plural. You know, that *little* voice.'

'Your shadow?' asked Seth, frowning.

'My what?'

'Your hidden parts.'

'Bad parts?'

TUESDAY

'Not necessarily. Could just be repressed parts of the true you.'

Who Dave really wanted to be and not what everyone else wanted for him?

'They teaching you this in school?' asked Dave.

'Watched a video on YouTube. Jung.'

'He got a channel like you, this Young?'

Seth broke into laughter. 'You still have the bad jokes. You'll be okay.'

Dave joined Seth, unaware what was making them laugh.

Seth set the computer on the bed and returned to his crisp eating. 'So, why do you need these emails?'

'This Dustin says I contacted him out of the blue, right? But he contacted me, I swear.'

'You want to take this situationship further but he's not sure?' asked Seth.

'What?'

'Kidding!' Seth threw a Hula Hoop at him.

'Just tell me why I can't find the emails!'

'Look, if you haven't deleted them, someone has.'

'Like who?'

'The Very Hungry American himself.'

'Dustin.' Dave rolled his eyes and laughed.

'Or anyone who can get onto the server. Rodric would be able to see what has been deleted. He can hack into anything but I haven't seen him for days. Think he's avoiding me.'

'Avoiding you?' asked Dave, having known all along the creepy beanpole wasn't Seth's usual crowd.

'Said he'd help me with Comp Sci homework. Only came over a couple of times and didn't do it all. Anyway, there's an easier answer to all this.'

'I'm not sure I can hack whatever it is myself.'

'I'm absolutely sure you can't, Dad.' Seth broke into laughter. 'Why don't you mail this guy and ask him if he sent you an email or not?'

Dave nodded at what was indeed an easier solution.

'Or ask your boss if Rodric can help?'

'Digby?'

'The other one.'

'Why would I ask the Chairman?'

'Doh. Cos he's Rodric's dad. I told you that.'

The realisation sent Dave's head bobbing. Seth hadn't said it in four clear words, but it now made sense why the Dr Double Barrel had turned up at the end of the barbecue. He'd been dropping Rodric and Seth off. The Chairman and Rodric's dad were one and the same.

CHAPTER TWENTY-THREE

Dave emerged from a light slumber and reached for his telephone. Armed with the results from yesterday's MRI and EEG, Dr Bete would visit on his round that afternoon. Dave had traded Hula Hoops to learn the results sooner, Craig happy to take the crisps off his hands but declaring himself 'one of the great uninformed'.

It was half past ten.

'Ah!' Dave stabbed the end of the bed with his clammy feet, trying to loosen the hospital corners Maureen had tucked and re-tucked hours earlier.

'Tight sheets don't cure nothing, do they love? But them's the rules,' she had said, squeezing his shoulder.

Them's the rules, thought Dave. Like Digby's 'rules' that made him think, as a gay man, his accusations of sexual harassment wouldn't be taken seriously. Like the social rules that had pushed Dave into marriage and a middle-class existence. Who made all these 'rules' that microstructure existence? If there were someone to point the finger at, it would be a darn sight easier than navigating a nebulous series of tacit agreements.

Dave's attention came back to the phone in his hand, the usual screensaver of the Millennium Stadium now black and housing the words: DUSTIN GREAT BRAKES. Phones silenced across the hospital, Dave took a moment to realise it was an incoming call. He pressed on the green button and activated the speaker function.

'David, Dustin here. Better after your little turn?'

Dave stared at the phone, knowing it wouldn't elucidate his confusion. 'Still at the hospital,' he replied.

'But—'

'Just a bit of mercury poisoning. Not in intensive care or anything.' Dave wondered whether he was downplaying the situation for Dustin or himself. Either way, he sounded sarcastic.

'Mercury poisoning? Jesus Christ. What are the chances of that?'

'What do you mean?' Dave froze.

He remembered Dustin talk of Adrian's Creek in the car, silently requestioning his insistence on nothing having been proven. Dave's head ached. He had trouble regrouping everything that had happened over the last few weeks, not to mention the discovery that Rodric was the Chairman's son. All that time spent at the house, never really helping Seth with his homework, and now the beanpole had disappeared.

Dustin coughed, breaking the silence.

'I'm just saying, not many people get mercury poisoning, do they?' he said.

'Suppose not,' said Dave, deciding he had been downplaying it and maybe Dustin knew no more than him.

'Listen, I'm not gonna be around for a while.'

Dave sat up in bed. 'Not around? But you just closed the deal.'

'Not mine to close, David. The CEO is up in Canada sorting a few things. It's better this way.'

'What way?'

'Can I give you some advice? Take the time you need to get better.'

'Time?'

'No rushing back. Look, I have to go.'

Dave frowned. He had assumed Dustin was getting back to him after he'd followed Seth's advice and emailed him.

'Aren't you calling about my email, Dustin? It's just I can't find the original message you sent about wanting to consider Wales for your factory.'

'You can't?' There was a long pause before Dustin coughed up a laugh. 'You know *you* mailed me, right? No offence. I thought whales were those big animals that live in the sea. Had to look you guys up on the map when I got your mail.'

'I'm telling you, Carol. There's something fishy going on.'

Remembering himself in a rowboat with Sal, Dave regretted his words. All those dead fish. He shivered. He'd known all along something wasn't right with the Great Brakes project. Now Dustin was denying emails Dave was sure he'd received. He'd not been with it lately, but that was a stretch.

'Rhys says we could be in Paris by the autumn.' Carol picked up the *Beautiful Homes* magazine she had dropped on his bed as a gift and started to flip through it.

Too busy trying to save his own marriage. That's why he hadn't acted sooner. Dave had been trying to tell Carol about his doubts around Great Brakes since her arrival that morning, hoping she would help him stop the project. Dave stared into her parting. She worked with the Chairman, after all. If there was something odd going on, he also had a right to know. Dave didn't like old Rhys, but polluting Welsh waterways was bigger than both of them.

'Are you listening to me, Carol? Those emails I got in the beginning, they were never sent.'

Carol's head rose from the glossy pages to frown at him. 'You can't receive something that was never sent.'

'So, someone else sent them?' said Dave, finding his own answer in her sarcasm.

'Why would someone send you an email that didn't concern them?' Carol sighed and dropped the magazine into her lap. 'When are these results in? You really aren't making much sense.'

Dave looked to the door. No sign of Dr Bete. Maureen hummed on the other side of the room as she milled around the empty bed. Carol was right. It didn't make sense. Seth could get Rodric to help. Hack whatever needed hacking. Even if the little creep was showing a bit of backbone by not doing Seth's homework, he'd come back to help if he knew his dad's reputation was at stake.

'Is Seth coming today?' asked Dave.

'Well thank you, Carol, for coming to see me.' Carol rolled her eyes.

'Don't be like that. Listen—'

'Dave!' Her hands sprang into the air. 'Stop with all this crazy talk. The one time you manage to impress everyone—'

'Pardon?'

'Look, what I meant to say is . . . accept your good fortune. Focus on getting better, the future, Paris. Rhys says the Great Brakes project should have the green light soon. He's working directly with the First Minister.'

TUESDAY

'But what if this project isn't all it seems.'

Dustin's call earlier that morning still didn't make sense. It had felt like a warning. If the emails hadn't come from him, they had to have been sent by someone who wanted the project to come to Wales. But who? And why not be open about it? It was like it was being fast tracked.

'You don't think the Chairman could somehow—'

'Jesus Christ, Dave. You're getting bloody para—'

The door swung open and Dr Bete entered. The backing group of interns harmonised a good morning.

'Mrs Welch? A pleasure. Dr Bete.' He stretched out his hand as Carol stood.

Doc, doc, doc, doc, Doctor Bete.

Dave tracked Carol's face for a sign of amusement.

Nothing.

'Please, take a seat.' Dr Bete pointed to Carol's vacated chair. 'We have some news.' The backing singers froze. 'Let's start with your scans, shall we? No reason for concern but we found a lesion on your brain.'

'A lesion?' asked Dave, his stomach somersaulting.

Dr Bete extended an arm to one of the interns, inviting them to speak.

'It's damaged tissue, Mr Welch.'

'I have brain damage?' Dave scrunched his hands into balls.

'Well, of sorts, yes.' The intern nodded.

'Let's start again, shall we?' Dr Bete rolled his eyes. 'You have some damage to brain tissue.'

'Because of the mercury?' asked Carol.

'I don't think so. Such lesions can be caused by a tumour or a stroke but rest assured we found no sign of either. I can only put this lesion down to your recent bang on the head . . . coupled with a career of many bangs on the head. Had some headaches recently, haven't you?'

Dave nodded.

'You told me yesterday my head looked big? And your hands.'

Dave's head dropped into another nod.

'It's rare that we see this, Mr Welch, but I believe you may have a case of Alice in Wonderland Syndrome.'

'Like the book?' asked Dave.

'Named after the book. The tissue damage causes altered body image in yourself and others. Seeing someone with a very large nose for example.'

'Or ears,' muttered Dave, looking up to the ceiling.

'Indeed,' said Dr Bete. 'Ears if you prefer. People may appear larger—'

'Or smaller,' finished Dave.

Carol pinched his toes and mouthed, 'Pay attention.'

Dave *was* listening. He was hearing every single word and starting to replay the last few weeks in his mind. Big ears, little people, huge noses.

'This might not have been your experience, Mr Welch, but losing the sense of time is another common symptom. It often leaves patients with the wrong impression about situations and events.'

'You okay, Dave?' asked Carol.

'Will I get better?' asked Dave, tears dripping from his chin.

'We can give you medication, as we would migraine sufferers. It will help. Let's not forget your mercury poisoning though.' A chirpy tone inhabited Dr Bete.

Dave lifted his head. 'How could I?'

With all the talk of seeing big noses and little people, Dave *had* forgotten the mercury poisoning. It was the least of his worries when a big rabbit could be on the loose, inviting him to tea parties.

'The high levels of mercury in your body can also

TUESDAY

cause confusion,' continued Dr Bete, 'hallucinations and anxiety, all leading to a sense of paranoia.'

Carol's stare filled with knowing.

'Double trouble?' asked Dave.

'You could say that,' said Dr Bete. 'Do you eat a lot of fish, Mr Welch?'

'I told you, it's not right eating all that sushi.' Carol said to Dave, providing Dr Bete with a reply.

'The human body can handle low levels of heavy metals. It eliminates them over time. I believe your body stocks them. We are also running some urine tests. It happens sometimes. Again, very rare. Funnily enough, all that weight you have lost is what has accentuated your symptoms of poisoning.'

Dave had trouble finding the humour.

'Won't you help him, Dr Bete?' asked Carol, filled with sudden concern.

'Now there's the good news.' Dr Bete smiled.

Hope flooded Dave, lifting him from his pillow.

'We can do something about the mercury. It's a process called chelation. We administer drugs to which the mercury sticks.' Dr Bete brought his hands together. 'Then everything evacuates in your urine.' His hands splayed to demonstrate a waterfall of pee.

'So, if you lower the mercury—'

'Yes, Mr Welch. If we lower those levels, it should ease all the symptoms. We'll start here at the hospital with an IV so we'll be keeping you in a few days. Once we have you more stabilised, we can probably send you home with oral medication.'

'Thank you.' Dave shook the doctor's hand.

With a whoosh of coat, Dr Bete turned, Dave remembering the presence of the backing group of interns as they parted to let him pass. Dr Bete stopped in his tracks.

'One last thing.' Dr Bete turned back to face them. 'You only have one son, don't you?'

'Why?' asked Carol.

Two, thought Dave.

'Let's test his blood too. Just in case.'

'Blood test?' asked Carol, her voice rising.

'For his own good.' Dave replied, trying to emulate the look Carol had been giving him all morning.

'He hates needles,' said Carol.

'Does he?' asked Dave.

'Just one thing after another. I've got to go.' Carol stood. 'The Chairman's back from Canada this afternoon.'

CHAPTER TWENTY-FOUR

'So, what is it you do then?'

'Heating technician,' said Dave, admiring a pair of striped pyjamas in the bed opposite and noting what appeared to be well-proportioned ears, nose and hands.

'Not your lucky day, is it?' Maureen had said earlier that morning, slamming a tray of cornflakes, yoghurt and diced pear on the table and explaining Dave would have to share his room. 'Bit of a shit show, the NHS nowadays. Poor sod's been waiting months for a hip replacement,' she had continued, divulging all of Mr Jones's medical history.

Dave swallowed his yawn as he waited for more questions from his new roommate. He had wanted to persuade himself company provided distraction, his mood darkening on meeting incessant conversation. Morning drizzle drummed the window, washing Dave deeper into despair. He was tired from a sleepless night trying to unravel what over the past few weeks had been real, rather than misread, exaggerated or plain imagined.

'Heating technician? Bit like a plumber, is it?' asked Stripy Pyjamas. 'I used to be a bit handy, but I've been waiting years for this operation. It all started back in two thousand and ten . . .'

Noticing months had become years and, thanks to Maureen's briefing, already familiar with many unsuccessful steroid injections and physiotherapy sessions, Dave's attention floated into the car park. Alice in bloody Wonderland Syndrome! Only Dave *Weltch* could have a condition named after some madcap story of a girl falling down a rabbit hole. That was what happened in the book, wasn't it? It explained the visits to Iceland, Sal and his hairy ears, the lost hours. And yet, it had all seemed so real. So very real. Couple that with mercury poisoning, from sushi of all things, and there you had it. Sal had spoken to him about fish, all those dead fish. Dave shivered. If Sal was a figment of his imagination, a hallucination, everything they spoke of during those trips to Iceland had to be things Dave had known all along. He shook his head. That was a rabbit hole darker than the one into which Alice had fallen.

Dave exhaled. Chelation therapy starting that afternoon, life should soon become less confusing. Those emails that were never sent, the confusing call with Dustin and his untimely disappearance, not to mention ideas Dave had entertained about how the Chairman's visit to Canada could somehow be linked to the Great Brakes CEO being there. The Chairman may have studied there but it was a big place. Paranoia, Carol had called it. She was right.

'Ten years she's been gone.' said Stripy Pyjamas.

Dave's attention came back to the room, his stomach dropping. His new roommate's verbal diarrhoea was symptomatic of a decade without conversation. The old man was lonely. Carol was still very much alive, but Dave knew that feeling. He hoped she would visit today. Seth would soon, in any case.

TUESDAY

'You have children?' asked Dave, remembering Dad suggesting investing in others' lives made your own feel less worrisome.

'No, son. Barb couldn't. Couldn't do much about it back then. You?'

'One,' said Dave. He thought on Jedd. He'd been close to telling Carol but she'd been like a coiled spring since the barbecue. What the hell, he needed to talk to someone. 'Maybe two.'

'Maybe?' Stripy Pyjamas fumbled with the remote control, bringing himself to a more upright position.

'He turned up a few weeks ago. An old rugby tour.'

'I knew I recognised you. Dave Welch isn't it?'

'One and the same.' Jazz hands splayed before dropping to the bed. 'Probably not what you remember.'

Stripy Pyjamas laughed. 'None of us are what we remember, son. So, your wife found out and that's why you're in here?'

Dave half-cracked a smile. 'Haven't told her yet.'

'Might want to do that before she finds out for herself.'

Dave sucked in his tummy before letting it splurge. 'I feel such a failure.'

'You're not proud of one time on tour. We all feel like failures if we define ourselves by a single mistake. And they say mistakes aren't mistakes, you know.'

'You what?' asked Dave.

'Acting out of character can teach us we don't want to do it again.'

Dave nodded.

'A marriage is built on many things.'

'I'm beginning to think mine is built on very little, apart from Paris.'

'Full of French, son. Don't want to go there.'

Dave laughed. Stripy Pyjamas was quite funny. There

was something that reminded him of Dad. His pyjamas hung loose. In a face carved by years of laughter, sat blue eyes that shone with curiosity. Not so bad to have a bit of company in the room, after all.

'You retired then?' asked Dave.

'Sort of, son.'

He looked sprightly, a man that needed to keep his hand in. One of those manual professions that finds it difficult to sit down. Dad had been like that. Every day out in those fields come rain or shine.

'Anyway, what are you in here for, if it's not feeling sorry for yourself?' asked Stripy Pyjamas.

'Alice in Wonderland Syndrome.'

'Like the book?'

'And mercury poisoning.'

'You're joking?'

'Why would I joke about that?' Dave straightened himself.

'No, I mean that's a bloody coincidence. A lot of my research is in mercury cycles in the environment.'

'You're a researcher?'

'Professor. Was Head of Biochemical Engineering at the uni. Retired now, but I still dabble. I've got an invention, see. You know forty percent of Europe's rivers and lakes have dangerously high levels of mercury.'

Dave did know, Jolene having sent him an article on the subject. Stripy Pyjamas was a professor, who would have thought? And he'd researched mercury in the waterways. What were the chances of that? It wasn't simply that he reminded Dave of Dad, there was something familiar about him. They must have met before.

'Did you say mercury cycles?' asked Dave.

'Think of the water cycle,' said Stripy Pyjamas, 'and how all water on Earth is connected.'

TUESDAY

Dave frowned. This was getting weird. He double-checked the old man's nose, his ears. All were of normal proportions. Dave inspected the room. Same four flecked beige walls.

'Geothermal activity releases mercury vapour into the environment. It disperses and this *elemental* mercury vapour undergoes photochemical oxidation to become inorganic mercury that then combines with water vapours to travel back to the Earth's surface as rain.' Stripy Pyjamas' finger drew circles in the air.

'Elemental mercury?'

Stripy Pyjamas nodded. 'But where it gets dangerous is when it converts to methyl mercury and makes its way into the food chain. The little fish eat the plankton, the big fish eat the little fish and—'

'People like me eat the big fish,' finished Dave.

'People like us all.'

'But you say this is a natural cycle?'

Stripy Pyjamas' head bobbed up and down. 'Excellent question. It is, but most mercury in our water comes from human activity like fossil fuel combustion, smelting and other industrial activities, not to mention—'

'Stuff that's dumped into the sea.'

Stripy Pyjamas frowned. 'You seem to know a bit about this?'

'A little.' Dave sat up in bed and rubbed his face.

He had to stop feeling sorry for himself. The last few weeks had been all over the place, but whatever conversations he'd had – or hadn't had – with Sal, it was time to tell the truth. His recent paranoia hadn't invented the doubts around Great Brakes. They were printed in black and white in the press. Dave had reread Jolene's string of emails from the day of Dustin's visit. He had to get better so he could engage with the Chairman and the First Minister. The other thing that held true from the past few weeks was his absolute shameful ignorance to do the right thing. Regret, if he was totally honest, had only been provoked when that same ignorance had come to bite him on the arse. He was living – thankfully still breathing – proof of what mercury pollution could do. He reached for his phone.

'You alright, son?'

'It's this big project I've been involved in. I've messed up there too.'

'Tricky things them radiators.'

'What?' Dave looked up from his phone, belatedly remembering having reverted to his typical subterfuge when it came to his occupation. 'You're not wrong there. Pesky things.'

Dave dropped his phone in the bedsheets. He couldn't call the Chairman yet. He had to get his ducks in a row, do more research. He really needed to speak to Jolene but she'd been refusing his calls. He knew she was mad at him but thought she might have come around now he was in hospital. What was that Gandhi quote she was always citing about forgiveness being an attribute of the strong? Anyway, even armed with proof, he couldn't make the call with Stripy Pyjamas listening. To all intents and purposes, Dave fixed leaky radiators and installed boilers. He'd email her instead.

'Remember what I was saying about acting out of character?' asked Stripy Pyjamas.

Dave's head rose from his phone. 'Teaches you to not do it again?'

'Sometimes we act in a way others see as out of character while we try to find who we really are. Who we have become can feel a far cry from who we want to be. I get that feeling about you.'

TUESDAY

Dave stared across the room, fixated by the glint in Stripy Pyjamas' eyes. It wasn't curiosity he could see, but a mix of wisdom and contentment. That calm sense of knowing that accompanies experience.

'Tell me, is there a way of getting mercury out of water?' asked Dave.

'Funny you should mention that.' Stripy Pyjamas pressed the button on the remote control to raise his backrest. He lowered his voice. 'I've been working on a new coagulation system, see. Can't say too much.'

'Coagulation?'

'It reacts to the mercury to make it solid and then you can extract it. Tried to speak to the government about it, but they said I needed a patent.' Stripy Pyjamas glanced towards the closed door, pressed another button on his remote control and closed the blinds. 'You know they work with the CIA now?'

Dave fell into his pillow.

'It's the Russians, see.'

'And the Chinese,' added Dave, deducing why Stripy Pyjamas seemed familiar. 'I'm not sure I asked your name?'

'Jones. Bryn Jones.'

CHAPTER TWENTY-FIVE

'Like the book?' asked Jolene, frowning.

It had been his own response to the diagnosis and would be every reaction thereafter. Dave simply had to suck it up. Only Seth had repeated 'Alice in Wonderland Syndrome' with a smile.

'Are you like tripping all the time?' he had asked, wide-eyed on visiting with various flavours of Monster Munch.

Seth had been in every morning for the past week, unlike the lesser spotted Carol. Whenever she deigned to visit, she came armed with one subject of conversation. If Dave was yet to divulge the mess that was Great Brakes or the six-foot tall secret accompanying Jolene, it was because Carol barely paused for breath when touring the City of Love's arrondissements. That and the fact that, as Bryn reminded him daily, Dave was an out-and-out coward.

'Jesus wept, Dave. How can you get that *and* mercury poisoning,' continued Jolene, repositioning her glasses to inspect him.

Dave shrugged. It was official. He was a circus act. A twenty-first century version of the bearded lady. He

TUESDAY

reached out a hand to Jolene who took it in hers. Dave had emailed Jolene with an apology, laid out all he knew about Great Brakes but heard nothing back. That was until she had floated into the ward during the post-lunch lull, Jedd trailing in her wake, in what Dave hoped to mean a laying of arms.

'Sorry we didn't come sooner,' said Jedd. 'Weren't sure we should.'

Dave straightened himself, his pyjamas straining at the neck. 'I waited for you at the stadium.'

Jedd looked at Jolene for support. 'I got the wrong bus. Left my phone at Jolene's. I wanted to talk to you at the barbecue. And then, well—'

'You went down like a sack of shit!' finished Jolene, lowering her voice to match that of Digby's.

Dave laughed. He searched for words as Jedd shuffled from foot to foot. Words to thank Jolene for her Gandhiesque forgiveness, words to explain he was happy to have another son, a promise they would make things work. What was hidden had to come to light, be it in his professional or personal life. Dave could see himself in Jedd. A younger, optimistic version ready to wrestle life. Jedd would have a place in his family whatever the cost. He owed him that much. He'd travelled across the world to find him.

'I could have handled things differently,' said Dave.

'Me too,' said Jedd.

'Me three,' said Jolene. 'How is Carol?'

'Carol?' asked Dave, realising Jolene would understandably think he'd told his wife about Jedd. 'Oh, she's fine.' Dave checked his phone to see two grey ticks still hadn't turned blue.

'Lots to take in, I suppose.' Jolene exchanged glances with Jedd.

All Carol was taking in was an imminent move across

the Channel. Dave couldn't blame her. He'd kept her in the dark about everything. Meanwhile, the Great Brakes project was moving forwards and Dave hooked to an IV drip doing nothing about it. That said, chelation therapy was going well, Craig slipping Dave the word there was talk of him being released soon. Dave could come back for further infusions and revert to tablets.

Debating how much longer Bryn would be in physio, Dave decided to cut to the chase. He'd dodged work conversation until now but his real identity would be unveiled if Bryn overheard him talking to Jolene.

'I'm sorry, I should have taken more notice of what you were trying to tell me,' Dave squeezed Jolene's hand. 'I had my doubts but the pressure was on.'

'Don't worry about that now,' said Jolene, understanding the urgency. 'Listen, I got your mail. We'd already started researching anyway.'

'You had?'

'You remember I'm a personal investigator?' said Jedd.

'Research journalist,' corrected Jolene.

Dave's stomach gurgled. Maureen had woken him from a light sleep with vegan meat loaf and an eye roll at about half past eleven. He'd kill for a Magnum now. He went for his usual joke, stopping himself. Seth had shown him around his TikTok channel that morning. As much about sea preservation as riding those waves, Dave had made a mental note to get closer to what motivated his son rather than linger on generational differences. It went for both sons. The dad jokes needed to go.

'It isn't all stakeouts and sleeping in cars,' said Jedd.

Dave frowned.

'Personal investigating, a lot of it happens online.'

'Researching.' Jolene laughed.

Dave frowned again.

TUESDAY

'He's a bit of a hacker,' said Jolene.

'What've you found?' asked Dave, straightening himself into a full garrotting from his pyjama collar. 'Can you help me?'

Jolene loosened the fabric, giving Dave's arm a squeeze and whispering, 'So glad you're not mad.'

He may have been a little upset, but it was more Jolene who had been mad at him. Dave went to speak but noticed Jedd in full flow.

'. . . a number of leads pertaining to possible leakages not only at Adrian's Creek but certain facilities in Asia.'

'I think I read something about that . . . but those facilities aren't on their website,' said Dave.

Of the limited due diligence Dave had undertaken, he had visited Great Brakes' corporate website before Dustin's visit, scouring it again earlier that day.

'These are operations ran by the group but not in the company name. Great Brakes is part of a much larger offshore holding company.'

Jolene beamed at Jedd.

'She calls me a hacker but all of this information is available online.'

'It is?' asked Dave.

'If you know where to look. Anyway, I need to dig some more to get a full picture. The news around Adrian's Creek and it being an accident, well I might need to get into some mails for that.'

'And that is hacking more than investigating, right?'

Jedd laughed. 'Technically.'

Dave thought back to the initial emails from Dustin Harris that were never sent. Seth had no news of Rodric, leaving him at an impasse. Small men with big ears had been hallucinations, but not the Great Brakes project. He hadn't been that out of it to have found a company out of nowhere, email them and serendipitously discover a multi-million-pound investment project. Let's face it. That hadn't happened in five years of being in post.

'Can you retrieve emails that have been deleted or recalled?' Dave asked Jedd.

'Can I?'

'I mean, is it possible?'

'Of course.'

'Would I still be able to see them on my computer?'

'What's going on, Dave?' asked Jolene.

Dave hesitated. Jolene had said it impossible for Dave to have pulled the Great Brakes project out of thin air, albeit formulating it more colourfully.

'In the beginning, I got an email. Thought it was for Essex at first.'

'Essex?' asked Jolene.

'Never mind. Anyway, it was Dustin mailing me out of the blue saying he had a project for the UK. Now those emails are gone and Dustin says he never sent them.'

'Someone had to have sent them,' said Jedd.

'Unless I imagined it all but—'

'Come on!' said Jolene. 'Pulled a project that size out of your arse, did you?'

'You got your computer here?' asked Jedd. 'There should be some trace even if they were recalled. I'll check it out for you.'

Dave pointed over to the bedside locker, relieved that Jedd and Jolene didn't put the last few weeks entirely down to paranoia.

'You've got Jaffa Cakes in here,' said Jolene.

'Take them. I'm allergic to oranges,' said Dave as the door swung open and Bryn was wheeled back in.

'He's back!' shouted Dave, widening his eyes at Jolene.

TUESDAY

'That he is! Fit as a butcher's dog!' Bryn shouted back. 'Don't mind me.'

'Take the computer with you,' Dave whispered to Jedd. 'Let me know how you get on. The password is pass—'

Jedd laughed. 'I get the drift.'

'Not your lucky day, is it, Bryn,' said Maureen, readjusting his pillows and pointing to the tray. 'All the sheep in Wales and you get one poxy bit of lamb in your cawl. Probably cold now too.'

'Listen, we're going to head off,' said Jolene, stuffing the Jaffa Cakes into her handbag. 'We'll be in touch.'

'Don't leave on my account,' shouted Bryn.

Dave beckoned Jedd. He had to talk to him before he left. 'Listen, I'm sorry I wasn't more welcoming when you first arrived. It was a bit of a surprise.'

'I get it. Suppose I was pissed at you not believing me.'

'He missed the bus on purpose,' said Jolene, squeezing Jedd's arm.

'That doesn't matter. I want to make amends. Be the father I haven't been.'

Bryn's bed whirred into an upright position.

'My mum wouldn't lie, but I understand you want to be sure. I did the DNA test.'

'You did?'

Bryn's bed whirred some more.

'Jolene convinced me it was for the best. Ellis said I'd missed you but his nurse friend was still there. Thought I was with some other American in town, some rapper.' Jedd laughed. 'Anyway, Ellis said he'd let you know. Like I said, I wanted to talk at the barbecue but with everything that happened.'

Dave remembered seeing a string of text messages as he had stood on his front doorstep, fresh from visiting an Icelandic volcano. Dave had assumed Ellis had been telling him about the lost wallet cover story. It's the one they used to use on tour. He'd never called Ellis back.

'The results are back?' asked Dave.

A number of missed calls from Ellis also came to mind. The ones Dave hadn't answered since he'd been admitted, too ashamed to tell his old teammate about the bump on the head.

'Not yet.' Jolene squeezed Dave's hand. 'That's why we haven't visited sooner.'

'Well, one of the reasons.' Jedd glanced at Jolene.

'To be honest, I wasn't sure how things were with Carol.' Jolene offered a shy smile.

'Carol?

'I'm so glad you're not mad at me.'

'Mad at you?'

'I'm sorry, but something snapped when she called me a woke little shit.'

'She called you what?'

'It was after Jolene called the Chairman a you-know-what,' said Jedd.

'Crikey,' said Bryn, plunging the room into darkness as he turned off the main light instead of adjusting his backrest.

'Whatever Carol called me,' said Jolene. 'I should never have told her Jedd was your son.'

CHAPTER TWENTY-SIX

Stood in the foyer at Cardiff House, Dave shuffled in front of the elevator, pressing out the creases in his trousers. For want of other options, he'd dressed in the suit he'd been wearing when admitted to hospital. Craig true to his word, Dave had been released at ten thirty. On arriving home, he'd walked straight back out on finding an empty house. The easiest way to speak to Carol was to go and see her at work, neither she nor Seth having replied to his texts that morning.

'Not your lucky day, is it?' Maureen had said, handing him the remaining Flamin' Hot Monster Munch from the bedside locker.

'I'm being released, Maureen.' Dave had gifted her a stare and the crisps.

'Pissing it down out there, love. You'll get soaked. Thanks for these though. Likes my crisps like my men, me.'

Dave had waited for a smile or sign of mirth, leaving before the silence became awkward.

The elevator at the sixth floor, Dave ran a finger under his shirt collar, unsure he wanted to set foot in it again.

None of it was real. He knew that now. He needed to prove there was nothing to fear. He gasped for air, thoughts of the confined space already triggering him and sweat pooling in his lower back. Deciding he already had enough medical conditions to deal with, he walked past reception and made his way to the stairs.

Duffy's 'Mercy' greeted Dave on arriving at the eighth floor. Images of hill, vale and puffin-dotted coastline filled the television screen in what had to be the Welsh Tourist Board's most recent promotional campaign. Begging Wales to release you? Transposing a lover's captivating spell onto that of a rainy country was tenuous. On the upside, Duffy marked a long-awaited deviation from Tom Jones and Bonnie Tyler. Dave stretched over the desk to look for Carol before reminding himself adults rarely hide under furniture. Noticing the Chairman's office door firmly closed, Dave strode over and knocked.

'About time, Carol. Come in!'

Dave pushed at the door. 'Chairman.'

'David . . . you . . . I was expecting . . .' The Chairman rose and sat back down again. He placed the lid on a Montblanc pen. 'Just signing some papers.' He slid them under a file on his desk. 'You're out then?'

'Seems my treatment is working.'

Dave hovered at the door as the silence between them allowed Duffy to enter the conversation. He diverted his attention to a panoramic photo of Swansea's Three Cliffs Bay above the Chairman's head.

'Come in, come in. Where are my manners. Can I get you a coffee? Ca—' The Chairman stopped mid-shout. 'You don't know where Carol is? She's normally in by now.'

If Carol's boss was as unsure of her whereabouts, Dave might not be as paranoid as he feared. Carol knowing

TUESDAY

about Jedd would also explain recent tension, even though Dave couldn't understand why she hadn't mentioned it. The thought had tickled him since Jolene's departure from the ward the previous day.

Dave closed the door behind him and pulled out a leather chair to sit facing the Chairman. Whatever Seth had said to reassure him that night on the bench, Dave still wondered if Carol might have a thing for old Double Barrel. Jolene certainly didn't. That much had been cleared up at least.

'Actually, it's you I need to talk to,' said Dave, diverting his focus back to the perilous cliffs on the wall.

He had come to talk to Carol but, the Chairman alone, it was as good a time as any to relay his concerns. Jedd hadn't come back with further information but Dave knew enough to sound the warning alarm. The dossier had been fast tracked. There was no time to waste.

'It's about Great Brakes,' said Dave.

'Well done on that again, David.' The Chairman sat back in his chair. 'The First Minister is more than delighted we finally have something *green* to plop into the docks. That toilet paper company was a fair few jobs, but hardly high-end.' He burst into laughter. 'More *bottom* end of the market when you think about it!'

'About that,' Dave pinched his thighs, trying to squeeze out some courage. He'd been fearless on the pitch in front of thousands of fans. Here he was letting one little man drowning in upholstered leather intimidate him. What was Rhys? Five foot five? Five foot six at most.

'It's all well underway. No need for you to worry.' The Chairman pushed on the leather armrests to stand. 'Shouldn't you be resting?'

'I believe Great Brakes is intentionally dumping mercury,' shouted Dave.

The Chairman fell back into his chair. Bringing his palms together, his fingers pointed to the ceiling. 'Mercury poisoning? But that's what you have, isn't it? That and what was it?'

'Alice in Wonderland Syndrome.' Dave waited for the usual refrain. It never came. Instead, the Chairman pulled open a desk drawer and produced a bottle of whisky and two glasses.

'Seeing things bigger or smaller than they really are,' mumbled Dave, feeling the weight of the silence.

'Splash of Penderyn?' The Chairman waved the bottle at Dave. 'You seem tense. Could you be seeing that one allegation in Adrian's Creek as *bigger* than it is? By all accounts, it was an accident. I read about it in the press. Unfortunate, yes, but not intentional.'

A crystal-cut whisky glass was pushed towards Dave despite a shake of the head. Brown liquid sloshed the sides. He grabbed the glass, hoping for Dutch courage in the Welsh liquor. He slugged.

'It's not only that, Chairman.'

The Chairman's hand paused as he poured his own glass. 'It's not?'

'There have been other incidents, mostly in Asia.'

'Where in Asia?'

Jedd hadn't gone into detail. Dave rolled the whisky in his glass, kneaded his thigh with his free hand.

'Great Brakes is part of a holding company.'

'And what do you know about this holding company?'

Dave knew very little. Jedd was researching more. He should have waited to have more information before talking to the Chairman. He slugged the whisky.

'Look, I wanted to give you a heads-up. It's hardly green, green tech if they dump into the Bristol Channel is it?' Dave took another gulp of the whisky. 'Poisoning our

TUESDAY

fish. Everyone's fish. The mercury cycle infesting the water cycle.'

'You seem quite upset for something you don't know much about. What *do* we know? I can't go to the First Minister with supposition.'

Dave's mouth opened, the dearth of words irrelevant in the face of a stream of rehearsed rhetoric.

'What we do know for sure is that this project will create three hundred jobs here in Wales, and at a time of rising costs and likely unemployment as other companies close. It's an investment in today and tomorrow.' The Chairman smiled. 'It's what we are employed to deliver, you and me included.'

Dave reached for his head. The room span.

'Can you flag it up with the First Minister so there are no nasty surprises, for him or us?' said Dave, needing to get out of the office.

'Shall I tell Carol you passed by?' The Chairman stood. 'I'm afraid I'm busy catching up on things since getting back.' He waved his hands in the air. 'I'm late, I'm late! For a very important date!'

'Sorry?'

'Bet you're excited about Paris.' The Chairman guided Dave to the door. 'For now, I suggest you go home and rest.'

As the door closed behind him, Dave exhaled. Important date, what was that about? All that waving of arms. It was good to get out of there. He'd ballsed up a bit, could have been more prepared, but it had gone better than expected. It was probably the nicest he had ever seen the Chairman.

Dave paused in front of the TV screen, watching a puffin dive-bomb an unsuspecting fish. The Chairman had been too nice. *I suggest you go home and rest.* He'd been patronising him, hadn't he? *I'm late, I'm late! For a very important date!* That was Alice in bloody Wonderland!

As feared, the Chairman hadn't taken him seriously. He never did; why would he start now? Dave pulled out his phone. No messages from Jedd or Jolene, still nothing from Carol or Seth. He pulled at his shirt collar, undoing the top buttons. Heat engulfed him. He shouldn't have had that whisky. Wandering towards the stairs, Dave stopped dead in front of the elevator, regretting the absence of Sal when he needed him most. Sal would know what to do.

'Sal doesn't exist,' he muttered.

Dave's shoulders sank. He missed the little fella. Could you miss a figment of your imagination? The trips to Iceland had been impromptu, confusing and painful but he'd come back with greater clarity. It wasn't that Dave doubted *what* he had to do next. He didn't know *how*. How could Dave Welch make everyone listen? He scoured the empty foyer as his finger edged towards the elevator button. It was Tuesday, after all. If he'd manifested Sal before, he could do it again. Where was the harm in that?

Ping.

Dave glanced around. Silence. Even Duffy had conceded two weeks in Lanzarote was cheaper than a waterlogged caravan park in Pembrokeshire. Dave stepped into the elevator. Letting the doors close, he examined the metal cube. The air carried an instrumental version of Radiohead's 'Creep' and a hint of lemon. He waited.

He waited some more.

Nothing.

He closed his eyes.

Nothing.

He squeezed his fists into balls. He'd seen it in a film.

Nothing.

He opened his eyes.

TUESDAY

The lift started to move. Dave held his breath.

It descended a floor and jolted to a halt.

He waited.

The doors opened on a collection of spotty and excitable placement students.

'This lift is taken!' shouted Dave, stabbing at the number eight button to take him back up a floor.

The doors tried to reopen. Dave jabbed any button he could see. The doors jammed shut. It was too hot. Dave took off his jacket, wiped his forehead. That whisky was strong.

The lift started to move.

He squeezed his eyes shut.

What had happened last time?

Had there had been a light?

Pain drove into Dave's head like a knife.

Then, all the lights went out.

'Bloody hell, Dave.'

Dave's head flopped out of the elevator doors, landing on Carol's black patent high heels. Chanel number something ambushed him.

'David, what *are* you doing?' The Chairman's head joined Carol's floating over him.

Looking for elves, thought Dave, but thought better of saying it out loud.

'You're out of hospital?' asked Carol, her eyes where her chin should have been. 'Why are you here?'

Dave's head span. Looking up his wife's skirt was not his idea of Iceland. He must have passed out. Damn it.

'Are you sure he should be out, Carol?'

'I sent you a text,' Dave muttered into the carpet, ruing

his bad luck at the Chairman being with Carol when she found him.

'He's been here talking conspiracy theories about the Great Brakes project and yet he was the one who found it. Is it this Narnia thing he's got?'

'Alice in Wonderland,' replied Carol, bending down. 'Brings on all kinds of paranoid hallucinations.'

'That's the one,' mumbled the Chairman.

'You shouldn't be here,' Carol addressed Dave. 'You can't think straight.'

'I'm sorry, Carol.' Dave brought his mouth to Carol's ear. 'About Jedd, I know why you've been acting odd.'

'Don't worry about that now.' She stroked his hair. 'We all make mistakes.'

'But I need to talk to you about Great Bra—'

'That man needs to be back in hospital, Carol.'

'Oh Carol,' whispered Dave.

The lights, as had become their habit, went out.

CHAPTER TWENTY-SEVEN

'Get stuck in the revolving door, did you?'

Laughter ricocheted around the four walls. Apart from Bryn's pyjamas now a mint green flannel, Dave was wheeled into the same configuration as earlier that day.

'Missing your scintillating company, wasn't he, Bryn.' Craig laughed, pulling back the covers. 'Drinking whisky when on medication if I'm not mistaken.'

Craig detangled Dave from the IV drip and helped him into bed.

'Take these,' he said, thrusting a cupful of tablets and a glass of water towards him. 'Doctor's orders. You need to rest.'

Dave wouldn't have chosen to return so soon but Craig wasn't entirely wrong. Seeing Bryn was akin to sliding into a pair of comfy slippers. As for the twenty square metres of unthreatening flecked beige, they reduced the risk of relapse. The door closed behind Craig and Dave fell into his pillow. He'd only searched for Sal because he needed to talk to someone who understood him. Now he was back on a high dose of chelation drugs.

'What happened, son?' Bryn's bed whirred into a fully seated position. Bright blue eyes waited on an answer.

Dave debated starting with the fact he wasn't a heating technician. Convinced he'd never see the old man again, he'd abandoned any notion of confessing his true occupation.

'Releasing me early was an error of judgement according to Dr Bete,' said Dave.

'Sounds like one of them politicians caught with his pants down.' Bryn laughed.

Dave had felt more than fine. What if he did have PTSD on top of his other conditions? He'd have to invest in a notebook to write them all down.

'Something else is bothering you,' insisted Bryn.

Dave examined the old man. It *was* strange for Bryn to be a specialist in mercury and the water cycle and be plonked in the same room. With no further news from Jedd or Jolene, Bryn could be the ally he sought. Dave opened his mouth and closed it again. How could he confess to being that idiot on the phone fresh out of Langley?

'Them DNA results back?' asked Bryn.

Dave had forgotten about them. Of course, Bryn would have overheard the end of his conversation with Jedd and Jolene. Dave had no idea when the results would be in, not that there was much point now. Carol knew why Jedd was in town. Son or no son, Dave had cheated all those years ago. So, why no shouting and screaming? Dave thought back to lying on her feet, splayed between the elevator and the eighth floor, doors rebounding off his gut.

'We all make mistakes,' she had said, Dave intrigued by her state of calm.

Buying whole milk instead of semi-skimmed a few weeks earlier at Tesco's had provoked more of a reaction. Here was one full-fat illegitimate son and it was the most

TUESDAY

forgiving he'd ever seen his wife. She'd even accompanied him to the hospital.

'Let's get you better,' she'd said in the ambulance.

'I thought you'd fallen for the Chairman,' Dave had replied, the words tumbling out of his mouth to be met with mirth.

'I'm pretty sure he'd be more interested in you than me.'

He'd told her he loved her, not hearing her reply as the white ceiling fell in on him. Siren wailing, they had zigzagged through traffic, Dave debating whether those three words held true for her, or him. Saying them was one of those things you couldn't stop once you'd started, like the eyebrow threading Carol spent a fortune on each month.

'Is it that project you were talking about?' asked Bryn.

'Project?' asked Dave, questioning whether he might have spoken to Bryn about Great Brakes after all.

'You said something the other day about messing up on a big project? One of those new heat pumps?'

Dave shook his head. So many lies made it impossible to keep track. He checked his phone. Still no news from Jedd and Jolene. He'd left messages on his way over to Cardiff House. If they didn't have any news, they could at least tell him as much.

'I'm sure it's not as bad as you think,' said Bryn.

'I think it might be,' replied Dave, debating how to elaborate on the mess consuming him whilst remaining within the metaphor of a leaky radiator. Bryn was, after all, an expert in such matters. Not leaky radiators, but mercury water pollution. His advice could be useful. Dave looked at the slumped, bony shoulders. He'd written him off as mad on the phone, when he was a bloody university professor! And here was Dave seeing elves. Who was the crazy one?

'*Happens every day,*' said Bryn.

'What does?' said Dave.

'Mistakes.'

'Suppose they do.'

'*No matter what you say.*' Bryn's sing-song accent became more melodic than usual.

Dave frowned. Was he—

'*It's not unusual,*' continued Bryn.

Dave's mouth dropped open.

Bryn smiled.

'You bloody well know I work for the CIA, don't you?'

'Not the FBI then?'

'Bryn, I don't know what to—'

'I'm not being funny, but the training they give you at Langley is piss-poor. I've known since they wheeled me in here.'

Laughter rumbled up from Dave's stomach, shooting out of his mouth like artillery fire. Bryn joined him, his head falling into the pillow and tears rolling down his cheeks.

'But how did you work it out?' asked Dave, wiping away his own tears and feeling lighter than he had in weeks.

'Used to love *Rugby Special Wales* on Sunday evenings. You were interviewed once. That presenter, Huw whatsisname made fun of you talking about the hooker because of how you pronounced your double 'o's but you had the last laugh when—'

'I slipped Tom Jones lyrics into all my answers and he didn't even notice!'

Bryn's face contorted once more in laughter. Dave was never invited back to *Rugby Special Wales* but the few times he'd been on the pitch, before the knee injury, the crowd had sung, *'Forgive me, Huw Jenkins, I just couldn't take any more!'*

Dave fell into his pillows. 'Oh Bryn, I'm sorry.'

'Don't be, son. Almost wet myself coming off the phone to you. Haven't laughed like that in years. Not since my Barb got on the bus forgetting she had her rollers in. Third bench down from Cariad Tea Rooms!' Bryn's laughter took control of him once more.

'Bit of a coincidence being thrown on a ward together, don't you think?' said Dave.

'Oh, life is made of happy coincidences, son. So, tell me about this project of yours. Part of that *Green, Green Tech of Home* thing, I bet?' Bryn wiped his eyes with the sleeve of his pyjama shirt.

'You know about that?'

'Keep an eye on these things. The worst thing they ever did was task the Welsh government with finding foreign investment like it was some kind of panacea. Felt the brunt of that when all those manufacturing companies left to go somewhere cheaper, didn't we? Now it's all green this, green that.'

Dave sat up in his bed. 'You don't agree with it?'

'Of course, I agree with sustainability. It's not compatible with capitalism and globalisation, that's the problem. They work on buying and selling, perpetual growth.'

'Like electric vehicles,' said Dave, remembering Jolene's attempts at educating him.

'Exactly. By claiming them as a green solution, we have also committed to everyone on this planet buying a new car. Can't tell me the automotive industry isn't happy?'

'This project is for a brakes company. I found it. Well, it found me but they've been accused of mercury dumping.' Dave checked his phone again to find nothing. 'I'm trying to undertake more research so I can warn the Chairman.'

Dave and Bryn looked to the door as it swung open.

'Not your lucky day is it?' said Maureen, pushing her way into the room.

'Well, I have been readmitted to hospital, Maureen.'

'And they choose today of all days to put a shocking picture of you in the *Western Mail*.' She read from the newspaper in her hand, 'Dave Welch, Head of America for the CIA says the project is an opportunity to put Wales on the sustainability map.'

'Let me look at that!' Dave wafted a hand at Maureen.

'Front-page news!' Maureen handed him the newspaper.

'Green car company to set up three-hundred-job EV brakes factory.' Dave read the headline out loud. 'Bloody hell! It's announced already! But I was only talking to the Chairman this morning.'

'The effing disgrace?' said Bryn.

'Easy, Bryn,' said Maureen.

'Sorry, Maureen, love.'

'He can't have checked it out,' said Dave. 'How is it in the paper? I bet the press release was what he was working on when I entered his office.'

Dave skimmed the article, reading that Great Brakes had applied for thirty million pounds in grant funding. Yet to be approved, it was odd to have announced it already.

'Don't go forgetting us when you're famous!' said Maureen as she left the room.

'Mr Llewellyn-Jones, I had a meeting with him,' said Bryn, lowering his voice.

'You did?'

Dave listened as he tried to read the rest of the article. The words blurred on the page, the doctors having doubled down on whatever they were giving him. Apparently, construction would start as soon as possible. The

TUESDAY

CEO of Great Brakes, a certain Laurent Richard, claiming it *a small step for his company and an even greater step for a cleaner world.*

'Tried to get some support for my coagulation technology,' continued Bryn. 'It's patented and ready to roll out. I wanted to start testing it by using it to clean up the Bay. I've even got research funding from an Icelandic Research Centre.'

Dave's head shot up. 'Iceland?'

'Scientists there are running pilots across the world to detect mercury in the waters. It links to the Icelandic fishing industry. Anyway, your Chairman said Wales wasn't interested. Said it wouldn't create any new jobs!'

'Not three hundred like a new brakes factory,' mumbled Dave.

The room span. Dave abdicated to the pillow. The doctors were right. The sooner he rested, the quicker he'd be out of here. He knew what he had to do. For now, rest. He lined up a row of fluffy, white sheep, told himself they were Welsh, not Icelandic, and started to count them one by one by one.

CHAPTER TWENTY-EIGHT

'Dave!' Former fullback and owner of calves the width of tree trunks, Ellis waddled towards him.

Dave threw his arms around his old teammate, relief flooding his limbs. Twenty-four hours after readmission, Dave had been released for a second time, defying Dr Bete's prognosis.

'See you in half an hour!' Craig had shouted after him.

Dave wasn't coming back. He had wrongs to right, his newfound clarity no doubt speeding up his recovery. He'd talked it all through with Bryn. There was a reason the mercury poisoning had happened to him. Its timing was no accident either. Dave had a plan. This was Take Two. He had a particular set of skills, skills that would make him a nightmare for Great Brakes.

'What's this thing you've got?' Ellis pulled away to scan Dave from head to foot. 'That Johnny Depp film, in'it?'

'*Fear and Loathing in Las Vegas?*' said Dave, knowing he'd told Ellis about the caution.

'Not that one, dipshit. You know what I mean. The one

with the bloody rabbit.' He stepped back and splayed his arms. 'My ears look big in this?'

'Hang on. What are *you* doing here?' asked Dave, curtailing his laughter on realising he hadn't told Ellis he had been readmitted, let alone that he was being released.

'Come to pick you up.'

Dave had only texted Carol and Seth. Again, no reply from either.

'But how did you—'

'Popped by yours. Seth told me you were getting out.'

'Seth was at home?'

Ellis nodded.

'But he didn't come with you?' Dave looked over Ellis's shoulder at a fairly empty main reception.

'He was with Jedd.'

The blood drained from Dave. In the ambulance, he'd asked Carol not to tell Seth about his possible half-brother. She must have decided otherwise. Or Jedd had taken it upon himself to turn up. After all, they had bumped into each other that evening Dave had woken up on a bench in Queen Street.

'But no Carol?' asked Dave.

Ellis shook his head.

'But why was Jedd at my house?'

'How should I bloody know? Saying goodbye?'

'But we agreed he'd get back to me once . . .' Dave hesitated. He hadn't told Ellis anything about Great Brakes. 'Once he knew more.'

'Mate, isn't it best to let it lie?'

Dave eyeballed Ellis. Someone must have warned him Dave was going a bit doolally. 'You been talking to Carol?'

'I told you, she wasn't home.'

'None of this makes sense!' Dave shouted at Ellis.

'Mate, let's get you home.' Ellis pushed on Dave's lower back, edging him towards the revolving doors.

A ping.

Dave stopped dead. He scrambled in his pocket for his phone and saw he had a new message.

Seth
Need some time to work things out

'Shit!' shouted Dave, entering the revolving doors. 'Seth knows Jedd's his brother.'

'Jesus Christ! Have you not read your emails?' Ellis shouted back.

The question reminded Dave that Jedd had his computer, making him wonder if returning it had been the reason for Jedd visiting the house. Not that it explained why Jedd hadn't been in touch about his research. Dave turned, noticing Ellis wasn't behind him. He pushed the door a full three hundred and sixty degrees and re-entered the foyer.

'Thought you were taking me home?' said Dave.

'You don't know, do you?'

'Know what?'

'The DNA results are in. Jedd isn't your son.'

―――

On arriving home, the only thing awaiting Dave was his computer on the dining table. Checking under it confirmed the absence of a note. Jedd lacking the decency to tell him to his face confirmed to Dave that he would never see him again.

He paced the house, two questions gnawing at him. Firstly, if Seth didn't have a brother, what had he left to

TUESDAY

work out? And secondly, the omnipresent enigma of the last few days: where the bloody hell was Carol?

Fur swept between his legs.

'Bloody ca—' He reached out to the sofa to break his fall.

Ringing filled the house.

Dave dashed back to the dining table to retrieve his phone. Talk of the devil. He dropped himself into one of the chairs, noticing the microwave said eleven thirty. Lunchtime at the hospital, he was a bit hungry. He pressed on the green button.

'Carol, come home, I need to talk to you. All that stuff Jolene said—'

'I'm not coming home, Dave.'

'Not—'

'I'm at mum's.'

'Look, I know I've been difficult but there's been so much going on.'

'Dave, listen.' Silence squatted the line, leaving no room for words. Carol coughed. 'There's no easy way to say this. Your son's not your son.'

'But I know about Jedd now.' Dave exhaled with relief.

'Dave, I'm talking about Seth.'

Dave pulled the phone away from his ear to look at the screen. He put Carol on speaker and pushed his back into the plastic chair until it pained his spine. Part of him had been waiting for this day, those very words. As time had passed, that part had shrivelled to microscopic but never disappeared.

'I'm listening,' he said.

'Remember my ex-boyfriend, Evan. Worked for S4C as a producer? You were away and we bumped into each other in the Rummer Tavern.'

Dave had a clear memory of a skinny introvert with a

romp of hair. Auburn hair like Seth's and a former Welsh swimming champion.

'Well, we—'

'Not sure I need the full detail, Carol.'

'Remember we'd been trying for ages to get pregnant?'

How could he forget? He'd tried but the doctor referring to Dave's semen as 'not entering the Olympics any time soon' had only fuelled performance anxiety.

'When I fell pregnant after that one night it felt like fate stepping in.'

'Fate stepping in? You had a one-night stand.'

'You're one to talk,' shouted Carol.

Silence. The chair pressed between two vertebrae.

'You're right.' Dave's voice was a whisper.

He was too tired to be angry. Too tired of the lies, the deceit, of every single thing being so bloody complicated. Too tired to be tired. Children here and there. Years of avoidance and the unsaid. Marriages that were never meant to be, jobs too difficult to master, mortgages impossible to clear. Man-made complication.

'Why are you telling me now?' asked Dave, wondering if Carol was done with all the lies too.

'Those tests at the hospital, the blood types showed there was no way Seth could be your son.'

'That's why you didn't get angry about Jedd?' Dave ran his hands through his hair, the past few days making more sense.

'Maybe. I dunno. I had a feeling it would come up. It's a rare blood type.'

'But where's he gone?'

'Gone?'

'Seth's not here, Carol.'

Silence regained the line.

Time, that was what Seth had said he needed. Seth, the

one thing that wasn't a complication. His son. The boy who was becoming a man of whom Dave was so proud wasn't his son, after all. Didn't change anything? It changed everything. He hadn't even come to talk to him. Dave thought back to what Carol had said.

'What did you mean when you said *maybe* that's why you weren't angry about Jedd? Me and you, it's over, isn't it?'

'It's been over between us for a long time.'

The line cut.

Dave stared at his phone until the screen blackened. His body slid down the chair as the scaffold supporting his life fell away. His wife, his son, the almost other son. He looked at the cornices, realising the house would have to go too. Once the truth came out about Great Brakes, that would be his career up the swanny. Dave reached over to his computer and powered it up. He couldn't believe Seth would leave in silence.

He scrolled endless emails. Nothing. He fell upon the DNA results from the hospital, clicking on them to be sure he was as seedless as he had always known. Seth being conceived had felt like a miracle. That non-Olympic seed a reflection of him: the rugby player that never made it all the way, the default husband, the drawling Mancunian unable to sell Wales . . .

Ping.

Dave scrolled to the top of his inbox.

Chairman's Office
Presentation by the First Minister
Dear All, With the completion of the audit . . .

Dave clicked.

Dear All,
With the completion of the audit, the First Minister has confirmed his presentation to the Cardiff Investment Agency this afternoon to talk about upcoming changes and future announcements. Everyone is convened at the auditorium at the Senedd at 2pm.
Yours sincerely,
Rhian Davies

The First Minister never presented to CIA staff. Dave assumed this Rhian Davies must be covering Carol's absence. Weirdly, she had the same name as the girl he'd been seeing in Swansea before meeting Carol but he doubted it could be the same one. Dave sat back in his chair. Carol might come back to her job one day but not to him. She was right, they'd fallen out of love. Had they ever really been in it? Dave had known deep down about Seth. Dates coinciding with a rugby tour and Carol insisting Seth was early when he popped out bang on his due date. Auburn hair that Dave would stare at for hours as he nursed him to sleep. And yet, they'd bonded. Seth was the one person that gave the rest meaning. He'd lost him in recent years to TikTok but those hours at the hospital had reunited them. He'd said he would help him sort out this mess of a project, talk to that creepy little Rodric.

And now he was gone.

Not a word.

Dave checked his phone. He clicked into his last message from Seth and reread it. *Need some time to work things out.* Work out if he ever wanted to see Dave again? Dave threw his phone on the table, misjudging the distance. It teetered on the edge, rocking back and forth in indecision before clattering to the floor.

'Shit!' Dave shouted at an empty house, pushing himself out of the chair and noticing a blue suit hanging on the back of the living room door that he hadn't seen on entering.

Everything was leaving him. His job was the only thing left. He checked the microwave. One o'clock.

There was no point trying to stop the project now. A few media scares, Great Brakes would be more careful in Wales. In any case, the project had been approved by the First Minister. How was Dave single-handedly going to turn that around? Instead, he could accept the single iota of good fortune the universe had handed him.

Dave shook off his jeans and sweatshirt, looked back at the microwave. No time for a shower. He slid into the red shirt hanging next to the suit. Red for Wales. Freshly pressed, he tried not to crease it as he pushed the buttons into their matching holes one by one by one. End of audit announcements, that was worth a listen in any case. He'd never seen the First Minister in person.

Trousers and jacket on, Dave searched for his shoes on the way to the front door, then squinted as sun flooded the transom window. A weight banged against his hip bone. He fumbled in his pocket. In his hand appeared a lump of pocked lava.

But he had never actually been to—

Dave's arm rose to shield his eyes, even though he knew the lights were about to go out.

CHAPTER TWENTY-NINE

Wind tickled the water, rippling his face as he leant over the stream. Dave shuddered, his body evacuating all air. Lupins chased buttercups up the opposite riverbank, the wind lifting a white sheet to reveal a pair of well-laced walking boots swinging from the boulder next to him.

'Jesus Christ! Why are you wearing that?' asked Dave.

'I am the Ghost of Yesterday Dave,' said the sheet. 'Ooooh!'

'I know it's you, you know.'

Sal ripped the sheet off his head, straining to keep his red hat in place.

'How?' He dropped the sheet to the floor.

'Call it an educated guess.'

Today of all days, thought Dave. He'd be back in that hospital quicker than—

'Don't you know why you're back?' asked Sal.

—Quicker than he could finish his own thought.

'Hang on. Did you say the Ghost of Yesterday Dave?'

'The sheet too much?' Sal shrugged.

'It's all too much!' Dry laughter bounced down the

TUESDAY

river as Dave pushed at the ground, his fingers disappearing into downy moss.

'You can't leave,' shouted Sal. 'I told you, I'm the—'

'It's entirely pointless me trying to fight this, isn't it?' Dave stared at Sal. 'So, let's get it over with. I want to hear what the First Minister has to say.'

Sal raised an eyebrow.

Dave went to speak, closing his mouth as quickly. Sal wouldn't approve of his motivations to be at the presentation, especially if he knew Dave was considering the possible you know what.

'Ready for the big promotion, are we?'

Dave lowered his gaze. Hiding things from Sal was like trying to push jelly up a hill. Impossible, utterly pointless and always messy.

'Thinking of taking it, are you? Wife and son gone and this other son you never knew you had not yours either, this promotion is the only chance you have at holding on to something? Kudos, recognition, a last ditch attempt at respectability.'

Dave stared at Sal. That about summed it up. No point in insisting otherwise. The chelation treatment obviously wasn't working.

'You ever stopped to ask yourself *when* you see me?' asked Sal.

'When I see you?'

'Rather than *why* you see me. People are so tied up with why.' One hand wafted through the air as the other gathered the sheet at his feet. 'But combine why with *when*, or *who*, or *how* and you get a different answer.'

'You're starting to give me a—' Dave turned to see Sal covered once more. 'Not the sheet, please.'

'Need to get on if you want to make that presentation. Look into the water.'

'What?'

Sal lifted the sheet and peeked out. 'I told you, I am the Ghost of Yesterday Dave. Now look into the water.' The sheet dropped back down.

Dave shook his head. One thing after the bloody other. He looked into the river as it sliced his face.

'The past shapes us,' said Sal.

'You what?'

A finger prodded Dave. 'Look into the water!'

The endless blue abyss echoed with whistling wind. Dave leant in, his fingers clutching at the grass beside him. As the shards of his face floated away, an empty rugby pitch replaced the river, Dave now crouching some thirty metres from the posts. He frowned. He'd been transported from Iceland to a rugby ground and hadn't felt a thing. That wasn't how it happened in the films. In front of him, he noticed a ball waiting to transform points into more points. Dave stood. A pair of blue socks reached his knees. This was Heywood Road.

'Come on, Dave. Focus.'

Dave knew that voice too. Eight years his senior and thanks to a Jamaican mother, Chris was Carrington's answer to Michael Jackson. The rising star of the English team, he would help out training the Under-16s when visiting his parents. Dave's eyes revisited the empty stands. Heywood Road, back where his rugby career had begun. A pair of scrawny knees confirmed he was fifteen again.

'What's up with you today?' asked Chris.

'Up with me?'

'You don't have your eye on the game.' Chris kicked at the ball. It wobbled from the tee to lie in the grass.

'I'm no good!' Dave sank to the floor. 'I'll never be any good.'

'This 'cos your dad wasn't at the match on Saturday?'

TUESDAY

Dave shrugged. Dad wasn't at any matches.

'Busy?' said Chris.

'Busy getting pissed.'

'Aye. Heard about that.'

Dave's heart dropped into his stomach. All the lads at school had heard about it too. Dobs and Griff had cornered him in the toilets.

'You piss yourself on benches too, Welchie?' They'd taunted, prodding at his groin.

Dave's eyes welled. Everyone knew. Dad was a laughing stock. Playing the way he was, Dave would never amount to anything either. Not that Dad would care. He'd shouted as much when trying to sober up after the police had brought him home, annoying Mum not with his comments, but by waking Maya. He wanted Dave to do something proper with his life.

'Fed up of being picked on,' Dave said to Chris.

'And you think I wasn't at school?'

Chris had never spoken to him directly about the nicknames that had become kicks and punches, the reasons he'd turned to rugby and the comments that had followed him into the locker room.

'He's such an embarrassment.' Dave swallowed back the tears.

'That's your dad you're talking about.'

'Why can't he be like other dads?' asked Dave.

'My dad's messed up too.'

'Why you telling me off for dissing mine then?'

'Still your dad. Parents mess up too, you know.'

Dave studied Chris's face, now a picture of calm. 'What's with yours then?'

'Lost his job, didn't he. Not the same since. Sits at home all day, watching shit on telly. Mum's got two jobs, cleaning up other people's mess.'

'He misses work?'

Dave thought about Dad, toiling the land for a pittance.

'Does he heck. Hated it in that factory. Always wanted to be a carpenter.'

'Why doesn't he do that now?'

Chris shrugged. 'He got tired.'

'Suppose it's hard work.'

'Nah. He got tired of life, not work. Your dad's different.'

'He is?'

'Ted the Turnip King?' Chris smiled. 'He's fighting the good fight, believes in what he's doing. And he's not wrong. What do you think will happen when we don't produce any more of our own food?'

'Suppose so. Maybe he's getting tired too? Tired of the fight.'

'Don't diss your dad. Learn to be different.'

'That what you're doing?'

'Too right.' Chris stood wrenching Dave by the arm. 'Now get up off your sorry arse and mark this penalty.'

Dave laughed. He fetched the rugby ball. Placing it back on the tee, he angled it to expose the sweet spot, ready for his foot to make contact. He twisted the ball a nudge, aiming the seam slightly to the right of the posts.

'Right, now step away and prepare your run-up,' said Chris.

Dave took three long strides backwards, checked he was lined up correctly and took another two long strides right. He was a left footer.

'Preparation is one thing, but the key to success is in focusing,' said Chris.

Dave swung his arms, clapped his hands together. He could do this. He would do this. No one would tell him

TUESDAY

otherwise. He would do exactly what he wanted to with this one life. He'd show Dobs and Griff. He'd show Dad. Dave Welch believed. He would be someone. Life wouldn't slow him down or tire him. He ran to the ball. Weight shifted to his right, his left leg thudding into the ball. A bolt of electricity juddered through him.

His foot hung in mid-air as the ball traced a perfect arc through the two posts.

'That's more like it!' Chris slapped him on the back. 'You'll make it. Just got to believe. And stop listening to everyone else. Your life is yours to define.'

Dave smiled. 'I get it. Thanks, Chris. And for the other stuff, you know, about my dad.'

'Be kind to him. You won't have him forever.'

Chris rubbed his face, failing to hide a sudden sadness.

'You're here a lot at the stadium lately,' said Dave.

'Lung cancer, doctors said. Need to be with me dad right now. And me ma.'

'But the World Cup?' The words shot out, Dave knowing Chris had been working for years to get on the national team and this was training time.

'If following your dreams was easy, they wouldn't be dreams.'

The stands started to spin, slowly at first before blurring into a blue haze. Dave closed his eyes. When he reopened them, his aging reflection stared back at him from the river.

Chris Beckinsdale. He hadn't seen him for years. They'd kept in touch at the start of Dave's career. Mum said he'd been at Dad's funeral. Away in New Zealand, Dave had made it home for the end of the wake but Chris had already left. Dave had felt only relief at not having to face him. Chris's dad had had a prognosis. Dave couldn't have known in advance about his dad's heart attack.

'You knew he wasn't doing great though?' Sal stared at him from the boulder next to him.

Dave jumped. 'I don't want to be here!' he shouted.

'Tired are we? Like Ted the Turnip King. About to throw in the towel.'

'Shut up!' Dave placed his hands over his ears.

'How about pissing more taxpayers' money up the wall with your new inflated salary?' Sal's words filtered through Dave's fingers.

'Shut up, shut up, shut up!'

CHAPTER THIRTY

'You alright, love?' Set in a maze of wrinkles in the seat opposite, a pair of blue eyes examined him.

'Where am I?' asked Dave, his gaze bouncing around a sludgy orange decor and stomach somersaulting in the rattling plastic.

'Three, love.'

'Three?' He frowned.

'Three steps to heaven.' The woman winked, her voice undulating in song. 'That's if you play your cards right. Nice suit.'

'Pardon?'

'Number three bus, in'it!' Wrinkles fell into more wrinkles.

The bus full of otherwise empty seats and the lady's eyes disinclined to leave him, Dave pulled his phone out of his pocket to check the time. Twenty past one. Of course, he was on his way to the Senedd.

'Meeting the First Minister,' said Dave, remembering he'd been back to Iceland and fed with a need to re-establish his sanity.

'And I'm the Queen of Sheba, love.' The lady stood. 'This is me. If you're up for it, the offer still stands.' She winked again, slapping him on the shoulder.

Laughter rumbled through the orange walls and chequered upholstery. The front doors clapped shut and the bus pulled off. Dave ran his hand down his trousers, rolled his shoulders to readjust his jacket. Back in bloody Iceland, now of all times. Whatever they had pumped into him at the hospital wasn't working. This was an important meeting. He had to hold it together. He straightened, focusing on the chewing gum-spattered pavement rolling past the window.

You ever stopped to ask yourself when you see me?

That's what Sal had said. And no, Dave hadn't. Well, in the beginning he had decided it was only Tuesdays until that theory had fallen apart. Dave rechecked his watch. It was probably another five minutes to the Bay. At least he was on time for the presentation. Didn't do to be arriving late. It was at the Senedd, wasn't it? Dave checked the phone still in his hand, a calendar entry alleviating his fears. He rubbed at his sweaty brow. Sal hadn't wanted him to miss the presentation either. Jesus Christ! He had to stop thinking about Sal! Who pays attention to little men who don't exist? Dave slid two fingers under his shirt collar, pulling it away from his neck. Cotton clung to his armpits. He'd worn red again. Idiot.

The bus doors opened and clapped shut, Dave's gaze fell on an amber traffic light ahead. A man approached, reaching for the handrail as the bus, having barely resumed its journey, ground to a halt at the next lights. One red light on this road and you got them all.

'Dave?' said the man, barely a metre away and tugging at a less than enamoured French bulldog.

'Chris? Chris Beckinsdale?'

TUESDAY

Smiling eyes sat in a dreadlock-framed face. 'Dave Welch, it *is* you!'

Dave slapped his hand into Chris's.

'Bloody hell! It's been so long!' said Chris.

Dave's eyes bounced around the empty bus, knowing that for him it hadn't. Releasing his hand, he tugged again at his shirt collar. Red light, red shirt. Red for bloody Wales. The number three, this was the number three. He hadn't gone anywhere. The bus darkened. On emerging from under the railway bridge, Dave spotted Cardiff Central, his shoulders dropping with relief. They weren't in Iceland.

Chris took a seat in front of him, twisting to talk. 'You okay? You look like you've seen a ghost.'

A sheet flapped in Dave's mind. The Ghost of Yesterday Dave. He had thought of Chris for the first time in how many years and now here he was.

'I was just . . . it's weird. How long has it been?'

Dave knew the answer. Once Dave had left Sale, his career taking him to Wales, they'd kept in touch for a while. The fame and television interviews, the tours, the booze, the women, Dave had dived headfirst into a new life. He jerked his foot back as a warm tongue licked his ankle. Seemingly exhausted by its endeavours, the dog flopped to the floor and stared at him. Jesus, it was ugly.

'Not long after your dad's funeral, wasn't it?' said Chris.

Dave refocused his attention, remembering what had been a short chat, him too much of a coward to put words on the guilt weighing him down, unable to admit not having been there for Dad. They hadn't spoken since. He'd followed Chris in the papers, of course. Everyone had. Right up to that episode with the International Rugby Board.

'Lost touch once I moved to Wales,' said Dave.

'Lost touch with a lot of people.' Chris stared at him.

'There was a lot going on,' said Dave, remembering ignoring his calls.

The bus ambled through traffic. Dave checked his phone for the time, Chris's eyes never leaving him. How did you come back from letting down the one guy who had supported you, your friend, your mentor? One of the few people who had believed in you.

'Anyway, what are you up to now?' asked Chris.

'I work for the Cardiff Investment Agency.'

'What's that then?'

'We bring investment into Wales, create jobs.'

'From outside Wales?'

Dave's head dropped into a nod. He could see Ted the Turnip King in Chris's eyes. Could see the look that said, 'waste of taxpayers' money.'

'Sustainable investment,' added Dave. 'In fact, I have a presentation now. Pierhead Street. This is me.'

Chris looked up. 'Ah, me too.'

'Meeting the First Minister.' Dave waited for an indication Chris was impressed with what he had become. It never came. 'So why are you here? You live here now?' asked Dave.

Chris shook his head, turning to alight the bus and dragging a reluctant dog behind him. 'Sort of holiday with the wife.'

Air flooded Dave's lungs on exiting the bus. Seagulls screeching overhead, he glanced up and down the street. This was definitely Cardiff Bay. He shook his foot, a wet nose exploring his ankle.

Dave pointed up the street. 'I'm this way.'

'Looks like we're going the same way.'

The two men walked towards the government offices.

TUESDAY

Dave sought words in the silence, the only vocabulary he found, feeble, vain attempts at excuses, or reasons to show how he'd changed. There were no excuses. He'd let Chris down. He'd let himself down. He always let himself down.

Ahead, a woman in a yellow dress waved, Chris lifting his hand to return the gesture.

'Isn't that the Minister for Sports?' asked Dave.

'Well, Arts, Sports and Tourism to give her her full title.' Chris laughed.

'You know her?'

'We're meeting for lunch. I'm an Ambassador for the Rugby Board.'

Dave stopped dead. 'You . . . but they?'

'Hung me out to dry?' Chris smiled. 'Weren't the only ones, were they?'

Chris's dog sat on Dave's shoe, eyes boring into him.

'The World Cup was approaching, everyone was told to keep a low profile.' Words rushed out of Dave. 'You know, if we wanted to be in the team.'

'I know exactly what happened, Dave.'

Chris had tried to rally support, denouncing the racist remarks from the changing room that had spread into the crowds. It was the World Cup, everything Dave had been training for.

'I never thought you'd leave,' said Dave. 'I thought it would die down.'

'All be brushed back under the carpet, you mean?'

'I'm sorry,' said Dave, the words emerging as a whisper. 'I really am. I should have stood by you.'

'Look, it's all water under the bridge, mate.' Chris grabbed Dave's arm. 'The past shapes you but it's what you choose to do here and now that defines you.'

The past shapes you.

Dave bent down to stroke the dog, its demeanour softening as it rubbed its back on the pavement.

'Don't stroke the lazy bugger. He's been known to bite if you indulge him.'

Dave pulled back. 'What's he called?'

'Sid.'

'Sid?' Dave laughed.

'Kids love the sloth in those Ice Age films.' Chris slapped him on the arm before ambling towards the yellow dress. 'Keep in touch.'

'I will,' mumbled Dave, wondering if he would ever see Chris again.

Fearing he'd be late, Dave pulled out his phone and darted to his left. A scooter swerved to miss him, a bag of chips flying into the air.

'Out of the way, mate!' shouted the driver, a ketchup-sodden lump landing in front of Dave and splattering his feet like a crime scene.

'Watch what you're bloody doing!' shouted Dave.

'Watch where you're bloody going!'

Sweat carved a path between his shoulder blades as Dave stood motionless. He had no idea what was happening anymore. Iceland, Sal, Chris, soggy bags of chips, was any of it real? Could he have thought of Chris only to bump into him again after all these years? Someone calling after having thought about them out of the blue, that's been known to happen. Or maybe Chris was another hallucination? A mind that took him to Iceland could make up anything. Dave prodded at the chips with his shoe, vinegar attacking his nose. They seemed real. His shoulders dropped, his lungs evacuating their contents. Overhead, seagulls shrieked.

Dave rechecked his phone. Ten to two. Time for the presentation. He had to pull himself together. This was it.

TUESDAY

If the First Minister was here to talk about Great Brakes, he'd mention Dave's role. He might even talk to him directly, offer him the Paris promotion in person. Dave wasn't Chris, he'd already proved that. Dave hadn't been sent to change the world. He was here to keep it turning in his own little way. Three hundred jobs. You couldn't say Wales didn't need them. What was Chris trying to achieve by becoming an Ambassador? He'd soon learn he had to play by their rules. This job was the only thing Dave had left now. If a hallucination is a false perception of events, maybe life is one big hallucination.

Dave dropped his phone into his jacket pocket, a scratching sound causing him to pull it back out. A piece of pocked lava fell to the floor. Dave looked heavenwards and covered his ears as the screeching overhead reached a crescendo. Seagulls crisscrossed the blinding sun, one by one by one, dive-bombing the vinegary delights at his feet.

CHAPTER THIRTY-ONE

Unsure of where he was, Dave inched open his eyes.

A clear river rippled a silent reply.

'No!' His gaze met a familiar dance of lupins and buttercups. 'Absolutely bloody not!'

'Prefer the number three bus to this natural beauty?' asked a white sheet.

'Come on! This is getting annoying.'

'Isn't it just.'

Pulling at the mound of cotton revealed Sal.

'*You're* annoyed, are you?' asked Dave. 'So very sorry.'

'You wouldn't be here if you didn't want to be!' Sal battled with the sheet's folds.

'But I *don't* want to be here.'

'It was you trying to find me in that lift.'

'Enough talking,' said Dave. 'I get it. We've done Ghost of Christmas Past.'

Sal rolled his eyes, his face framed by the draping sheet. 'Look like Christmas to you? Where's the snow?' His hands met in prayer. 'Where's the baby Jesus?'

'Okay, okay. We've done the Ghost of Yesterday Dave.

We know the present me that's everything that happens when I'm not being dragged to Iceland. Let's call him—'

'Now Dave?' said Sal.

'So, it must be time for Tomorrow Dave? Take me to my lonely grave. No wife, kids or friends mourning me. A sorry box of forgotten bones and a headstone wishing me good riddance.'

'Pity doesn't suit you, you know.' Sal rolled his eyes. 'Now will you shut up and look in the water.'

'Okay, okay. Let's get this over with.' Dave leant towards the river.

'Ooooh,' said Sal, voice muffled. 'I am the Ghost of Tomorrow Dave.'

'For—'

Dave lurched forward, gulping as he entered the blue abyss headfirst. Somersaults left his stomach rattling in his ribcage. His teeth clenched as the contents of his insides battled to spill out. Closing his eyes, he started to pray, for what he wasn't sure. In any case, he had no sooner addressed the big guy in the sky when he landed with a thud, his eyes springing open.

Dave grabbed the edges of the seat beneath him, rattan digging into his palms. Packed like sardines, chequered red-and-white tables surrounded him, all empty. A machine slammed onto the table. Dave jumped. He slid his wrist across the screen, frowning at the waiter and wondering when he had started paying with his watch.

'*Je sais, Monsieur, je sais*. We all miss the old days.' The waiter sighed.

Dave looked past the velour-shrouded windows to a cobbled street and a group of Japanese camera enthusiasts. 'I'm in France?'

'I ask myself the same thing, Monsieur.'

'No, I mean . . .' Dave scoured the restaurant, the only

other patrons cancan dancers furling legs out of dusty pictures. From a yellow ceiling, a speaker purred '*Joe le Taxi*'.

So, Tomorrow Dave *was* in France? Dave's stomach pushed at his belt. The taste of steak lingered on his tongue but a filmy layer on the roof of his mouth made him doubt his certitude. To be in Paris, he must have accepted the promotion, but that certainly didn't explain the shitty restaurant. He checked his watch. Twelve thirty.

'Where is everyone?' he asked.

'*La finale, Monsieur,*' replied the waiter, mumbling into his moustache.

La finale. He was on his way to see the match. He remembered now. He always rushed a steak and chips pre-match because he hated those verrines served at the Embassy. Minuscule portions of indistinguishable layers. Dave frowned, wondering how he could know about the match and the steak and chips but have been surprised he was in France.

'Ooooh,' said a familiar voice, drowning out Vanessa Paradis. 'I am the Ghost of Tomorrow Dave.'

Bloody hell, that's right. He was here, but not really. Dave rubbed his temples trying to decipher an in- and out-of-body experience rolled into one. That had to mean he was only privy to what he wanted himself to know, but that would mean hiding things from himself, which was surely impossible. His finger dodged a clump of encrusted mustard as it traced a slow line down the tablecloth in front of him, confirming it wasn't the pressed white linen of *La Table*. He grabbed the glass pitcher, sniffing its acidic dregs and noting it far from a 2028 Margaux.

Dave's wrist vibrated. A new message. He opened it.

See you at The Dubliner

TUESDAY

Of course, he wasn't going to the Embassy. Those days were over. He *had* been trying to hide certain things. Pushing back his chair, Dave searched for the absent waiter before making his way outside. As the wind lifted his coat, he moved left and right, legs aching as he dodged swarms of people ambushing him like flies. On arriving at the pub, he grabbed the brass handle, took a deep breath and entered a carpeted den of lager-laced adrenalin and well-known haven for homesick Brits in Paris. His attention immediately fell on the screen that filled the back wall, the odd taste that had accompanied him from the restaurant elucidated by a sponsorship advertisement for meat-free meat.

Words replaced the image of a double cheeseburger and fries.

Rugby World Cup Final
France versus Wales
Tbilisi, 2039

Dave hadn't thought to question his age. He searched for a mirror in the crowded bar. 2039, that made him sixty-one. Dad had been sixty-one when he died. Dave looked back at the screen. Tbilisi? The Welsh team had gone to Georgia to train before the 1999 World Cup, the Georgian lads not qualifying that time around. Dave's knees had gone by the time Georgia had played in 2007 but he'd watched them struggle from the stands. Thrown into a pool with the French, arrogant and boisterous on their home turf, the Georgians had had little chance. Times had certainly moved on, with Georgia now the host country and Wales in the final. Dave smiled at red dots lining up next to blue dots, the camera zooming in on an unknown generation.

'They turned up anyway?' A guy shouted to his friend over Dave's head.

'The Rugby Board's always been a farce,' another voice shouted back.

'Leave that stuff to the politicians.'

'Farce?' asked Dave, cornered by the two men's stares.

'You think World Rugby gives a shit about racism, let alone Slaughter-free Sam.'

Dave frowned.

'That what they're calling the fake meat guy?' The other guy laughed.

'Why do we make everything into a joke?'

'Mate, it's a game. They take the knee. What else can they do?'

'Not take blood money. You heard the working conditions that man condoned to build that stadium? As long as he doesn't consider them *his* people, he doesn't give a shit.'

'It's starting,' said Dave.

'Who's that old fella?' said the man to Dave's right.

'Where are the anthems?' asked another.

A hush descended on the pub.

'You won't all remember me.' The voice rippled around the crowded bar sending a chill up Dave's spine. Dave fixed the bald head that filled the screen, swimming in eyes that had believed in him all those years ago. 'The older amongst you might.'

'Chris Beckinsdale,' mumbled Dave.

'I started playing rugby when I was twelve because Steve Wilkins told me darkies didn't belong in Carrington.' Whispers danced around the almost silent pub. 'A sport that rallied people as a team, I thought rugby could offer me a path to acceptance, to belonging. And fans did shout my name in joy, fondly called me Becksie, until occasions when I missed a conversion or a penalty. Then,

TUESDAY

I was told to piss off back on the boat.' Eyes exchanged nervous glances across the pub. 'I'd never been on a boat, never been out of Greater Manchester, not until I started touring with the England team. Whilst touring, I realised my face didn't quite fit when it came to my teammates and coaches either. The face of England was white, mine wasn't. "That's what it's like in other places, Chris," they told me. "Not for us. You know you're one of us." But the day I challenged the Board, I was silenced. Equality and fairness were quintessentially English and not up for debate, I was told, as was not making a fuss over a little banter here and there. And so, I left the game, felt sorry for myself. I drowned in the legal fees thrown at me by the institution known today as World Rugby and of which I became Chairman a few weeks ago. I'm happy to stand here before you today acknowledging that times have moved on.' Tension leaked from the room. 'But as much as times move on, it is our collective responsibility to make them move in a positive and fair direction. That's why I came back to work for the sport that had abandoned me. I never gave up on rugby. I never abandoned the fight against racism. I never stopped believing we can live in a fairer world. But to do that we have to stop compartmentalising racism into different areas of life. We can't sanction it in the locker rooms, on the pitch and in the stands, only to finance our sport by money that comes from inequality and injustice. Taking the knee is laudable, no longer singing Swing Low, Sweet Chariot is progress, but it's not enough. We are all accountable.'

Whispering recirculated in the pub.

'Jesus Christ! He's doing it!' said the guy next to Dave.

Bustling occupied the screen, cameras bouncing from face to face in the crowd. The camera panned up to the sponsorship boxes and the mouthing of non-discernible expletives. Transmission cut.

'Where's the match?' shouted someone.

'It's lighting up X.'

'Look at this live feed! The players are all walking off the pitch!'

The screen resumed its coverage, it now connected to the barman's social media account.

'The past shapes us,' said Chris. 'The present defines us. The future awaits us.'

Amidst a flurry of swipes, flashes and shares, Dave stood motionless.

The Ghost of Tomorrow Dave had taken him right back to Chris. Achieving dreams by abandoning what you believe to be the right thing is the stuff of nightmares, that's what Chris had said in Iceland. Not in Iceland, a long time ago back at Heywood Road. And Iceland didn't exist. Well, it did. Dave simply hadn't been there, not really. But all the stuff Sal had been telling him was the same as what Chris had tried to share back then. Lessons on how thoughts, words and actions should align, words he had been quick to ignore.

Dave pushed through the crowds to the bar, craving the support of century-old mahogany and the relief of any liquor.

The past shapes us, the present defines us, the future awaits us.

A double whisky landed in front of him. Knowing he hadn't ordered it, Dave snatched and drank it anyway, the brown liquid scorching his throat. He'd been transported to Paris to see Chris's future but had no idea what *he* was doing at sixty-one. Fallen from high places, it seemed. Something told him the promotion hadn't panned out. He slugged at the whisky. If he didn't know what his life had become, he had to still be keeping something from himself.

TUESDAY

'*David! Putain! Je te cherchais partout.*'

'Pierre,' said Dave, turning towards the perfumed scent of money and a cashmere sweater draped over taut shoulders.

'I wasn't sure you got my text. No one's heard from you since, well you know. Did you see what just happened!'

Whisky licked the sides of Dave's glass. He knew it. At sixty-one, he wasn't with the Welsh government anymore. He'd been ousted, lauded for bringing in Great Brakes and hung out to dry when it all went wrong. Chris was everything Dave had wanted but failed to be. That's why he had been seeing Chris's life and not his own. He'd been right, you can try to hide the truth from yourself but it will always find you.

'*Ca va?*' asked Pierre.

Dave gripped the tumbler in his hand, suddenly remembering that none of what he was experiencing was real. A projection of the future, everything happening to Tomorrow Dave could be decided by Now Dave. Tomorrow was in his hands, it always had been. His life had just been waiting for him to decide how it would pan out. Dave *could* change the world.

Dave closed his eyes, emboldened by his epiphany.

'*T'es bizarre, t'es sûr que ça va?*'

'Give me a Guinness,' shouted Dave, 'and make him go away!'

When Dave reopened his eyes, he cradled a perfectly pulled pint of stout and the 'little French prick', as Jolene had fondly christened their former placement student, was nowhere to be seen.

CHAPTER THIRTY-TWO

'Why are you in the middle of the road?' Mouth forced into a smile, perfectly white teeth gleamed at him.

Dave caught sight of the Senedd building as a cologne and vinegar breeze caught his throat. He coughed. Attempting to steady himself, he skidded on a mound of ketchup-smothered chips. 'What the...'

A hand caught Dave's arm. 'You're as white as a sheet.'

The two men stared at each other.

Dave wondered if they had ever been so close and how there was never a single hair out of place on the Chairman's head. He shook potato remnants from his shoe, realising he was exactly where Chris had left him.

'Not having one of your Narnia turns, are you?' asked the Chairman.

'Narnia?'

'The other one then, you know, with the rabbit.'

Dave shook his head. Double-barrelled dickhead. Some things never change, he thought, remembering he'd been in France. He glanced at his watch, happy to still have ten minutes to spare. He'd hardly been away. In the beginning, he would lose hours. It had to mean the chelation therapy was starting to take effect. He couldn't let on he'd been on one of his 'trips' though.

'I'm fine,' said Dave. 'Everything's fine.' He recalled the last time he'd seen the Chairman, having fallen out of an elevator at Carol's feet. 'The whisky got me in your office last time, that's all.'

'Are you sure you should be out and about though?'

Dave started walking, knowing what he had to do. 'They've upped the dose at the hospital,' he shouted behind him.

The Chairman tugged his arm, stopping him in his tracks. 'No one is expecting you at this presentation.'

Dave knew otherwise. It was his chance to meet the man at the top. He'd come to the Senedd believing his job and promotion were the only things left to cling to, forgetting righting the wrongs he had discussed with Bryn. One didn't have to mean forfeiting the other. Dave could change things from the inside by climbing the ranks, like Chris in that vision. Seeing Chris in years to come demonstrated another way, one where Dave could succeed without compromising himself, or the Bristol Channel.

'Did you speak with the First Minister about the accusations?' Dave eyeballed the Chairman.

The Chairman lowered his gaze. 'It's not easy, David. I have always tried to keep my personal and work lives separate.'

'Sorry?'

'You don't believe Digby, do you?'

'Digby?' asked Dave, memories of Pinot Grigio ranting returning.

Dave hadn't even confronted the Chairman with Digby's sexual harassment accusations that day they'd met in his office. Dave rubbed his head. He really hadn't been with it. That bloody whisky.

'Sour grapes because he wasn't offered Paris,' continued the Chairman.

'Paris wasn't on the cards then, was it?' replied Dave, trying to recall the exact timeline of events.

'You didn't know it was, but *he* did. Ask Carol.'

Dave wouldn't be doing that. Carol had left him. He scraped his shoe and the last clumps of recalcitrant potato onto the road.

'Why do you think Digby's gone and I'm still here?' continued the Chairman. 'You can't believe everything you hear now, can you?'

Dave knew Digby would have jumped at the chance to live in Paris but wasn't so sure he would have lied to get there. He tried to oust thoughts of unwanted advances, wondering why the Chairman was bringing it up now.

'Does my sexuality offend you?' insisted the Chairman.

'Of course not!' replied Dave, a final morsel of chip taking flight from his shoe and landing within inches of the Chairman's leg.

'You know our policy on diversity and inclusion.'

'About our meeting—' said Dave, confused with a conversation that had gone so off-piste.

'No need to apologise.'

Dave hadn't been intending to. The accusations he wanted to talk about were the ones levelled against Great Brakes. The problem was he still hadn't heard from Jedd with the proof needed or further information on the mysterious holding group. Jedd probably wouldn't bother either, not now the news was out he wasn't Dave's son. You'd expect a text at least, to say goodbye if nothing else.

The Chairman tugged him. 'Are you sure you're okay, David? Wouldn't you be better resting up?'

TUESDAY

Dave shrugged off his arm. 'I was talking about the accusations of mercury dumping.'

'Accusations, David.' The Chairman smiled. 'You said it.'

'At least flag my concerns.'

'Of course. Your concerns are everyone's if there is any proof behind what you say. Tell me, do you have that proof now?'

Dave felt the phone in his pocket, knowing there was no point in checking. 'No.'

'One doesn't flag concerns with the First Minister. One brings him solutions.'

'Solutions?'

'Jobs. A solution to rising unemployment. Exactly what you have brought.'

Dave nodded. He wasn't sure how, but he had. Wales hadn't seen a project like this in years. The two men resumed their walk. A heavy silence falling upon them, Dave's thoughts returned to his bus journey there and the chances of seeing Chris Beckinsdale in Cardiff.

'The First Minister is a busy man, David. Let me give you some advice . . .' said the Chairman.

Dave turned the corner, the red bricks of a looming Pierhead building and the smell of the sea greeting him. The Senedd's undulating roof hovered like a sail. Chris would be at his lunch now. Working for World Rugby as an Ambassador, who would have thought? He was spitting feathers back in the day, losing that lawsuit against the *Daily Mail* when they ran with the headline *Lie-half kicked out of England 15 accuses IRB of racism.* Could real-life Chris – the one he had just seen in Cardiff –have become an Ambassador to try and influence things from the inside, like in that vision of the future? No, not vision. Hallucination, that's the word Dr Bete—

'Are you listening?' The Chairman grabbed Dave by the shoulders, bringing both men to a standstill in the foyer. 'It's okay but whatever you do, don't bring it up today.'

'The accusations against Great Brakes?' asked Dave.

'Jesus Christ! No! Of course, not them. You really aren't listening are you? I was talking to you about the promotion. It's definitely yours.'

'It is?' Dave stared at the Chairman as he pressed the button to call the lift.

Dave had seen himself in Paris, in that forgotten restaurant, but that was only one outcome. He was in charge of his hallucinations; he'd learnt that much. He was also in charge of his own destiny. He could make Paris work for him, for everyone.

'The full restructuring won't be announced until next week,' concluded the Chairman. 'That's all.'

The lift binged, announcing its arrival.

'Let's take the stairs.' Dave made for the door to the left of reception.

'Stairs?' The Chairman chased after him. 'As I was saying, the First Minister is a busy man. He won't have time to talk to you. Probably doesn't even know who you are.'

'David? David Welch?'

Dave's attention had been momentarily consumed by the multicoloured verrine in his hand. The waitress had said it contained prawns, avocado and rutabaga, the latter *a bit like leeks*. Rutabaga was another name for swede; Dave knew as much. He'd simply resorted to small talk to observe the First Minister. Now here was the man himself bounding towards him.

TUESDAY

'First Minister.' Dave went to shake hands, performing an impromptu dance to alleviate himself of a plate of finger food, a glass of water and range of miniature cutlery on a nearby bookshelf.

'Hate these verrines, don't you? No idea what's bloody in them,' the First Minister whispered. 'Dying to meet you. No one has forgotten that try in the 1999 World Cup. Rhys told me you were incapacitated?'

Dave smiled, knowing old Rhys hadn't betted on him being there. From the corner of his eye, he could see the Chairman cornered by a ravenous Minister for Agriculture, who, absent from presentation, squatted the buffet as he ranted about the price of milk between mouthfuls of panko-encrusted prawns.

'Delighted to meet you.' Dave stretched out his hand, knowing this was his chance, even if he still hadn't received any further proof from Jedd.

'Great Brakes, that was all you?' The First Minister took Dave's hand in his.

The size of a shovel, Dave looked twice. Please, not now, he thought, his shoulders dropping on remembering a recent Wales Online article. The tallest leader Wales had ever seen, their new First Minister measured a whopping six foot four.

'About Great Brakes . . .' said Dave, trying to focus. He could do this. Tomorrow Dave could be like Tomorrow Chris. 'It has come to my attention that the company may not be as green as they say.'

'What do you mean?' The First Minister frowned.

'I mean, they may have been dumping—'

'*May* not be as green, *may* have been dumping. That's a lot of *mays*.'

It was only two, but Dave could tell the conversation

wasn't going well. 'I mean, they've been accused. It's just—'

'I've read about the Adrian's Creek allegations.'

'You have?' Dave's head shot up.

'Of course, we researched the company.'

Encouraged it wasn't going as badly as he had first thought, Dave assumed the First Minister must have also read that the Adrian's Creek allegations were judged unfounded.

'But there's more—'

'Greenwashing is everywhere nowadays, isn't it?' said the First Minister.

Despite having been interrupted, a response akin to something Jolene might say buoyed Dave. Feeling the First Minister open to discussion, he congratulated himself on having decided to broach the subject. Now, all he needed to do was find his words and formulate his concerns in a less wishy-washy way.

'Some of it true, some not.' The First Minister leant in.

'Sorry?' said Dave.

'A company is like a small country,' continued the First Minister, forgotten spinach peppering an unfaltering smile.

'Is it?'

'Take Wales.' The First Minister's hands rose in levity. 'Being entirely green and competitive don't always go together.' He slapped Dave on the back. 'You're right to come to me with concerns but leave that with the politicians.'

That *wasn't* something Jolene would say. Ill-prepared, Dave had been put in his place. Of course, he didn't appreciate the intricacies of running countries, or companies. There was a reason the First Minister had the position he had, and Dave his. One thing he now knew for sure

TUESDAY

was that the First Minister was ready to turn a blind eye to whatever he revealed.

'So, you've met the man of the moment?' asked the Chairman, red-faced and sliding into the discussion.

'Indeed, I have, Rhys.' The First Minister trapped Dave in a stare. 'I was about to explain that sustainability is *above all* about the people of Wales having a livelihood. And this fine man has got us there.'

'That he has,' said the Chairman, frowning at Dave.

'I was also telling David about the research you undertook on Great Brakes before we pushed it over the line.'

Dave frowned back at the Chairman. He'd been sure he hadn't taken him seriously. Dave felt for his pocket as his phone vibrated, knowing he couldn't answer it now.

'Well, once you came to me with your concerns, David. I felt it important,' said the Chairman, making Dave wonder if his desired absence at the presentation had less to do with the Chairman fearing Dave would voice doubts about Great Brakes and more to do with taking all the credit.

'Thanks again, Rhys. We got it all over the line in time,' said the First Minister.

'In time?' mumbled Dave, reaching to the bookshelf for his glass and drinking the water in three gulps.

He'd thought he was doing right by talking to the First Minister but everyone had aligned on Great Brakes being a perfect fit for Wales, even happy Dave had pushed it through without the proper due diligence. Why were ghosts of past and present sent to him today, if not as a pertinent reminder of how Dave Welch had always messed up? And would have continued to mess up without the Great Brakes project, the Chairman's ultimatum failing to make him a sacrificial cow. He'd seen Tomorrow Dave but tomorrow wasn't decided. Dave was the man of the moment but that didn't mean he could single-handedly change the course of events. He didn't run a big company or a small country. He was Dave Welch.

'Listen, you don't seem incapacitated to me, David.' The First Minister glanced at the Chairman. 'And you're used to the limelight. I think it only right you go to this conference with Rhys.'

'Conference?' Dave's head lifted.

'Sustainability conference. In Iceland, wasn't it, Rhys?'

The Chairman nodded, Dave wondering if it was the same one he had been invited to weeks before.

'Sustainable investment in a time of growth or some such. They want us to announce Great Brakes,' said the First Minister, convincing Dave the conferences were indeed one and the same. 'You've taken Wales to victory in the rugby and now again by bringing in hundreds of jobs. It should be you, don't you think, Rhys?'

The Chairman shuffled. 'Of course, First Minister.'

'Ah, there's Geraint. Please excuse me.' The First Minister crossed the room to greet the Minister of Agriculture, splayed hands parting the crowd like a snow plough.

Dave's pocket vibrated for the second time. He pulled out his phone and read two texts. The first was from Carol telling him her lawyer would be in touch shortly. The second eight-word missive from Jedd confirmed everything Dave knew to be true.

'Count me in for that conference,' he said, on realising there was only one course of action left and clinking glasses with a less-than-enamoured Chairman.

CHAPTER THIRTY-THREE

'And then I realised,' Dave addressed Bryn on the bench next to him, morning sun illuminating a shock of white hair. 'I'm Dave Welch. How am I going to change anything?'

'Know the feeling, son. If you ask me, no one cares how much mercury is in our water, let alone want to clean it up. Where's the money in that? I've pretty much given up getting my invention out there. What's the point?'

'None at all,' replied Dave, his meeting with the First Minister and follow-up discussion with the Chairman having offered enlightenment.

'Hywel is a pragmatist,' the Chairman had explained. 'You know what that is, David?'

Dave had assumed it meant someone practical, not that that explained the 'g'.

'It's the opposite of an idealist,' the Chairman had continued, illustrating the only thing that had made working for the government easier: everyone was trained in answering their own questions. 'His job is to make sure the people of Wales have roofs over their heads, places in schools and . . . *jobs*.'

Clean water and a future for their children, Dave had wanted to add but had stopped himself, knowing the die were cast.

'With the elections brought forward, they'll have wanted to get the news out before purdah sets in,' said Bryn, bringing Dave's attention back to the park.

'The elections, of course.'

Thanks again, Rhys. We got it all over the line in time. Dave nodded, realising the project announcement had been fast-tracked to anticipate the moratorium on pre-election promotional communication.

'Anyway, extracting methyl mercury is focusing on the problem not the cause,' continued Bryn. 'What we actually need to do is—'

'Stop it getting into the water in the first place,' finished Dave, straightening his back and pushing himself into the bench's wooden slats.

'That's why you've invited me down here? Roath Park, third bench down from the Cariad Tea Rooms. Over.' Bryn burst out laughing, torso rattling in his University of Wales t-shirt.

'Exactly that.' Dave smirked, remembering their first telephone call. 'Over.'

'But you know the Welsh government refused to support me. They have no time for an old fart wanting to clean up the sea.'

Dave pulled his phone out of his pocket. 'Jedd sent me this.'

'Jedd, your American son?'

'Jedd, my not so American son.'

'Thought he was from California.'

'He *is* American. I mean, he's not my son.'

TUESDAY

Bryn's eyes widened. 'Well, you do get yourself into them, don't you?'

Dave shrugged. That he did. Even if Jedd was not Dave's son, he was as keen a surfer as Seth. Having researched the accusations of sea pollution levelled at Great Brakes, he was determined to help out. The information had taken more time to get hold of than expected, the holding company having recently changed names.

'A story for another time,' said Dave. 'The important thing is that he says…' He read the eight-word message he had received whilst talking to the Chairman at the Senedd the previous day, '"I have what we need about other allegations."'

'What's that then?' asked Bryn.

'He won't tell me over text. I'm seeing him later.' Dave took Bryn by both shoulders. 'Listen, I've been invited to this conference in Iceland.'

'Iceland? But it's them who—'

'Agreed to fund your research project, I know. It's all a bit much to explain right now but it can't be a coincidence. The Welsh Assembly has been invited to announce the Great Brakes project there. Well, they've asked me to do it.'

Bryn's eyes lit up. 'And you're—'

'Going to use the opportunity to denounce the mercury dumping.' Dave gripped Bryn's arm, the old man's hair dropping into his eyes.

'That's great!' Bryn scraped back his fringe. 'But I don't get it. Your son, well, your not son, he's got more stuff on these allegations. Sounds explosive enough if he won't text it. Why do you need me?'

'Because whatever Jedd might have, what we still don't have is concrete evidence of mercury dumping. I can't risk our information being labelled as anti-greenwashing rhetoric. I need you to go to America.'

'Bloody hell! America?' Bryn's lips rattled as he exhaled all the air from his body. 'I've never been further than Lanzarote.'

'Listen, Bryn. I'm a nobody. I'm not in a position of power like the CEO of Great Brakes or the First Minister.'

'But together we are strong?' finished Bryn.

Dave smiled. 'So, will you help me? I need you to go out there and prove there is mercury in the water at Adrian's Creek. Jedd has already found confirmation they've been acquitted of dumping charges but no one has actually tested the water. Sounds like a Senator was paid off.'

'*Plus ça change.*'

Gauging Bryn's facial expression rather than relying on linguistic comprehension, Dave decided it a good thing he was about to blow the Paris promotion into smithereens. He'd be hard pushed to order a coffee and a croissant.

'Are you in?' asked Dave.

'Of course I'm bloody well in!'

'Forgive us, Welsh Assembly,' sang Dave.

'*We just couldn't take any more!*' Bryn's tenor notes rid the path of a gaggle of geese. 'Always moves in flocks, geese.' He pointed to the disgruntled honking making its way back to the lake. 'You don't want to cross them either. Nasty pieces of work. Got teeth on their tongues.'

'Leaving Sunday,' said Dave. 'Gives you time to get everything done before the conference on Tuesday.'

Tuesday. He hadn't realised. It had all started on a Tuesday. What were the chances of it finishing on one? Dave sighed. One in seven, he supposed.

'Flying, the safest form of travel? How many people survive a plane crash?' asked Bryn, pointing a finger to the sky. 'But I'll get there by hook or by crook. Just need to find my big boy pants.' He waved, his new hip cutting him a spritely departure. 'Over and out, son.'

TUESDAY

Dave stopped under the shade of a drooping tree, noting it as tired in appearance as he felt. The sun rippled the lake's surface as a daisy chain of schoolchildren marched towards the playground. Dave didn't have time to be tired. The conference was in two days' time and the Chairman was convinced Dave would deliver some greenwashing guff about the *Green, Green Tech of Home*. His vision, hallucination, whatever it was, of Chris confronting the International Rugby Board's contradictions by placing himself within the organisation had made sense during the chat with the First Minister. He might only be Dave Welch, but with the right teammates, he could position himself. No try was ever scored by one person alone.

But who else could he trust?

The Chairman?

Dave didn't buy the Chairman's explanation about Digby. The only grapes his former boss had ingested were in that cheap Pinot Grigio at the barbecue. Too many, yes, but not sour. Dave held his breath, for the first time realising the connection.

Lie-half kicked out of England 15 accuses IRB of racism.

On speaking out, rather than being heard, Chris had been painted as someone bearing a grudge. The same thing was now happening to Digby. What plagued the Chairman could be the truth about his personal life coming out. He came from the private sector but he had all the makings of a career politician desperate for the limelight. If you asked Dave, the man was not to be trusted and Digby's accusations were true. He was in no way an ally.

They would have to go it alone.

Dave checked his watch. He only had an hour before meeting Jedd and Jolene. He walked towards the park gates, eager to use the time to book his and Bryn's flights and bemused by the idea that all roads led to Iceland.

As he made his way home, he thought on the many coincidences since that first call from Helga inviting him to the conference. The discussion itself had been odd enough, all that talk of opposing forces. Then, opposing forces had taken hold. A conflict between what Dave thought he should do, what he could do and what others deemed necessary. Every time he had met with Sal, he'd been on the point of going against his inner knowing.

Dave shook his head, remembering the silvery gloop coursing his veins and addling his mind. He'd had the diagnosis and yet all those 'trips' were starting to make sense. He'd been forced to face himself, and not only during the more recent trips as Yesterday Dave and Tomorrow Dave. Right back in the beginning on top of that windy hill, he had been asked to make three wishes. It had started then. Laughter trickled out of Dave on realising he was going to Iceland for real. How would it feel to set foot on that lonely rock he had so wanted to avoid?

He kicked a stone in front of him. It inched up the path. He kicked again. It disappeared into the herbaceous border. Dave was impatient to learn what Jedd's research had unravelled. The string of texts had also alluded to Jedd knowing about Seth's blood test results. Seventeen texts in total, Dave's upper thigh had vibrated non-stop on bidding the Chairman goodbye at the Senedd. Why these youngsters couldn't write one long comprehensive message would forever be a mystery.

Dave sighed, wishing Seth would also send him a message, however long or short. He was okay, that was the main thing. Jedd had said as much, also explaining his own belated response as leaving Dave time to digest. Dave hadn't told Bryn everything. An illegitimate son turning out not to be yours was one thing, let alone a seemingly legitimate one not your flesh and blood either. The deceit hurt but, most of all, Dave missed Seth. Seth had always been his son and Dave his dad. That didn't have to change.

He checked his phone for messages. Nothing.

CHAPTER THIRTY-FOUR

The doors slid open and Dave entered Cardiff Airport's departures hall. Last time, he'd left for Vegas and returned with a caution. This time, he was going to Iceland to return without a job. His eyes following a snaking queue, peppered with at least three men sporting wigs and wedding dresses. Dave glanced at the departures board. It had to be the flight to Ibiza, even if Monday was an illogical day to start a stag weekend. Dave ran a finger over his wedding ring, flesh bulging over a lifetime of marriage. That was over too. A headed letter had arrived that morning from a certain Dewi Cheatham.

Dave checked the board for the KLM check-in desk and wandered over to the less populated end of the hall where Bryn would have also checked in the previous day, flying via Amsterdam to Detroit.

'I've got several paper bags,' Bryn had explained, as Dave had bid him goodbye in the car park, exorbitant stopping charges preventing a protracted goodbye.

'Bags?'

'To breathe into if I think I might pass out. Maureen gave them to me.'

'You went to the hospital?'

'Bumped into her in Iceland.' Bryn had frowned at Dave on understanding his confusion. 'The shop, son. Not the country. They had an offer on cottage pies.'

Sidestepping to avoid a yellow-and-black striped suitcase, a toddler clinging to what were supposed to be the bee's antennae, Dave approached the check-in queue. He thought back to his conversation with Jedd and Jolene a few days earlier. Skirting around the subject of genetics, it had concluded with an apology, Jedd slapping Dave on the shoulder and offering a shy smile.

'Sorry about the mix-up. Mum gets carried away. She spent three years when I was younger trying to link us to the Apache. Had ravens all over the house. Said it was her totem animal or something.'

Jedd had then shared everything he had been able to dig up on Great Brakes. The factories in Asia pre-dated the one in Adrian's Creek. After twenty years in operation, Jedd had found a raft of buried allegations of mercury dumping in both Vietnam and Malaysia but also several detailed witness statements talking of ruined fishing catches, a rise in congenital defects and sudden illness in the local populations. As Dave had anticipated, however, no testing had been done. The holding company in question was called Greentech Holdings. If that wasn't a blatant attempt at greenwashing, Dave didn't know what was. The problem was Jedd hadn't uncovered much more, apart from the holding company's much-publicised support for local higher education and reforestation projects and a recurrent pattern of investing in local community projects where there was any whiff of accusation. Dave had been right to send Bryn over to the States. Politics were getting in the way. What was it the Chairman had said about the First Minister? *His job is to make sure the people of Wales have roofs over their heads, places in schools and jobs.*

Dave glanced around. The Chairman nowhere to be seen, he yelped as a suitcase rammed into his shin. The mop of blond hair at his knees offered him a wide smile, it fading to a frown when the boy's mother joined them.

'Kids gotta play, don't they?' she said.

Pain shot up Dave's leg, inviting him to reply that kids should be educated to grow up thinking about those around them. Instead, he left his thoughts in the queue and made his way to a nearby empty desk, remembering they were travelling business class. The compliance team usually reserved the luxury for flights over six hours, but the First Minister had insisted. Dave pushed his passport through the hole in the perspex screen.

'Mr Welch?' said the assistant behind the counter. 'Travelling with Mr Llewellyn-Jones, I believe? Here's your boarding pass. Feel free to use our business lounge. Have a nice flight.'

Dave made his way through security, sure of where he would find the Chairman, as voices gained in volume behind him.

'You don't stop him, he'll keep doing it,' said someone.

'And what if everyone minded their own bloody business!' replied Suitcase Kid's mum.

'Better we all shut up, is it?' muttered Dave.

He entered the business lounge, his footsteps echoing from its limited occupancy.

On the far side of the room, a full head of hair peeked above a copy of *The Financial Times*. Dropping the newspaper, a hand reached for a glass of whisky.

'David! There you are.'

TUESDAY

Dave chicaned through an army of black leather armchairs towards the Chairman. He'd replayed their discussion after the presentation at the Senedd more times than he cared to remember. Bryn didn't like the man either but thought the Chairman being new to politics *could* play straight into their hands. After all, he *had* researched Great Brakes, meaning Dave's concerns hadn't gone unheard.

'Fish out of water, son. Excuse the pun.' Bryn had doubled over laughing. 'He's not a career politician. He's a businessman trying to swim in the right direction. If you ask me, your Jedd, well, not your Jedd, had to do some serious digging to get this new information. Rhys whatsit thinks he's clever but what did he uncover with his research? Nothing. Think about it, he's got a business reputation to consider before three hundred jobs. Will he want this shit flying back at him when it hits the proverbial fan?'

Dave had frowned, wondering if shit hitting a fan was more of a simple expression than a proverb.

'Exactly,' Bryn had replied. 'He doesn't. The First Minister will turn a deaf ear, what with elections around the corner, but not the Chairman. You ask me, you should tell him what we've found. Make him see this is a chance to save his skin. We need a voice like his.'

'David!' shouted the Chairman, bringing Dave's attention back to the business lounge. 'You're miles away. Not having—'

'A Narnia turn?' Dave shook his head. 'Listen, I'm glad we have some time before the flight. I need to talk to you.'

'Jesus Christ!' said the Chairman, falling back in his seat.

Dave played with the wrapper that had emptied itself of sugar into a potent espresso.

'And how did you find all this out again?' asked the Chairman.

'A private investigator.'

'Like Magnum?' The Chairman laughed. 'Seriously, but who?'

'You remember that American, claimed to be my son?'

'Claimed?'

'Long story.'

'And how's Carol?'

'Carol? She's at her mum's.'

'Right you are.' The Chairman slugged his whisky. 'Anyway, this American, can you trust him? Sounds like he turned out to not be your son, after all. Could he be lying about this too?'

Dave shrugged, never having considered the possibility that Jedd could have been lying about everything. 'We don't know who's behind the holding company, but the papers show clear ownership of other factories in Malaysia and Vietnam.'

'Where we have more allegations of dumping?'

'More than that. Years of what water pollution does to local communities.'

The Chairman stood.

Dave jumped.

'I need another whisky. Don't know about you, David?'

Dave nodded even though it was half past six in the morning. Cologne engulfed him as the Chairman darted to the bar. A passive reaction had greeted Dave's revelations, interspersed by the odd nod. Still unsure of the Chairman's loyalties, Dave hadn't revealed the plan to uproot the Great Brakes investment project at the conference, nor had he mentioned Bryn was on his way to Detroit with a wad of paper bags and his water treatment technology. He had

TUESDAY

delivered a curveball. The question was, what would the Chairman do with it?

Two tumblers landed on the table. Dave reached for his and slugged, warmth flooding his chest. Words Dave was unable to decipher danced in the Chairman's eyes. He slugged again.

'You were right to bring this to my attention, David,' said the Chairman, breaking the silence.

'Being associated with this would not be good for your reputation, Chairman.'

'Absolutely not.'

Dave felt himself relax, realising Bryn may have correctly gauged the Chairman's motivations.

'The question,' the Chairman continued, 'is what we do with it?'

Dave pulled the tumbler away from his mouth, noticing at least a double serving and his head starting to fuzz. What they intended to say at the conference was work in progress, Jedd researching meat to add to the bones. How they would communicate it was another worry. Before attempting to teach Bryn how to use FaceTime, Dave had learnt there were other hurdles to cross.

'How can you have an iPhone and never text people?' Dave had asked him, wide-eyed in the corner of Costa.

'Who am I gonna bloody text, son? My cat?'

'David! Focus!' said the Chairman, tugging his arm.

'Is it me or is it hot in here?' replied Dave, glancing around and remembering he was in the business lounge.

'I said I need to speak to the First Minister.' The Chairman drummed his fingers on the leather armrest.

'All he wants are the three hundred jobs.' Dave raised his hands. 'It's election time.'

'Think about it, David,' said the Chairman, his eyes

wandering the room in search of answers. 'You blow this thing wide open . . . that is what you're planning to do?'

Dave hesitated before nodding.

'At the conference?'

Dave nodded again.

'Well, that's not going to win anyone an election now, is it?' The Chairman's voice rose an octave.

'Err.'

The Chairman leant in. 'We need to back the First Minister into a corner.'

'Blackmail?' asked Dave.

'Come on, David. I never said that. I mean, we have to inform him of what you have learnt. As a pragmatist, what will be his main concern?'

'Ensuring the people of Wales have a livelihood?' replied Dave, once again debating how a 'g' had found its way into a word he'd heard more during the past week than the rest of his days combined.

'No, David. He'll want to ensure his career doesn't get spattered when the shit hits the proverbial fan.'

The Chairman checked his watch, Dave deciding the expression had to be a proverb after all.

'The funding should have been voted yesterday but it was pushed to today,' the Chairman continued.

'I've been meaning to ask how it was already in the paper, without funding secured?' Dave watched for a reaction to indicate the Chairman having leaked it.

'You know journalists, David.' The Chairman rose, pulling his phone out of his pocket. 'Approval will be announced at the conference. *Green, Green Tech of Home* and all that. It's as good as done and the very reason we set up the Welsh Technology Accelerator Fund. That leaves us a small window . . .'

TUESDAY

'Window?' Dave tried to focus as the Chairman's face blurred.

'To get the First Minister to desist, of course. Once the funding is through, he won't get behind any narrative of mercury dumping. I'll call him now.'

'At half past six in the morning?'

The Chairman picked up the tumblers. 'Another Penderyn?'

CHAPTER THIRTY-FIVE

Muffled voices became louder. His forehead pushed at something cold and sticky as the sickly scent of lavender flooded his nostrils. Dave opened one eye.

'There he is.' The voice lisped the 's'. 'Slouched over the loo.'

Dave coughed, wrenching up his head.

'Dad?'

Dave twisted to stretch his legs. His back fell onto the porcelain. 'Seth?'

Seth slid down the wall to sit next to him. 'What happened?'

'You're here?' Dave smiled, picking scraps of toilet roll from his knees. 'Ouch.' He screwed his eyes shut. 'Feel like I've gone several rounds. Where am I?'

'This one of your turns, Dad?'

His tongue stuck to the roof of his mouth, Dave decided it didn't feel like a turn. No Iceland, no Sal. In fact, he couldn't remember anything other than being in a business lounge with the Chairman. His finger traced a ridge on his forehead, searching a reason for having fallen asleep on a toilet seat.

'The Chairman left me to call the First Minister. I felt dizz—'

'You're travelling with Rodric's dad? I haven't seen him.' Seth searched the toilets.

Dave placed his arm on Seth's. 'What matters is you're here. I thought—'

'Don't worry, Dad.'

Dave smiled. 'You called me Dad.'

'I said, don't worry. I don't care what a bunch of tests say. You'll always be my dad. We've got other problems.'

'Problems?' asked Dave, remembering Seth's unanswered question. 'Where's the Chairman?'

'Long gone,' the voice Dave had heard on waking lisped as a woman came into view in the doorway. Half-tamed by a blue beret, fuzzy hair nested above plump cheeks and a large nose.

Dave pointed at her. 'It's you!'

'Dad!'

'Me?' she said, a waft of gin flooding the cubicle.

'The cleaner from Cardiff House!' Dave waved his hands around his head. 'You look different but it's you!'

'Dunno what you're talking about, love.' Her head fell back in laughter as she steadied herself against the wall. 'The name's Gwen. I works for KLM. Calling you for over half an hour before your flight took off, I was. Then your son here arrived. Found you on his phone.'

'Shit!' Dave checked his watch. 'My flight has gone?'

'Yes.'

Dave examined what seemed to be the same nose as the one he'd seen at Cardiff House and Cardiff Bay Visitor Centre. Without the headscarf it was hard to tell.

He rubbed his head. 'And Mr Llewellyn-Jones, the man I'm travelling with?'

'Left on the half past seven to Amsterdam as planned,' said Gwen, rolling her eyes.

Dave fixed Gwen with a stare, now sure it was the cleaner and wondering why she was there. The Chairman wouldn't have left without him. On returning from calling the First Minister, he would have wondered why Dave had disappeared. He would have looked for him.

'Look, Dad,' said Seth, shaking his arm. 'I know what happened with those mails now.'

Dave retched, Penderyn bile rising into his mouth. He pulled at the dangling toilet roll and spat into it.

'The ones you got but never got,' continued Seth.

Dave rubbed his head. 'The ones from Dustin at Great Brakes, you mean?'

'Except they weren't from him. Rodric sent them.'

Dave's mind flashed back. *Good evening, Mr Weltch.* 'The creepy little beanpole?'

'His dad told him to send those mails.'

'The Chairman?'

Seth nodded.

Dave wiped his brow with the toilet paper in his hand, throwing it in the bowl as stench of vomit overcame him. There was no reason for Rodric to send an email for his father, posing to be Dustin, let alone two. Dave dropped his hand into his lap. Of course, Rodric must have slipped up first time around by mentioning meeting in Detroit, the Chairman having no idea Dave had never made it there. And to think, Dave had been sucked into believing they were in competition with Essex.

'But that means the Chairman sent me an ultimatum, only to deliver the Great Brakes project on a plateau?' asked Dave. His eyes widened as they bounced from Seth to Gwen. 'So, it's him driving this project coming to Wales?'

'Well done, Sherlock,' said Gwen.

'Bumped from my flight?' shouted a man behind them, as Gwen strode across the airport, Seth and Dave trying to keep up.

'Not you as well?' said another.

'Extremely sorry. There seems to be a bit of a glitch in our system,' replied a perspex-muffled voice.

'Glitch! I've got to get home.'

'Computer errors happen.'

'It's the bloody Russians if you ask me,' shouted the man, 'or them Chinese.'

As the two men continued to argue in front of the KLM desk, Dave wondered how Gwen had been able to rebook him and Seth seats on the very same flight, facilitating an easyJet connection to Reykjavik.

'You *are* one of them, aren't you?' said Dave, rushing to catch up with Gwen.

'I told you, I works for KLM.' Gwen stopped at the entrance to fast-track security. 'How else would I have got you on this flight?'

'I mean, one of *them*.' Dave lowered his voice.

'Dad!' said Seth. 'You can't talk like that.'

'Talk like what?' Dave frowned.

He'd seen her at Cardiff House and then down in Cardiff Bay Visitor Centre. Well, heard her lisp and recognised her nose the second time. It had to be her.

Gwen placed a hand on his arm. 'There is no them and us, Mr Welch. That's how all problems start.' She pushed him in the direction of the security guard. 'Now you know what you need to do.'

'Wh—'

Gwen walked away.

Dave stepped forward to allow the security guard to scan their boarding passes.

'Why were you so weird with that KLM woman?' asked Seth. 'She was good enough to help us. Does it matter to you who or what she is?'

Dave stared at Seth, unable to confide he had doubts about her being a Welsh elf – if that was even a thing – and deciding to ride with presumed intolerance.

'Don't suppose it does, Son.'

'You've got to work on that, Dad.'

They stepped, one by one, through the security arch, neither of them setting off the machine. Waiting for their cases to spew out the other side of the baggage scanner, Dave rubbed at his throbbing head.

Seth stared at him. 'You're not having—'

'I told you, no,' snapped Dave, fearing the opposite.

If Gwen *was* an elf, it could be one of his turns. Dave glanced around a room filled with grumbling at having to remove shoes and belts. Covered by that ridiculous beret, Dave hadn't seen Gwen's ears. He examined Seth's hands, followed by the security guard's and his own. Everyone appearing normal, he decided Gwen had to be telling the truth about working for KLM. Her nose ugly but not out of proportion, he must have confused her with the cleaner.

'You were planning to come all along? To Iceland, I mean?' asked Dave, noticing the baggage scanner had stopped spewing cases.

'Jedd's been sharing his findings with me,' replied Seth.

'Jedd?'

'Look, I know why he came to Wales. Now he wants to

help. We have to stop this company, Dad. You can't chuck whatever you like into the sea.'

'None of it makes sense though, Son.' Dave ran his hands through his hair. 'Why would the Chairman secretly push this project onto my desk? If it was for the fame and glory, he would have brought it in himself.' Dave checked his phone. 'Not even a message. I need to know what the First Minister said.'

'About what?'

'The Chairman was going to share Jedd's information with him before the vote went ahead to support the investment project with WTAF funding.'

'At six in the morning? What the actual f—.'

'Seth!'

'Think about it! He had no intention of speaking to the First Minister. If he wants this project to happen, he wouldn't find ways to get it stopped, would he? Jedd told me what you plan to do at this conference. That's why I'm here, to help.'

'How—'

Seth's eyes widened. 'Don't tell me you told the Chairman what you're planning?'

Retching more Penderyn, Dave thought back to the meeting at the Chairman's office just before he had been readmitted to hospital. He brought his hand to his mouth. 'Jesus Christ! The whisky.'

'What whisky?'

'He drugged me!'

A security guard's head peeked out from the side of the baggage scanner.

'Keep your voice down, Dad!' Seth pulled Dave aside. 'You're not making sense and I need to talk to you about Mum.'

Dave took a deep breath, wondering how to convince

Seth he'd been drugged not once, but twice. His readmission to hospital finally made sense. Nothing to do with his treatment not working, his drinks had been spiked.

'Dad, are you listening? I need to—'

'Look, I wanted to tell you about the divorce but you weren't talking to me.' Dave stared at Seth. 'You needed—'

'No, Dad, I—'

'I can't talk about your mum. Not now, Son. We both love you very much, it's just—'

'Dad—'

'It doesn't really matter. To be honest, me and your mum have been over for years. You can't build a happy lifetime on lies, hers or mine.'

Seth's shoulders dropped. 'Okay.'

'We don't have much time. We need to think. Why would the Chairman not bring this investment project himself? Why all the smoke and mirrors?'

Dave jumped. His phone vibrated in his hand.

'Jedd,' said Dave, activating his phone's speaker.

'You haven't left yet?' asked Jedd. 'Listen, I've tried all I can to get info on the holding company.'

'Greentech Holdings?' said Dave.

'Owned by a certain Laurent Richard.'

'The CEO of Great Brakes.'

'Clean as a whistle from what I can see. Born in Montreal . . .'

'Montreal? Hang on a minute,' said Dave, fragments of information sliding into place. The Chairman had links to Canada, had even returned there recently. 'The holding company was called something else before, wasn't it?'

'Yes, that's right.' Papers rustled. 'RWLJ Holdings.'

'Rhys-Wyn,' said Dave.

'Llewellyn-Jones,' said Seth.

CHAPTER THIRTY-SIX

Doors had been switched to manual and cross-checked. Whatever that meant, they hadn't opened. Dave drummed the wall as he and Seth headed up the queue to exit the Airbus A320neo.

'Wouldn't rock up here without a coat,' said the air steward, observing them from head to foot as Dave stared at a badge that revealed Fabien was happy to help in any of four European languages.

The door wrenched open and horizontal rain blew Dave's suit jacket inside out.

'*Oh mon Dieu!*' shouted Fabien, ducking inside the cockpit. 'You're on your own.'

Dave and Seth dashed for the bus at the foot of the trembling stairs, crossed the terminal and, thanks to a flash of passport and a swiftly bought ticket, were soon on a bus to Reykjavik.

'Jesus, it's cold out there,' said Dave.

'There's a reason it's called Iceland, Dad.'

Dave and Seth had made it to Amsterdam in time but

a delayed connecting flight had meant a later arrival in Iceland than planned.

'Big Bird flew into the turbine,' Fabien had announced in an impromptu translation, Dave assuming he wasn't referring to the yellow one from *Sesame Street*.

Dave checked his watch. 'It's started,' he said, drumming the window frame.

'Will you stop doing that!'

'Doing what?'

'We'll make the conference,' said Seth. 'Don't worry.'

'But what if the Chairman has already delivered the presentation by the time we get there?'

'Send an email. Tell them we're on our way.'

'What about the element of surprise when we arrive?'

'Focus, Dad. We'll work it out.'

Preparation is one thing, but the key to success is in focusing. Dave smiled at his son. All their preparation thrown up in the air, focus was more important than ever.

'We need those papers on the holding company,' said Dave, wondering if Jedd and Jolene's direct flight from Heathrow would land on time in about an hour.

'They'll get them, Dad.'

Jedd had been struggling to find any paperwork on RWLJ Holdings, meaning the proof they needed of the Chairman's involvement in Great Brakes was yet to surface. It was the one thing to swing the First Minister. He might turn a blind eye to possible mercury pollution in the name of Welsh jobs, but thirty million pounds of Welsh taxpayers' money given to the Chairman by the Cardiff Investment Agency was incompatible with winning the next election.

'Well, at least it's given Bryn a bit more time,' said Dave, eyes bouncing between aging lava fields and shiny, new factories. 'Let's hope we hear something soon.'

TUESDAY

There had been complete radio silence from Bryn since his departure. Dave had tried to call and send emails, regretting his haste at sending him all the way over to the States on his own. He checked his phone again. Nothing.

Dave rolled his eyes as he stared out of the window. 'Thought it would be prettier if I'm honest.'

'You can't judge a country by the airport road, Dad.'

Dave shrugged. Cardiff Airport could raise its game but the A48 passing through Bonvilston wasn't a bad drive.

'Listen, Dad, I think we need to talk about—'

'Seth, I've told you. Not now.' Dave fell into his seat, eyes resting on a smouldering horizon. 'Bloody hell, what's that?' He pointed out of the window.

'Wow, that's it!' Seth pulled out his phone and leant over Dave to film. 'You not read about it? They've been having tremors for weeks, then a volcano erupted in the night. Fa-something.'

'Fa-gra-dals-f-jall,' said Dave, hovering over every syllable. 'It means "beautiful valley mountain".'

'So, you do know about it?' Seth frowned at Dave.

Smoke and lava spurted into the morning sky. Dave stared until his vision blurred, thinking on how Sal would be encouraging him on if he were there . . . if elves existed. Hard to believe the Chairman had been tapping into public money under their noses to fund his own business ventures, and through a fund he had set up himself. Funding approval had gone through, Dave had read an email that morning. Old Rhys-Wyn was a cut above. He really didn't care about the impact of his greed on other people's livelihoods, their health, the sea. Dave couldn't wait to see the double-barrelled snake in the grass's face when it all burst open.

Wait for the tremors. Sooner or later, they always come.

'Bus stop five. Harpa Concert Hall,' shouted the driver as the bus shuddered to a standstill before an imposing façade of geometric glass panels.

'This is us!' Seth jumped up.

Dave looked at his watch. Five past three. The presentation was scheduled for three o'clock. He snatched his carry case from an overhead shelf and raced after Seth. Sea air tickled his nostrils and a wide-open bay beckoned from behind the looming concert hall.

'David Welch?' A blonde-haired woman with startling blue eyes stretched out a hand. 'Hel-ga Gun-nars-dót-tir.'

Dave remembered the line dancing syllables. 'You're the—'

'Mr Llewellyn-Jones told me you weren't coming. Follow me.'

The trio raced through the foyer, light flooding the building's facade.

'Beau-ti-ful, isn't it?' said Helga. 'Inspired by naturally forming basalt columns found in many parts of the country. You've been to Iceland?'

'Ne . . .' Dave paused.

Helga stopped and frowned.

Dave scoured her features. He tried to see her ears but they were hidden under too much hair.

She pointed to a broad staircase and resumed walking. 'Our largest conference hall is on the second floor.'

Dave mounted the stairs, Seth striding alongside him. Helga seemed to know he'd been to Iceland before. Well, sort of been.

'Hang on a minute,' Dave addressed Helga on reaching the top of the stairs, out of breath. 'If you

TUESDAY

thought I wasn't coming, why were you waiting for me at the entrance?'

'It's you we need.' Helga's mouth broke into a broad smile. 'We always knew you'd make it. Come with me.'

Seth's eyes widened behind Helga's back.

Dave shrugged.

'Has the presentation started then?' shouted Seth.

'It has.' Helga exchanged words with a security guard. 'Listen, he'll get you in the side door.'

Dave examined a man who was five foot at best and started to fear another turn. He moved his attention to Helga, deciding she was of a normal height. He examined Seth, confirming his features all normal. Dave pulled at his shirt collar. Sweat cascaded down his back. Red for Wales. Shit, he'd worn the same shirt.

'Side door?' he asked.

'You can join him directly on stage,' replied Helga.

'You okay, Dad?' Seth pulled Dave aside. 'This is your chance.'

'I can't do it!' whispered Dave.

'You have to.'

'But we don't have proof yet.'

'We have enough to sow the seeds of doubt. Jedd will be here soon and Bryn will come through. They have to.'

Dave had tried calling Bryn. His phone not ringing, data roaming must have failed.

'You said it's a thirty-minute presentation, starting with *Green, Green Tech of Home* before he announces Great Brakes,' said Seth. 'We can do this.'

Helga smiled. 'It's definitely you we need.'

Dave followed Helga to the side door. Before he knew it, he was stood squinting at the stage lights. In the darkness, heads turned as the Chairman stopped speaking.

'Rhys-Wyn, sorry I'm late.' Dave moved centre stage.

'David . . .' The Chairman smoothed his jacket and addressed the audience. 'May I introduce you to David Welch, our Head of Americas—'

'Head of America, singular.' Dave smiled.

'Excuse me, introduce our Head of America for the Cardiff Investment Agency . . . and now the short video I promised you about our wonderful country.' The microphone switched off. Lips barely moving, he whispered, 'David, you're—'

'Here?' replied Dave as, in the background, Duffy begged the crowd for mercy.

'Did you get my messages?' asked the Chairman.

'What messages?'

'I was worried. Not one of your turns again? I looked everywhere.'

'Don't you worry about me, Rhys-Wyn Llewellyn-Jones.' Dave lingered on the last four words.

'Sorry?'

'We know all about you.'

'I've no idea what you're talking about.'

'Oh, I think you do. Getting your creepy little son to send me emails.'

'Are you sure you're feeling alright?' The Chairman touched Dave's arm. 'These drugs they have you on. Not hallucinating again, are you?'

Dave shook off the Chairman. 'Don't patronise me. If I got sick, it's because of greedy arseholes like you polluting our seas!'

A collective intake of breath sucked the room of air, Dave realising Duffy had finished her pleading and the microphone had switched back on. Lights went up on an ashen audience.

'David, is this something to do with the Paris job not happening?'

TUESDAY

'What do you mean not happening?' said Dave, caught unawares before remembering his reasons for being there. 'Anyway, I never wanted to go to bloody Paris.'

'It's not the right time for promotions, what with the audit results in. Taxpayers' money and all that.' The Chairman lifted his notes to cover his mouth. 'I suggest you leave now!' he whispered.

'I'm not . . . Hang on, yes, let's talk about taxpayers' money, shall we?' Dave addressed the hall. 'Let's talk about the thirty million given to Great Brakes.'

'Let's.' The Chairman flipped to a slide entitled: *Another great break for Wales*.

Dave rolled his eyes.

'The thirty million given to your holding company you mean?' Dave tried to focus on the matter at hand and not the fact their marketing team was on its knees.

'Greentech Holdings?' said the Chairman.

'RWLJ Holdings,' replied Dave, pulling at his shirt collar. Sweat pooled at his temples. 'Maybe everyone here would like to know how the latest so-called sustainable investment in Wales is lining your pockets whilst polluting our seas.'

The hall inhaled once more.

The Chairman dropped his notes onto the podium. 'I'm very sorry about this. David is visibly upset and I am to blame. I must admit to something I am not proud of. The thing is, sometimes things happen, things we can't control.'

'But this is all your doing,' said Dave.

'I know it makes you sad, David, even a little angry.'

'Of course it bloody does.'

'But it's no reason to spread lies about me or,' the Chairman stretched an arm towards the screen behind him, 'this new *great break* for Wales.'

Shy laughter rippled through the room.

'Once Carol told me you were separating, how we felt about each other became obvious.' The Chairman tilted his head. Not a hair moved. 'I know her moving in must seem quick.'

'Moving . . .' Dave frowned, searching the auditorium for his son.

'Sorry,' mouthed Seth.

Dave realised what Seth had been trying to tell him since leaving Cardiff. 'But Carol said—'

'Your marriage had been over for a long time, I know.'

'She said what?'

'What with your son never being yours.'

The audience gasped, eyes dropping to the floor.

Dave swallowed the lump in his throat.

'I fell in love with your wife, David. For that, I cannot apologise. But please don't let this axe you have to grind get in the way of a tremendous opportunity for Wales and an even better opportunity for a sustainable transport future. An opportunity that wouldn't have been possible without you.'

CHAPTER THIRTY-SEVEN

Whispers danced their way on stage. The ceiling inhaled Dave as his eyes left Seth to search solace in the looming darkness. Damn, shit and blast. Dr Double Barrel had him well and truly cornered. Any allegations had lost credibility, the audience unsure of the bitter, soon-to-be ex-husband.

'Let me finish the presentation,' said the Chairman. A smile framed whiter-than-white teeth and a hand dug into the small of Dave's back. 'Why don't you take a seat.'

The room span. Sweat flooded Dave's underarms as he battled to understand what the hell Carol was doing with the Chairman. She'd laughed at Dave the day he'd challenged her. She must have been pushing the Great Brakes project to Dave all along, promised by the trappings of a better life. That meant she was also aware of the mercury dumping. *Stop listening to everyone else. Your life is yours to define,* that's what Chris would say. He'd pulled himself out of the quagmire of newspaper headlines. Dave belched, peaty bile filtering into his nostrils.

'The whisky.' Dave's eyes met the Chairman's. 'You—'

The Chairman smiled.

Dave looked out on a sea of concerned faces. No one would believe he had been drugged. Seth hadn't.

'Could this trip be proving too much for you, just out of hospital?' The Chairman tugged at his arm, the audience echoing his words in a harmony of concern.

Dave thought back to *The Dubliner* in Paris. A World Cup in Georgia wasn't out of the question, nor Chris heading up the Rugby Board. So, who was Tomorrow Dave? Probably as the vision had suggested, a washed-out has-been in some bar. Dave wasn't born to be a success. He'd failed at a rugby career, failed at his marriage. Pretending to know what he was doing promoting investment into Cardiff, his only ever break was a dressed-up money-making scheme.

'Come on now, David,' said the Chairman. 'Don't want a relapse.'

But Dave wasn't going to Paris, was he? The Chairman had said as much. There was no Paris. The one thing Dave had retained from those weird visions of Yesterday and Tomorrow Dave was that the future wasn't yet defined.

Preparation is one thing, but the key to success is in focusing.

His torso tensed along with his legs. Dave closed his eyes, balled his hands, took a deep breath and found himself back at Heywood Road. Taking three strides backwards, he checked he was lined up correctly and took another two strides right.

This wasn't about him and Carol. His marriage *had* been over for years. This was about Great Brakes, about doing the right thing. He could do this and no one would tell him otherwise. He would be someone. Not someone everyone else wanted him to be, someone *he* wanted to be. Someone he could be proud of. He'd show everyone he *was* like his dad.

TUESDAY

'Is this one of your Narnia turns?' asked the Chairman, confused by Dave's silence and tugging at his arm.

More whispers performed a merry jig.

Dave screwed his eyes tighter. He ran to the ball. His right foot slotted into place, his weight shifting. Silence flooded the pitch, broken by the sound of his left leg thudding into leather. Past expectant faces and open mouths, the ball soared through the air, the crowd erupting.

Preparation is one thing, but the key to success is in focusing.

Dave opened his eyes, turned towards the Chairman.

'Wonderland,' he said with a smile.

'Sorry?' replied the Chairman.

'It's not Narnia, it's Wonderland.'

'You know what I mean, the one with the wardrobe.'

'There is no bloody wardrobe!' The microphone screeched and the auditorium covered its ears on a collective gasp. 'What I have is Alice in Wonderland Syndrome!'

A door creaked open and heads craned as Dave locked eyes with Seth's stare. From the darkness cloaking the back of the room emerged a pair of dungarees and an orange depiction of the evolution of man, from caveman to surfer.

Preparation is one thing, but the key to success is in focusing.

Dave straightened his suit jacket. 'Alice in Wonderland or Narnia, that's not why we're here though, is it?'

'Exactly, David, we are here to talk about Great Brakes and this exciting opportunity for Wales.' The Chairman grabbed his arm.

'Opportunity to line your pockets you mean?'

Feigned concern fell into a frown, the Chairman noticing Jedd and Jolene approach. His attention returned to the stage as his laughter echoed through the silence. 'I'm simply paid to do a job, David.'

'So, Rhys-Wyn Llewellyn-Jones, do you have something else to tell us?'

'I thought we'd been through all this?'

'We haven't spoken about RWLJ Holdings.'

'Why would we speak of one of my companies?'

Dave froze. 'So, it *is* your holding company?'

'Clue's in the name,' said the Chairman, smiling. 'Like . . . what's he called in that book? ... The Mad Hatter. Now are you sure you don't want to sit down? News of the divorce can't have been easy.'

'This isn't about the divorce and no, I don't want to sit down.' Dave wrenched his arm out of the Chairman's claw-like grip to face the audience. 'Yes, my wife is leaving me and yes, I've had moments mad as a bloody hatter, seeing . . .' Dave paused, his attention locked on the Chairman's floating eyebrow, '. . . seeing the truth. The thing is, I have been sick with a disease caused by mercury poisoning. Not naturally occurring mercury, but mercury entering our water cycle thanks to laziness and greed.' Dave extended an arm towards the Chairman. 'Flushed into our waters daily, a little bit here, a little bit there. People not seeing it as a problem, thinking it will get diluted. But a multitude of little things never dilute. They amass, grow, take over. Today in Europe, many of our rivers and lakes . . .'

'Forty percent!' shouted Jolene.

'Yes, forty percent,' said Dave, returning a smile, 'have excessively high mercury levels. Our planet needs this water to survive, to have a future. How much mercury before we say stop? How much longer will we turn a blind eye in the name of so-called sustainability, making *more* things in order to *reduce* our carbon footprint. Because behind it all is money, ladies and gentlemen, and that's what the Great Brakes project is about. It's a company deliberately polluting our seas in the name of profit and that profit is going to Greentech Holdings, formerly known as RWLJ Holdings.'

TUESDAY

The room gasped.

Dave drew breath.

The Chairman raised a hand. 'Can we call security please?' he shouted into the void.

Jedd and Jolene joined Dave via a set of stairs to the left of the stage. They shook hands with Seth in passing, his face hidden behind an iPhone, filming proceedings.

'Don't you think your time would be better spent getting your colleague some help?' the Chairman asked Jolene.

'Ex-colleague. Have you forgotten firing me for speaking the truth?' she replied.

'For being abusive.'

'None of that matters now,' said Jedd, waving papers in the Chairman's direction. 'These prove that Greentech Holdings was formerly called RWLJ Holdings.'

'That's right.'

'A company about to receive thirty million pounds from the innovation fund *you* created for choosing to build a brakes factory in Wales,' continued Jedd.

'You just admitted RWLJ Holdings was yours,' said Jolene.

'I did,' said the Chairman.

'So, what do you have to say for yourself? Covering your tracks with a name change, you can do better than that?'

'Changing the name or selling my shares?' A glistening smile blinded Dave. 'You see RWLJ Holdings *was* mine. It isn't anymore.'

'Selling your—' Jolene looked to Jedd.

'What Dempsey and Makepeace have failed to uncover —' said the Chairman.

'Dempsey and who?' mumbled Jedd.

'—Is that I sold my company some time ago to avoid

conflict of interest. As Chairman of a public-funded body, it is unethical to have a vested interest in certain businesses.' A smile slid across the Chairman's face.

The auditorium filled with relief. Dave's eyes pleaded with Jedd's as he took the papers from his hand. They couldn't let the Chairman get away with it.

'Making Laurent Richard the main shareholder?' asked Jedd.

'Making Mr Richard the only shareholder.'

Dave examined the papers, confirming there were no other named shareholders. 'But there has to be—'

'How come the project made its way to Wales then?' asked Jolene.

'Isn't the point it did?' replied the Chairman.

'But the emails that were sent by your son pretending to be someone from the company?' asked Dave.

'Whatever you think you're looking for, it's not here. You have to let Carol go.'

'This is nothing to bloody do with Carol. It's about . . .'

'Mercury pollution,' said Jolene.

'You're accusing me of water pollution now?'

'Accusing Great Brakes,' said Dave.

'A company I don't own?' The Chairman laughed.

Dave pinched at his thighs, knowing his only chance was slipping through his fingers. The project making its way to Wales was not pure coincidence. It couldn't be. The Chairman had to have an interest. He had to be connected to the company somehow.

'But you're responsible for bringing them to Wales,' said Dave. 'You approved the project, pushing it up to the First Minister in double-quick time.'

'After undertaking the due diligence,' shouted the Chairman, smoothing a lock of hair into place. 'We've been through this. There is no proof of Great Brakes dumping mercury. Unless you have something new?'

One by one, Dave, Jedd and Jolene dropped their heads.

Behind them the presentation was withdrawn from the screen. Dave's eyes bore a hole in the grey carpet under his feet. Black flecks merged to form an infinite abyss, Dave berating what had become an absolute shower of—

'You there, son?'

Dave turned around.

A familiar face filled the screen, frowning as it leant in.

'Reykjavik, this is Adrian's Creek calling. Over.'

CHAPTER THIRTY-EIGHT

'I'm with Dave Welch. Over.'

'Yes, you are.' Dave smiled in the silence. 'Over.'

'No, I'm *here* with Dave Welch.'

The screen panned. Dave frowned at a bony, white-haired doppelgänger to Bryn's left.

'Well, your emails are very similar,' continued Bryn. 'Sorry for the radio silence. Lost my phone, didn't I? You know Dave here has had a hip replacement too?'

'Colchester Dave?' said Dave.

'One and the bloody same!' The skeletal head fell back in laughter.

'But—'

'You can't make this shit up,' said Colchester Dave.

'Not even if you tried,' added Bryn.

'Got called aht of the blue for a conference in Detroit, insisting it was definitely—'

'You they needed?' Dave addressed the auditorium, spying Helga next to Seth.

Colchester Dave frowned. 'Anyway, all my friends was livid. "Detroit?" they said. "You bloody lucky bastard."

TUESDAY

Lucky? I get 'ere and the conference is only bloody cancelled. Then, this one 'ere contacts me aht of the blue. "Geh'aht of it," I said, didn't I, Bryn?"

'That you did!' Bryn slapped Colchester Dave on the back. 'Here's me confusing his address for yours and then I finds out he's only down the road.'

'"Course, I'll bloody help," I said, didn't I, Bryn? What with my role in WANGA.'

'The World Anglers Association?' Dave remembered the misdirected emails in his inbox.

'One and the bloody same!' replied Colchester Dave.

The Chairman coughed. 'Well, this is a delightful little reunion but can I suggest we move on? It seems to me we've already lost enough time.' He looked to Helga, her face motionless.

'Mr Llewellyn-Jones. Nice to see you again,' said Bryn.

'Have we met?' The Chairman sighed at the screen.

'We have indeed. Bryn Jones is the name.'

'I'm sorry, I . . .'

'Don't remember me? You will do once we're done.'

Dave smiled. Bryn so sure of himself, he had to have done the testing.

'The Michigan WANGA delegation has been up in arms about Adrian's Creek,' continued Colchester Dave. '"Shu'up," I said. "Can't be that bad." Then I saw 'em. Hundreds of the buggers floating around, dead as you like. Who wants to see that? Not me, I can tell ya. Bloody criminal.'

'Criminal,' repeated Bryn, shaking his head.

Glassy fish eyes floated past Dave in a memory.

'Long and the short of it is, got Bryn 'ere access and we've done the tests.'

'Tests?' The Chairman looked at Dave, then the screen. 'Did you say Adrian's Creek?'

'Helga, can you let me share my screen, love,' asked Bryn. A photo appeared of a cockapoo in a festive jumper. 'That was his last Christmas,' said Bryn. 'Ate too much turkey and was sick in my slippers, poor fella. Where was it . . .'

The sigh expelled by the Chairman wafted over Dave like a clammy summer breeze. 'You want to explain to me what this charade is?' he spat under his breath.

A series of charts filled the screen. 'So, as you can see from our water analysis, the mercury in the lake is at dangerously high levels,' said Bryn.

'That means nothing,' said the Chairman. 'Mercury can come and go, can't it? Can we please get on with what we're here to do.'

'The concentration is its heaviest in proximity to the Great Brakes factory.'

'So, there's *some* mercury near the plant, who cares?' said the Chairman.

The audience gasped.

The Chairman straightened his suit and smiled. 'What I meant to say is, it doesn't mean it came from the factory.'

'Mercury doesn't come and go, Mr Llewellyn-Jones,' said Bryn. 'It infiltrates the water cycle, slowly poisoning our natural ecosystem and anything that lives in it.'

Dave's chest tightened. He spread his legs to steady himself as the Chairman's gaze fell to the floor. The on-screen charts disappeared, Bryn and Colchester Dave returning.

'Where you do have a point, however, is that these tests don't conclusively link the mercury to the Great Brakes plant,' said Bryn.

'Ah!' said the Chairman, lifting his head.

'But these signed affidavits from several ex-employees do.' Bryn pushed a handful of papers towards the screen.

TUESDAY

'Affidavits? Who are these people? Ex-employees you say. Laid off, I bet, with some—'

'Axe to grind?' finished Dave. 'That's your thing, isn't it?'

'Like an octopus, WANGA,' said Colchester Dave, winking. 'Got its tentacles everywhere. That's what I said when we first met, wasn't it, Bryn?'

'Tentacles?' shouted the Chairman. 'WANGA never wants any industrial development, full stop. This project *has* to happen in Wales. Think about it, it's three hundred jobs.'

'You're going to investigate further?' asked Jolene. 'Bryn has actual science backing up dangerously high levels of mercury, not to mention these affidavits. Water pollution is the price to pay for three hundred jobs, is it? You're Chairman of the CIA for Christ's Sake!'

'What, like the FBI?' came a whisper from the audience.

Jolene locked eyes with the Chairman. 'Surely what's best for you is what's best for Wales. Why are you so insistent on this project happening?'

'Someone else might have the answer we're looking for,' said Bryn. 'Over.'

Dave's head shot up. The screen split into two, Dave squinting as a yellow suit, tie and matching Stetson blinded him like the first rays of morning sun.

'Been keeping quite a few things from everyone, ain't that so?' An American voice slid out of the speakers.

'Dustin?' said Dave.

'One and the bloody same!' said Colchester Dave.

'How are you, sir?' said the ruddy face, dropping a bacon sandwich onto a plate in front of him. He chewed. 'Sorry, started breakfast as we were running late.'

'But—' Dave frowned.

'As it happens, I'm part of WANGA too.'

'Tentacles,' said Colchester Dave, waggling his fingers at the screen.

'Heard your fine sir, Bryn, was out here. Listen, I wasn't completely straight with you, David. I left Great Brakes because I had my suspicions about what was going on. Even challenged Laurent, the CEO. Then was asked to leave.'

'Why didn't you speak up sooner?' asked Dave.

'They threatened me with lawsuits. I'd signed NDAs.'

'So, why now?'

'Well, I may have signed NDAs with regards to factory processes.' Dustin thrust a photo at the screen. 'But not about this.'

Dave peered at the faded image. A couple of young men, glasses in hand, posed in togas. He'd recognise that whiter-than-white smile anywhere, even if the face in which it sat was forty years younger.

'Is that—'

'With Laurent Richard,' said Dustin.

'The CEO of Great Brakes?'

'One and the bloody same.' Colchester Dave snorted.

'Both studied at McGill,' said Dustin.

McGill in Montreal, of course. They hadn't met recently, they'd been friends since university. Dave's suspicions had been right! Next to an open-mouthed Jolene crouched Jedd, tapping furiously on his laptop.

Dave addressed the Chairman. 'So, you and the CEO of Great Brakes have been friends for years?'

'We may have known—'

'May have known? You sold all your shares in Great Brakes to him. Sold them to a friend. And helped that friend access the Welsh Technology Accelerator Fund.'

The audience gasped.

'Thirty million in taxpayers' money,' shouted Jolene. 'I knew you were a piece of—'

'Not sold, sold.' Jedd rose like a phoenix from the ashes. 'Laurent Richard is named minority shareholder in another holding company. My money is on you not selling your shares but circulating the money in another way.'

'What is this nonsense!' shouted the Chairman.

'Do you or don't you still do business with Laurent Richard? Were you not in Montreal with him a few weeks ago?' asked Dave.

'Okay, okay, I know Laurent. Maybe I pulled a few strings.'

'Purse strings'!' shouted Jolene.

'What's wrong with you people?' The Chairman stamped his foot. 'Green, green tech of home this, green, green tech of home that. You want development or not? Stop putting it out there if you don't.'

'Putting it out there?' asked Dave.

'You think Wales would have a sniff at this kind of investment if it wasn't for me?'

'So, you did help it along?'

'It's called networking, David. I wouldn't expect you to understand. What would your friend here call it?' The Chairman wiggled his fingers at the screen. 'Tentacles! *Green, Green Tech of Home*? For Christ's sake, no bugger Stateside knows Wales exists.'

A gasp swept through the auditorium.

Dave smiled. 'Oh, I understand perfectly, Rhys. You used your old boy network. Makes sense.'

'Exactly.'

'Tentacles,' echoed the screen.

'Good on you. You're right, we need that.' Dave smiled.

The Chairman straightened his suit.

'So, if this is all above board, why didn't Laurent approach the CIA directly.'

'Sorry?' said the Chairman, moving from foot to foot.

'If your tentacles reach the heart of the automotive industry in Michigan, why not make that intro to the First Minister?'

'He's tweeting!' shouted Seth.

'The First Minister?' asked Dave, watching Seth jump up and down next to Helga.

'I've been livestreaming to my followers.'

'Followers?' asked the Chairman.

'Tentacles,' echoed the screen.

'That's two million people who love the sea and don't want you lot chucking whatever old shit you want in it,' shouted Seth. 'It's all over TikTok and X. The First Minister has just tweeted, "*We must rage, rage against the dying of the sea.* Great Brakes will not happen in Wales."'

Dave frowned again, wondering if Digby could have resurfaced as some kind of media advisor to the First Minister.

'Hashtag WasteFreeWales is trending,' shouted Seth, Dave recognising the same hashtag the Welsh Assembly had been trying to push around the audit and admiring the chameleon-like ingenuity.

'Not happening?' shouted the Chairman, jumping off the stage and marching towards Seth. 'Show me that now!'

Seth thrust out his phone. 'See for yourself. They're calling you the sea snake.'

'But it has to happen! They agreed yesterday we'd have the money.'

'We?' asked Dave.

'We?' Bryn and Colchester Dave echoed out of the screen.

'Thought you'd sold your shares?' said Dave.

'Thought you were just networking?' said Jolene.
'Tentacles in too many pies?' Colchester Dave laughed.
'This is an absolute disgrace!' shouted the Chairman.

Pushing past Seth, he marched the length of the auditorium, a hand trying to regain control of his hair. The emergency exit door slammed shut behind him, silencing a wide-eyed, weather-beaten audience.

A hand in the second row climbed into the air. 'A question if I may?'

Dave nodded.

'I'm not sure I understand. Why is the CIA working with the Welsh government?'

CHAPTER THIRTY-NINE

Dave bent to take off his shoes and socks, the weather surprisingly clement.

'This beach is famous for its sneaker waves,' said Helga.

'Sneaker waves?' Dave lifted his head, remembering a yellow sign depicting a person facing a towering wave. He'd assumed it promised excellent surf in Icelandic. 'That doesn't sound great.'

'More a question of not trying to outwit nature.' Helga winked. 'No news from Mr Llewellyn-Jones?'

Dave shook his head as he stuffed his socks into his shoes. He hadn't seen hide nor hair of old Rhys, not since his swift departure via an emergency exit. Probably on a plane to Montreal, licking his wounds.

'That standing ovation really was something, wasn't it?' Helga smiled.

Dave stood and inhaled the sea air, remembering people rising out of chairs, clapping and stamping. The social media storm went off the Beaufort scale, an embold-

TUESDAY

ened First Minister stating, 'there wasn't a canary's hope Wales wouldn't answer the call of duty.'

Dave let out a laugh, recognising one of Digby's many Welsh proverbs. Something to do with mining, he couldn't quite remember. If his old boss was now some kind of public relations advisor, he was an unwittingly good one. In a series of GIFs, the First Minister's shovel hands had transformed into yellow wings, armed with an AK-47 and ready to take on a band of suited American corporate types.

'Well-deserved in any case.' Helga put a hand on Dave's shoulder, a shiver coursing the length of his spine. 'You really have been persistent in getting to the truth.'

Helga's smiling eyes danced in the sun. Dave sucked in his stomach. Thanks to Bryn's tests and the series of affidavits, Great Brakes' pollution of the seas had been revealed, and to great fanfare, but she was talking about another truth. Dave's own truth. The elusive music of his soul that had hummed in the background all these years as he had danced to everyone else's tune. Dave kicked the sand, staring over Helga's shoulder to an endless ocean. Her perfume played with his nostrils as he rued the time wasted, trying to not be like his father, trying to run from himself.

'What will you do now?' asked Helga, as if reading his mind.

Dave's cheeks flushed, wondering what being true to himself meant. It had never meant moving to France. The French and their bloody *French flair*, pulling it out of the bag in the second half and strutting around the pitch like oversized cockerels. The promotion and a new office in Paris had only ever been figments of the Chairman's imagination, but it was time Dave admitted he wasn't cut out for inward investment.

'Not what I'm doing now anyway,' said Dave. 'But we're all too busy asking for what we don't want to happen, rather than what we do, aren't we?'

Splashes of orange dotted the sky as puffins sought the cliffs behind them. Dave locked eyes with Helga. He'd never got to the bottom of her contacting him for the conference or her knowing when he'd arrive at the hall. Her azure eyes glimmered. He searched her face, blonde locks covering her ears. Something in her manner reminded him of Sal.

He hadn't thought of Sal in a while. Dave smiled, remembering his silly red hat. He'd popped up whenever Dave had floundered, pointing him in the right direction. Oddly, he missed the little fella. But he was better now, that's why he wasn't seeing elves anymore. Helga ran her hands through her hair, Dave straining to see her ears.

'I'm not cut out for what I'm doing now, but I've no idea what I would like to do,' said Dave, chiding himself for still entertaining doubts around Helga. He *was* better.

'Stay in government?' she asked.

Dave shrugged. Something in the past few weeks had made him see Dad hadn't been completely crazy. His fight to keep British agriculture alive had fallen on deaf ears when nowadays terms were being reinvented to return to what had been abandoned. Food independence, food security . . . from what he'd read, France had it about right. Fought tooth and nail to hang on to their agricultural production. Bloody annoying but you had to admire them.

'If I believed what I was doing could make a real difference,' said Dave. 'You know, not just a strapline on a brochure.'

'Funny how the future always intertwines with a notion of change,' said Helga. 'What if some things are good as they are?'

TUESDAY

'Exactly,' said Dave. 'What if a country like Wales could consider what it *needs*, not what it can *get* thanks to a pile of glossy brochures and a coherent SEO strategy . . . whatever that means!'

Dave had sat in a forty-five-minute meeting not verbalising that very question to the numpties who'd come up with the *Green, Green Tech of Home* campaign, not to mention their recent tourist videos.

'Remember we're writing for readers, but also for search engines.' A twenty-year-old in his grandad's sweater had chirped.

'Let's hope these search engines are fans of geriatric Welsh singers then,' Digby had mumbled, writing in large letters on his notepad to research new media agencies.

Dave's thoughts bounced to his sister. There was no one better than Maya at pleasing clients with her straplines, but whether she was truly happy was a question he'd often asked himself. Too caught up in himself, he'd just never asked her. That was another thing Tomorrow Dave would do differently.

'Come,' said Helga. 'Let's walk a bit. You haven't seen the best bit yet.'

Dave followed Helga, stretching his toes on every stride and watching black grains of sand trickle through them. The cliffs cawed a welcome as towering columns came into view. At the foot of the cliffs, loomed a gaping cave waiting to devour them.

'Remember the concert hall. This is what inspired the architecture,' said Helga.

Dave's eyes trailed the geometric formations, the cliffs above offering refuge to the orange feet he'd seen earlier.

'Think I've seen this on Netflix,' he said.

Helga laughed. 'It's been in a few series. Very popular on Instagram. The name means three trolls. In modern legend, a troll steals a wife from her husband but she turns into stone.'

'Now that sounds familiar!' Dave laughed. 'Well, apart from the stone bit.'

Helga tilted her head. 'I'm sorry about your wife.'

'Don't be.' Dave dropped his gaze, digging his feet deeper into the blackness. 'We had some good times, but Carol and I were finished a long time ago. Neither of us really wanted to admit it.'

Dave looked out to sea, surprised not by the sentiment behind his words, but their vocalisation. Whether Seth was his biological son or not didn't matter. He would always be his son. So what if Carol had lied? Dave had dissimulated who he was their whole marriage, caught up in what he was supposed to be doing. Getting married, having kids, a 'proper' job . . . Maybe Carol had too.

'The Chairman was just a catalyst,' said Dave. 'I know it's not really about him.'

Silence blanketed the beach. Dave sketched a life without Carol and one where Seth would soon leave home, realising the one thing more terrifying than Groundhog Day was infinite possibility. You always asked children closed questions for that very reason, to not overwhelm them with choice. *Do you want sausages or fish fingers?* rather than *What do you want for tea?* Oversized kids, the same fear held true for adults.

'You might prefer the original legend about these cliffs.' Helga brought Dave's attention back to the beach as she pointed up past the cave. 'Three trolls were trying to pull a ship to shore. It took so long, at sunrise they turned into rocks.'

'Trolls are different to elves?' asked Dave.

'It's all connected but they say elves are invisible whereas you can see trolls.'

TUESDAY

'You've seen a troll?'

'I had a few doubts about an ex-boyfriend.' Helga laughed. 'Seriously, elves are smaller than us and trolls very tall. Then there are the Hidden People. They're like us but live in a parallel world. They get confused with elves.'

'I read online loads of people in Iceland believe in this stuff?'

'Elves and Hidden People, they hold on to values and former ways of doing things. Other countries have similar creatures linked to their past and heritage but have let them go more easily.' Helga's eyes bore into Dave.

'But they *can't* be real, can they?' Dave kicked the sand that buried his feet.

'Who are we to say what is real? From the moment we think of something, doesn't it take on some kind of existence?'

'But these elves and the like aren't running around the place?' Dave's eyes scanned the empty beach. 'Anyway, you said they're invisible?'

'If lots of people in Iceland believe in them, it's because they want to believe. We walk around, as if in a dream, thinking we can't change anything. Isn't it comforting to think there are forces of good fighting for us.' Helga laughed. 'Who knows, maybe they're better versions of ourselves. Like that niggly voice guiding us—'

'In the right direction?' finished Dave.

The puffins cawed.

Helga's eyes locked with his, Dave falling into a blue so nuanced it contained sea and sky and everything in between. A memory of seeing and being seen returned. He reached for her face, his hand brushing her cheek before tucking blonde locks behind her ear, one by one by one.

One look. Just to be sure.

'Well, you're a bit fresh today,' she said.

CHAPTER FORTY

'But if you insist.' Helga's voice became gravelly.

Laughter smothered Dave, the smell of the sea replaced by disinfectant and what could have been a recently ingested Snickers.

'Craig?' Dave opened his eyes. 'Shit!' His hands fell to the bed on realising he was cradling the nurse's face. 'What the—'

'You've been out for the count, son.' The familiar voice carried across the room, confusing Dave even more as Bryn was supposed to still be in America.

'I'm back in hospital?' Dave asked Craig.

'Back in the land of the living!' shouted Maureen, battling to park a squeaky trolley at the foot of his bed. 'You missed lunch.'

'Not my lucky day,' mumbled Dave.

'Well, I'm all out of custard creams,' replied Maureen with a shrug. 'All I've got is some excuse for tea.'

Dave's eyes wandered the room. He must have been readmitted after the conference. It was the same ward, same configuration, but he couldn't remember flying back to Wales. In the bed opposite he recognised a shock of white hair, confirming the voice he had heard was Bryn's.

'Why am I back?' Dave stared at Craig, who busied himself with a chart unhooked from the foot of the bed.

'Drinking that whisky,' replied Maureen. 'Now I likes a drink like the best of 'em but mixing drink and drugs is never a good idea.'

Bloody hell! He *had* been drugged at the airport. Seth hadn't believed him but he'd been right about the Chairman and his laced Penderyn.

'Milk and sugar?' asked Maureen, a mug landing with a thud on the bedside table.

Dave shook his head, the realisation dawning on him that if he had been drugged at the airport for a second time, Gwen hadn't got him and Seth on a later flight and he'd never left Cardiff. The conference must have happened, the Chairman making it to Iceland without him. Dave slumped in his bed, wondering if the Great Brakes project was going ahead or not. Entertaining the hope that the WTAF grant hadn't been approved, he scanned the room for any sign of the *Western Mail* as he rubbed his head. On trying to lift himself, his arms collapsed under his own weight.

The fall caught Bryn's attention, as a familiar figure edged past Craig and Maureen co-piloting the tea trolley out of the room. Carol wore a coat Dave hadn't seen before and an expression he often had.

'Before you start, it's fine,' said Dave, noticing Bryn revert to a corpse position in the latter stages of rigor mortis.

Carol sat on the edge of the bed. 'It's not fine, you being back here. You've got to stop this.'

'No, I meant I know why you've been acting odd,' said Dave, embodying Tomorrow Dave, New Dave. He recognised the timing as far from perfect but he was always avoiding the inevitable, hoping for a better moment. It was time to face things head-on.

'Me acting odd?' Carol laughed. 'You feeling better then?'

'Listen, Carol . . .'

Dave hesitated, impressed with his newfound determination but wondering if he really did know why Carol had been acting odd. After all, he'd only discovered Carol was moving in with the Chairman once on stage at the conference, a conference he hadn't attended. Unsure if that meant she was having an affair with the Chairman or not, Dave drew breath, resolving that it didn't matter. He knew what he had to say. He'd never been clearer.

'It's time we were honest with each other,' he said.

Carol's head shot up. 'You know?' she replied, but Dave wasn't listening.

Words gushed out of him, thoughts that had been too-long silenced. 'What I did all those years ago. The guilt made me want to be someone else, pushed us into marriage . . .' Carol went to speak, Dave raising his hand. 'Let me finish. I'm not sure I've ever been the husband you wanted.' He reached for her hand, remembering the order of events and her phone call before he'd left for the airport. 'I do understand if you want a divorce.'

Carol frowned. 'But we—'

'Need to stop holding each other back, I know. Let's stop trying to make each other into something we're not.'

'This is all very considerate of you.'

'Can we keep the lawyers out of it?' asked Dave.

'Lawyers?' Carol's eyes scaled the tube attaching Dave's arm to a sagging pouch. 'You're on a lot of drugs. Let's talk about this another time.' She squeezed his hand. 'But

TUESDAY

thank you. Something in me thought you knew about Evan.'

'Seth will always be my son, even if blood tests say otherwise.'

'The blood tests to check for mercury levels?'

'The ones you didn't want him to have,' said Dave, remembering her dashing off in a flurry as the Chairman was coming back from Canada.

'I told you, he doesn't like needles,' said Carol.

'Doesn't he?'

Carol frowned. 'Anyway, why would mercury tests prove Seth's not your son?'

'You said you thought I'd always known about Evan.'

'About me seeing him again over the last few months.'

A cough burst out of Bryn.

'You *have* been having an affair,' said Dave.

———

The bed motor whirred into action, giving Bryn the appearance of rising from the dead.

'Did it then, son?' he asked.

Dave nodded. The new hairdos, nights away, ticks that never turned blue. Not the Chairman but Evan, not that it mattered. Carol had left, insisting he needed to rest and suggesting they reconvene when Dave was thinking more clearly. Letting her hand trail out of his, Dave knew his thoughts were their clearest in years. Carol deserved someone who loved her and who she could love back. No doubt they'd revisit the conversation but it had been easier than expected. It was what they had both wanted for a long time.

'Sure you're okay, son?'

Dave smiled at Bryn. He felt lighter. Seth was his son,

after all. All he needed to work out now was how much of the last few days had been a dream. He ran his hands through his hair, staring at Bryn in the bed opposite. Narrowing his eyes, Dave tried to remember his assumed identity. Civil servant or heating technician?

'You know who I am, right?' he asked.

'Dave Welch from the CIA. Over!'

Dave's smile widened. Of course Bryn knew who he was. That's why they'd been at the airport together, heading to the conference when Dave had been drugged. It was all starting to make sense, and there was time to turn this ship around. Even if the Chairman's involvement had been fabricated, the truth remained that Great Brakes had been mercury dumping.

'We started talking about my research and that project of yours, then you sparked out,' said Bryn.

Dave's eyes darted around the room, knowing something still wasn't quite right.

'Before I was released for the first time?' he asked.

'You've only been released once, son.'

Dave eyed a metal walking frame next to Bryn's bed, realising there was no way a man barely out of hip surgery could attempt transatlantic travel. It hadn't made sense from the beginning that Bryn would be back in hospital in the exact same ward. Bryn hadn't been drugged.

'How long have I been here, Bryn? What did Maureen mean about me being drugged?'

'Not sure those were her exact words, son.' Bryn pointed to Dave's bedside table. An empty paper cup stood next to the water jug. 'Think she meant mixing drink with whatever drugs the doctors are giving you.'

'I didn't pass out at Cardiff Airport?'

'Airport? They brought you in from Cardiff House. After you'd been to see that Llewellyn-Jones.'

TUESDAY

The truth finally hit Dave that he'd only been released once. He'd gone straight to Cardiff House to find Carol, drunk a whisky in the Chairman's office, entered the lift, looked for Sal and passed out. But that meant . . . His gaze landed on the navy blue suit and red shirt on the chair next to the bed. Dave's head fell into the pillow, realising his readmission had immediately followed going to see the Chairman. They'd given him more tablets, said he needed a good rest. Ellis had never come to pick him up.

'How long have I been out like a light, Bryn?'

'Rest, son. We'll talk later.'

Dave brought his hands to his face. He'd only dreamt an early release. That meant no meeting with the First Minister, no uncovering of repeated allegations of mercury dumping, no conference, no disguised holding companies, no WANGA and its tentacles and no downfall of the Chairman and his fraudulent scheme. Thinking about it, money in offshore companies, a geeky son sending fake emails and Bryn accidentally bumping into Colchester Dave was a little far-fetched. Dave hadn't defied medical science by bounding out of hospital to save the Bristol Channel. Of course he hadn't. He was Dave Welch.

The feeling of achievement that had fluttered for the briefest of moments in his chest took flight. The one time Dave had been exactly where he needed to be in life, he'd woken to learn it was complete and utter fabrication. His eyes welled as they bore holes in the polystyrene ceiling tiles. Dave the bloody laughing stock.

CHAPTER FORTY-ONE

The sun was setting when the door creaked open later that day, Jolene popping her face through the crack. 'Up for visitors?'

A tall American surfed into the room behind her. Surfboard or not, Jedd always glided. Learning Seth was his son, Dave had debated whether Jedd was too, the DNA results he'd seen in his dream having been pure fabrication.

'How's it going?' asked Jedd.

'The results?' asked Dave, cutting to the chase.

Jedd nodded.

Dave smiled. He'd gone from two to none and back to two sons. Dave had always known deep inside Jedd was his. He remembered that evening, Grace, the raven tattooed on her shoulder and its condemnatory stare. It was time to face up to what he had tried to forget by marrying Carol all those years ago. He may have invented a lot of the last few days, days he now knew were hours, but there *was* something to glean.

Dr Bete had been around earlier.

TUESDAY

'Don't swim against it, Mr Welch. Let it guide you to the shore,' he had said, placing a hand on Dave's shoulder.

'Sorry?' Dave had wiped his eyes.

'Madness is merely an exaggeration of the truth.'

Dave had waited for the punchline, a quip about his name, a retort declaring Dave's livelihood a waste of taxpayers' money. Nothing came. Instead, Dr Bete had left with a whoosh of coat, bewildered interns following in a staggered two-four-two formation.

Reincarcerated in a hospital bed, Dave had been forced to sit with himself that afternoon, obliged to confront what he'd been trying to avoid. Great Brakes' destruction of the seas had been a figment of his imagination; Jedd wasn't. He'd found a way to be honest with Carol. He could also change the course of his future by making up for the past.

The past shapes us. The present defines us. The future awaits us.

'Welcome to the family.' Dave stretched out a hand.

Jedd's hand slotted into his. 'You up to talking about the lawsuits?'

'Lawsuits?'

'Remember we spoke about Great Brakes in Asia.'

'Just before I . . .' Dave remembered never travelling to the conference. There hadn't been a conference. The one he had been invited to wasn't until later that year. 'When did we speak about that?' he asked.

'Before you were released.' Jedd exchanged glances with Jolene. 'We agreed I'd investigate the other allegations.'

His dreams had taken a surprising trajectory, but Dave was buoyed to learn he *had* found further allegations of mercury dumping other than the one at Adrian's Creek before passing out. Behind Jedd, a bed whirred. Wondering what else he may have misremembered, Dave felt around his bed for his own remote control.

'Tell me, has the Great Brakes project been approved by the Senedd? Any money awarded?' he asked.

Jolene shook her head, passing him the handset.

'But that's great news!' Dave stabbed at a button and his bed whirred into an upright position. 'But I still don't understand why it got to the press so quickly.'

'I might have leaked it,' said Jolene, looking to her shoes.

'Leaked it?' asked Dave.

'To get some support behind us.'

'But how did you work out the company behind Project America?'

'Project America?' Jedd let out a laugh.

'You told me, you idiot, when you mistook Jedd for Dustin when he first turned up,' replied Jolene.

Dave nodded. That made more sense than the Chairman turning into a hirsute version of Blofeld and fast-tracking projects to line his own pockets and take over the world. Dave sighed. All that talk of purdah, when elections weren't until next June! Dave eyed Bryn suspiciously, before reminding himself the old man held no responsibility for his behaviour in Dave's madcap hallucinations.

'Tell me again about what Great Brakes has been up to in Asia then,' said Dave.

'You'll never guess,' said Jolene. 'Dustin reached out. Turns out you're not going mad.' She nodded at the drip, 'Well, apart from your Alice moments.' Jedd prodded her. 'You know what I mean. Anyway, Dustin *did* contact you right in the beginning but recalled his emails.'

'He did?' Dave straightened his bed further, catching Bryn's eye across the room and trying to recall whether Seth or Jedd had offered that as the most obvious solution.

'That's why he called, to check they'd been deleted,' continued Jolene.

TUESDAY

'Why's that then, love?' asked Bryn, pressing his own handset and accidentally closing the blinds.

Jolene frowned at Dave.

'It's alright, he's with us.' Dave smiled. 'Bryn knows all there is to know about getting mercury out of water.'

'Nice one,' said Jolene. 'We'll be needing you, Bryn.'

Bryn beamed.

'Dustin says he was being pushed to get the project across the line,' continued Jolene.

'But why in Wales?' asked Dave.

'They'd read about the Welsh Technology Accelerator Fund in the press.' Jolene tutted. 'Made a beeline for us, thinking we'd offer mega bucks. Thought if toilet rolls qualified as green, green tech, we'd take anything.' Jolene shrugged, staking her foresight on the matter. 'Turns out they wrote to Essex first by accident, having seen us both registered at that event in Detroit. There's a guy there with the same name as you! You couldn't make it up!'

'Colchester Dave . . .'

'Very confusing email addresses . . .' Jolene continued, pushing her glasses up her nose. 'Anyway, Dustin started to have doubts as he'd been talking to managers at the factories in Asia. They told him about years of health issues in the local populations, all paid off with community-led sustainability projects. He'd decided his only recourse was to keep a low profile, let the investment happen without his name on it. When he called to insist there had never been any mails, worried because you'd started looking for them, he was shocked to learn you had mercury poisoning and saw it as a sign.'

Dave lifted his head.

'Anyway, he wants to help us,' continued Jolene as she repositioned her glasses. 'You up for this, Dave?'

'Up for what?'

'Bringing down Great Brakes.'

Dave was seeing his own *signs* since waking up and already addressing his personal life. The madness attributed to Great Brakes was also based on some truth. Whatever he could dream, he could do. Maybe he could turn this ship around too.

'Look, Jolene, I haven't always wanted to listen, but you're right. I've had enough of this green, green tech bollocks. Just a capitalist wolf in greenwashed-sheep's clothing.'

'Not the most Vegan of apologies but accepted.' Jolene smiled.

Dave debated whether it was an apology, or even carnivorous, before deciding it didn't matter. It was time to right some wrongs. What had Helga said? *From the moment we think of something, doesn't it take on some kind of existence?* Okay, she hadn't said it as such. He'd never met her. But the haze of recent years was lifting, his previous lethargy making him impatient to get out of bed and change the world.

'So, what's next?' asked Dave. 'Made a tit of myself talking to the Chairman without proof last time. Won't be doing that again.'

'Actually, you *can't* do that again,' said Jolene.

'He's been kicked out!' shouted Bryn. 'Saw it in the paper.'

'Tentacles in too many pies?' asked Dave.

'You what?' asked Jolene.

'Nothing,' said Dave, deciding it better to simply listen than interject.

'Pat from HR convinced Digby to lodge a formal complaint,' said Jolene.

'Pontypool Pat?' asked Dave, thinking of a shadow of a man who did anything for a quiet life.

TUESDAY

'Apparently the Chairman also went for one of the cleaners in the lift.'

'Hang on, did you say cleaner?' asked Dave. 'Not that woman with the big nose in the stationery cupboard?'

'What *is* your problem with her?' Jolene frowned.

Dave bit his lip. He had to stop this nonsense. 'I meant . . . well, who'd have thought HR would lift a finger?'

Jolene threw her hands in the air. 'You think the suffragettes got women the vote by saying, "Don't think I'll bother burning my bra today, no one's gonna bloody listen!"?'

'Look, I'm all behind pulling down Great Brakes but we work with career politicians, Jolene,' said Dave, thinking back to his meeting at the Senedd. However fictitious, it was based on civil service reality. 'How do you think the First Minister will react to three hundred jobs not happening?'

'Won't know until we try, but what I can tell you is he was beside himself when he heard about Digby. Then they did some digging and turns out the Chairman never even went to McGill!'

'The lying . . .' Dave stared at Jolene, a comfort forming at having known all along there was something fishy about good old Rhys.

Madness is merely an exaggeration of the truth.

'First Minister even offered Digby a position at the Senedd,' said Jolene.

'As his PR Manager?' asked Dave, immediately regretting his hasty dream-based assumption.

'How do you know that?' replied Jolene, re-examining the drip.

'He's been getting Seth to help him navigate social media,' said Jedd. 'Talk of the devil.'

'Dad!' Seth entered the room, throwing several bags of Hula Hoops on the bed. 'You okay?'

'Right as rain. Just need to rest.'

Seth high fived Jedd and Jolene and smiled at Bryn. 'Found out when I got out of school. Would have got here sooner but that American rapper was back, signing something in town. Took ages to get here.'

Just telling Dustin he isn't the only American in town.

Dave thought back to his first meeting with the Chairman and Dustin, remembering hearing exactly the same line. His paranoia really had been playing turns on him.

'Then I bumped into Rhianna,' continued Seth.

'*The* Rhianna?' Jolene's eyes widened.

Seth laughed. 'A friend from school. Rodric kept coming to our house thinking he'd see her there. Turns out he really fancies her. Idiot only went and told her!'

Dave smiled at Seth. A simple crush was a more likely teenage boy motivation than hacking into emails for his father, but there was something left to address.

'Anyway,' said Seth. 'Before you pass out again, Jedd's been talking to me about the Great Brakes thing. You know how you've always pooh-poohed my—'

'Listen, we need you and your two million followers.' Dave looked at Jolene. 'He can reach the people who really care about the sea.'

'That's a great idea!' said Jolene.

Dave took Seth's hand in his. 'You do what you want with your life. No more pushing from me.'

Seth stared at the drip. 'You okay, Dad?'

Dave laughed. 'Will everyone stop asking me that! I've never felt better.'

'That's the spirit, son!' Bryn fist bumped the air.

TUESDAY

'I've got something to tell you.' Dave's smile faded. His eyes bounced from Seth to Jedd and back to Seth.

'He's my brother, right?' said Seth.

'How did you—'

'Rocking up out of nowhere, curls like yours. Well, like you used to have.' Seth laughed. 'Anyway, you seen the way he eats his Hula Hoops?'

Everyone watched Jedd place crisps on his fingers one by one.

'Right,' said Jolene. 'If we're gonna bring the bastards down, we need to get you better, Dave Welch. In the meantime, let's make a plan. How can we pull in more support?'

'How about an Icelandic Research Centre running pilots to detect mercury in water?' said the bed opposite.

'Now you're talking, Bryn, love,' said Jolene as she picked up Dave's clothes to make room on the chair.

Dave's jacket fell to the floor with a thud.

'Pass me that, will you?' said Dave.

Jolene handed Dave the jacket. He rummaged in its pocket and pulled out a piece of lava. One by one by one, questions rose within him, fighting to be heard. He squeezed the pocked rock, cold penetrating him.

A trolley laden with evening medication crashed through the doors.

'What's that in your hand?' Bryn shouted.

'Proof I'm not mad,' said Dave.

'Looks like it's your lucky day then,' replied Maureen with a smile.

'Or proof that I am,' said Dave, laughing.

'Isn't a little bit of madness what keeps us sane?' said Bryn. 'Over.'

'You're not wrong there, Bryn. Over and out.'

– THE END –

ENJOY THIS BOOK?

There are a lot of books out there. I write what I enjoy and hopefully you do too.

You can't please all of the people all of the time but if this book struck a chord with you, how about leaving a review?

Gaining visibility in a crowded market is hard, good reviews make it easier. If you have five minutes to spare and are happy to jump on Amazon or Goodreads, that would be great.

Many thanks!

GET A FREE NOVELLA!

This book is part of the **7 DAYS** series.

If you liked it - and are in no way fazed by a week not starting on a Monday! - join my Readers Club and be the first to hear when the next novels in the series are released.

Sign up at www.lougibbons.com and receive a free novella as a welcome gift!

OTHER BOOKS BY LOU

THE WORLD HAPPINESS ORGANISATION

Retirement in the South of France isn't all it's cracked up to be. After fifty years of marriage, the only thing Mavis and Jeff agree on is that it's too late to change.

Enter the maverick and flirtatious Rémy, sent to prove them wrong. When he asks the Toulouse Club for English Pensioners to help oversee clinical trials for a revolutionary happiness drug, little does anyone know he is a World Happiness Organisation (WHO) agent, armed with their files.

But Rémy also faces a dilemma. The new drug is part of a covert scheme to monetise happiness, violating the Organisation's founding principles, and his boss is about to find out …

ACKNOWLEDGMENTS

It takes time and belief to write a book and those things can be difficult to find when you're not surrounded by the right people. My heartfelt thanks go therefore to family members, friends and writing buddies who have got behind my writing projects from day one. I love you all.

Secondly, a mention for my readers. I tested the water with a first novel, knowing no story can please everyone but finding a group of people who like what I write. Thank you for accompanying me on this journey. It makes it all worthwhile.

A special shout-out also goes to the technical team behind this novel. To Vicki Heath Silk for another fantastic cover, to Rachel Eley and Jennie Taylor for their sharp-eyed editing and to Pierre Cabrol – Midiconcept – for the best website ever (and accommodating my endless updates).

Last but not least, a fond mention for the *small, clever country* of Wales and the economic development professionals I have worked with over the years. While the storyline is entirely fictitious, global water pollution unfortunately isn't. Humour features in this novel as a tribute to the joy my adoptive country and its people have always brought me, but also as an experimental vehicle for greater awareness.

ABOUT THE AUTHOR

Born in Manchester, Lou grew up in Wales and now lives in the south of France with her favourite people and cat.

For a large part of the week, she writes for multinationals on subjects ranging from medical devices to supply chain management. It's fun, but a couple of years ago, a question started to niggle her: what would it be like to write about some of the other - let's say more quirky - stuff in her head. After a year-long novel writing course, the World Happiness Organisation was born and she hasn't looked back!

When she's not writing, Lou loves nothing more than cycling, doing up old houses and - when the opportunity presents itself - hiking up smouldering Icelandic volcanoes.

lougibbons.com